3 HOUR TOUR

A DEE SANDERS ADVENTURE

LP SNYDER

3 Hour Tour is a work of fiction. Any references to historical events, real people, or real places are used fictitiously. Other names, characters, places, and events are products of the author's imagination, and any resemblance to actual events or places or persons, living or dead, is entirely coincidental.

2020 Sky Blue Stories Paperback Edition

www.skybluestories.com

ISBN: 978-1-7355084-0-5

Cover art by Vince Conti

CAST OF CHARACTERS

Dee Sanders
Jamal and Angelic Jones
Mike and Keno Williams
Gina Dubulgee
Tom Jones
Holly Smithson
Jim Satterfield
Daryl and Mrs. Johnson
Antoine Debaucher
   William, Anthony, & Kyle
Ben Donner
   Jared,   Egan, & Jamie
Captain Demetrius (Bozo/BJ) Beaujeax
   Snarly, Huggy, & Scraggly
   K5J-Kazaam and the 5Jams
Captain Ivan Perez

PROLOGUE

Somewhere in the South Pacific

Then I heard it, a faint rumble of thunder in the distance. The sky was blue and the sea was calm. But there was something out there. Now it was a matter of time.

The sky darkened. A cloudbank had formed and blocked out the sun. People were able to spread out on the decks again and move back to their seats.

The PA came on, "The ship says they are headed our way. It shouldn't be long now."

Jamal looked at me and asked, "You believe them?"

"I hope so."

"It does look like it could storm," threw out Mike as he looked to the horizon.

"It could, or it could pass us by, or dissipate. Hopefully the launch will be here soon," I answered.

The sky grew darker, and a small breeze picked up. The waves formed a light chop. We drifted faster. People moved back under the canopies and closer together. Everyone buckled in and adjusted their life vests.

"I don't think they're going to get here," said Angelic.

Keno nodded and said, "Something is not right."

"We don't know what kind of storm it is, if any," I said. "It could be wind, it could be light rain, maybe a few waves, we don't know."

"But we do know that it's going to be dark soon," replied Mike.

I looked at him and nodded. I pulled my scope and scanned the horizon again. I couldn't see anything but an approaching storm.

I held the scope across my leg. "The storm is coming. I can see it on the horizon." We were in the back third of the launch, well under the canopy, in as good a place as any. If we got swamped, we should get out. If we got flipped, it might be tougher.

People were milling around now. Nothing came from the PA. The crewmen were watching the sky.

Lightning crackled, and after a long pause, the thunder rumbled. The storm was here.

PART I

THE 1ST HOUR

1

THE CRUISE

Six Days Earlier

That's a big boat. I guess they don't call it a boat, they probably call it a ship, I thought to myself as the cab stopped at the dock.

I was taking a cruise on my own for the first time. I decided on the spur of the moment to do something new, different, have fun in a new way. I love the water, especially the Pacific, and I love boats, but then this is a ship, and I don't know much about ships! My first cruise was a three day thing that wasn't much bigger than a houseboat.

I've spent most of my time around the Atlantic, the Caribbean, the Florida Keys, mostly Key West. But, I have a special relationship with Hawaii. I spent several years there while growing up. I want to see Hawaii again. I want to see Tahiti and Fiji and the South Pacific!

I paid the driver, retrieved my luggage, and started toward the end of the long line that had already formed. It was five in the morning at the port of Los Angeles.

It was warm and promised to get hotter. It was late

summer or early fall. It's hard to tell in LA, the weather doesn't seem that different from season to season.

I flew into town the afternoon before, had dinner on the strip. I'm from Nashville, Tennessee, and involved in the music industry. No, it's nothing like that. I'm an accountant, not a singer. I look after other people's money, country music stars, and people in the industry. The public doesn't generally realize there's a lot of different music in Nashville, not just country music. The city is full of top-ranked musical talent. Everybody that lives there plays or sings or plays like they do.

Anyway, I'm around famous people on a regular basis, so LA's crowd doesn't really impact me, and I'm a pretty low key guy anyway, being an accountant.

I queued up at the back of the line. That morning I dressed casually and resisted the urge to wear a Hawaiian print shirt. Looking ahead of me there were people of all ages, sizes, and colors in the line. This promised to be interesting!

As we crawled forward, I remembered someone at the office told me an 8-day cruise is really a 6-day cruise. You should always subtract two days off of the brochure because you spend a day at the dock boarding before you leave, and a day at the dock deboarding when you return. That same person told me that a cruise was really just a big floating buffet. If I get hungry, I guess I'll be okay.

I looked back at the line of people working their way to the check-in. Ahead of me was a younger woman in short shorts and flip flops standing next to an older man in a navy blazer and boat shoes. This must be an equal opportunity cruise. I say that only in jest. You see, I'm also the human resource guy where I work. A few years ago, in a cost-cutting move—an accountant is only dangerous with a pencil—the company combined the HR function with the business and accounting functions. I earned a certification in HR, as well as the one I have in accounting. So, I'm a CPA and an SPHR. Yes, I'm a double threat. You can stop laughing now! It really was my job, and I was looking forward to taking a break and going on this cruise.

THE LINE MOVED SLOWLY, AND THE SUN GOT HIGHER, AND the temperature and the tempers got hotter. People were muttering and stomping their feet.

I detached myself by studying the harbor, the dock, the ship, anything but the line. As I looked back to shore, a black limo pulled onto the dock. It was three extensions long. I wondered how the driver negotiated some of the turns into the port. The car stopped. The doors opened, and three big, burly men in suits stepped out. They were followed by three women and a silver-haired older man.

Based on his uniform, an officer from the ship, hurried up to them. His cap had enough macaroni on it to remind me of the pasta bar at an Italian restaurant. There were all sorts of stripes and markings on his jacket and shoulders.

The officer extended an arm as if to indicate direction. He turned, and the group fell in behind him. They started down the dock. The back of the line was the other way.

The silver-haired man was in front. He was flanked slightly back and behind by two of the blondes. They were tall and thin with slender shoulders and big feet. They were wrapped in designer high fashion and skinny heels. Those three were followed by the remaining blonde, similarly attired, followed by the burly men in suits. They made a big wedge moving down the dock.

I looked past them and down the way, where there was an elevator tower like you might see on a construction site. It ran upward for six stories, halfway up the ship.

They boarded the elevator from the dock and ascended

to the summit. Several other people had noticed the group as well. I overheard, "who was that," and "apparently not everyone has to stand in line."

I grinned and thought to myself, *somebody's always got a backstage pass.*

I MADE IT TO THE FRONT OF THE LINE. "MAY I SEE YOUR ticket?" the attractive young woman asked. Smiling in return, I showed her my copies. She validated them and gave me a cabin assignment.

Like I said, I wanted to enjoy this cruise so I reached deep in my pockets and paid for an upper deck, exterior cabin with a small balcony on the starboard side of the ship. Now if I could just find it.

Walking along, trying not to run into anyone, I glanced around the ship. I was inside a large atrium, and I could see multiple decks. Looking at my phone I tried to find the way to my cabin.

Struggling for a moment I decided just to stroll. My luggage was checked, and I only had my shoulder bag. I was going to relax.

Climbing a deck I went back into the sunshine. There was a beautiful view of the harbor, but I hoped we would be leaving soon. Moving slowly, I soaked up the fact that I was off work, letting that relaxation seep all over my body. Walking on I saw one of the pools and a little beyond, a shopping arcade. There was a bowling alley, followed by a movie theater, another pool, a casino, and several gyms. At least I could get some exercise. No shortage of things to do, but there'd be no time for taking it easy. I hoped to spend some time on the water, feeling the breeze and the sun, no problems, no worries, and no work!

Walking further, I stopped and sat in a lounge chair

overlooking the pool. I immediately heard, "Can I get you something to drink, sir?"

Oh, yeah. I paused to think, before I said, "A beer—tall, cold?" The steward nodded and disappeared.

Sitting and waiting I looked through the information the concierge had provided. There were all kinds of shows, spas, casino activities, and then tours and excursions. I'd been an open water scuba diver for several years, with over fifty dives. A couple of the early ones had been in Hawaii. I was anxious to get back in the water, there, and to dive Tahiti and Fiji and points in-between. Dives were almost daily, out islands, parasailing, kayaking, board paddling, snorkeling, and windsurfing. I might sign up for at least one of everything, and more if I liked it!

My beer arrived. I sat, sipped, and enjoyed the view around the pool and out to sea. Setting the empty glass down, I went to find my cabin. Studying the map I had a good idea of how to get there. It was a couple of decks away, but I found the entrance, ambled down the hall, read the numbers on the doors and there it was!

I entered my code, and the door swung open. Nice, tidy, and a little tight, no wasted space, but I only planned to sleep there. Walking to the sliding door, and opening it, I stepped onto the patio.

That's what I'm talking about. What a view! High on the ship, a close look to the front and a long way to the back, fore and aft, I suppose. After seeing this, the boats we ran around the lakes on in Nashville just weren't big enough. I pulled out a deck chair and propped up my feet.

2

STROLL AND MEET

After unpacking and stowing my gear, I set out to sightsee and find some dinner. I knew we were departing late in the afternoon, and it appeared preparations were underway. Strolling to the port side of the ship I noted there was no longer a line or anyone frantically trying to check-in. It was an empty dock in the sunny late afternoon. The pace had slowed considerably. As I stood there watching, a couple walked by me and nodded. They stopped just down the railing.

He was a tall, dark-skinned, African American man. He was a good looking guy, but in that ordinary guy kind of way. I identify with that because I'm pretty ordinary myself. Anyway, she was stunning! She was slender but shapely with thick, dark curly-ringed hair halfway down her back. She had a wrap around her legs and a scooped neck pullover that revealed and flattered her neck and upper chest. She had big dark eyes, a bright smile, and was laughing at something he said. I saw all that because she was pointed in my direction. I was glad he had his back to me, so he wouldn't see me drool, which I was about to do. She looked like a young Chaka Khan. I expect she knew it. She radiated beauty and presence.

I couldn't help but hear them talk. The man said something about dinner and where to look, which deck, which dining room, too many choices. He turned partially in my direction and nodded again. I smiled.

"This is my second cruise. But I don't have any idea which dining room or what deck. I am so lost." I shrugged.

She giggled, he looked down. "We were just having that same conversation."

She stepped across and held out her hand before saying, "I'm Angelic Jones!" And she was angelic, if you will.

I took her hand and shook it quickly. "I'm Dee Sanders, very nice to meet you." So as not to make him mad, I turned and held out my hand and nodded again. "Dee."

"Jamal Jones," he replied and nearly crushed my hand. That man had a grip, and I noticed facing him straight on, quite a set of shoulders. Was he a pro athlete, bodybuilder, workout freak? I thought, *I don't want to be on his bad side.*

Then he smiled and said, "Sorry, I work in a corporate environment, and they're always big on playing who's got the strongest grip."

"I'd say you win most of those," I replied and pulled my hand away.

Angelic tapped him on the shoulder. "Jamal, let the man alone." She smiled. "We're thinking about trying to pick out a café, would you like to join us?"

He grinned back at me and released my hand. "You like steak?"

"Who doesn't?"

We stepped from the rail and turned. Angelic spoke up, "I think there's a small café and bar on the next deck. It should have a nice view, and we can order off the menu."

We sat at a small round top and ordered one of the best steaks I'd ever eaten. It was simple, well-cooked, with a potato, a salad, and wine.

Angelic sat with her back to the windows, and as the ship pulled from the dock, the light silhouetted her, and she was beautiful. I could see the way Jamal looked at her and how they quietly held hands while we talked. A happy couple, no doubt, at least today.

Angelic asked, "I 'm just nosy, what do you do for a living?"

"I'm an accountant and an HR guy. I'm taking a little time off."

"Us too," replied Jamal. "Angelic is an oncology nurse, and I own and operate a corporate fitness and wellness center. We needed to get away."

"Where y'all from?" I asked. They both laughed.

"The south, just like you," replied Angelic while Jamal grinned.

"We're from Atlanta, what about you?"

"Nashville."

"Country music?" asked Jamal.

"Only the money, not the music."

"You mean you don't like country music," prodded Jamal.

"Of course I like it, you can't live there and not like it. I just meant I don't make music, I just count the money for those that do."

They both grinned. Jamal tented his fingers and began," I help fat, out of shape, overworked and overfed but undernourished executives of both sexes to try and hold down their blood pressure."

Angelic grinned. "I'm just a caregiver!"

Jamal jumped in, "She's a nurse practitioner in Oncology, they have a huge practice and a lot of sick folks. It's sad to see them." He continued, "We decided on a cruise because we'd never done one before. I'm not sure how I'm going to like it. Why did you pick a cruise?"

"Same as y'all, I wanted to try something different. Do you scuba?"

"Only once in a pool in the Caribbean."

Angelic laughed as she said, "Jamal almost drowned, he really doesn't like the water. I can't believe I got him out here!"

WE SAT FOR A FEW MOMENTS AND WATCHED THE SEA AND the sky.

"You ever do any of that ancestry stuff?" I asked.

She grinned. "No, but I'm mixed French and Moroccan."

I looked at Jamal. "I'm just a brother from south Georgia," he replied and laughed.

"Middle Tennessee, outside Nashville, a veterinarian would call me an NPB."

They both looked at me, and Angelic started to giggle.

"No particular breed, a little bit of a lot of things, I guess." We all laughed.

AND ON WE WENT LIKE THAT FOR ANOTHER HOUR. I GLANCED beyond Angelic, and we were well out to sea, surrounded by water. It was growing a little dusky. I looked at both of them and said, "Well, I think it's time for a walk around the deck and a sunset. Since that sounds so romantic, I believe I'll let y'all do that on your own."

Angelic winked at me, and Jamal bumped me on the shoulder as he got up. We traded room numbers and made plans for the next day. I waved goodbye as they moved out of the café and on around the deck. I watched them walk away and felt happy for them. I did feel a little bit alone at that moment, but I came on vacation by myself for a reason. It was a good reason.

3

THE 1ST NIGHT

Strolling the deck I watched as the sun settled on the horizon. Deck lights came up, and people took in the sights. Many were dressed formally as they headed toward the sit-down dinners. Some men wore tuxedos while women dressed in formal wear, others donned Muumuus and flip flops and board shorts and sandals. What a crowd!

I stopped on the rail at one of the stairways. There was an entourage coming up from below. It was led by the older silver-haired man I had seen on the dock. He was escorted by his three beefy and menacing-looking accomplices. I didn't see the women. *A boss and three of his subordinates,* I thought, *no, those guys are too beefy for business, they must be security. I wonder who he is.* The group reached the top of the stairs and strolled past me, engrossed in their conversation and oblivious to all the people and sights around them. As I watched them go, I wondered why they had made the trip. All of this was lost on them.

As darkness fell, and continuing to roam, I heard sounds from one of the pools. A swim seemed like it might be nice. I wandered back to my room and found a swimsuit and a tee shirt. My biggest issue tonight would be which pool.

I strolled to one of the outer decks and looked over the ocean. Waves crashed against the hull of the ship and moisture hung in the air. The deck lights behind me were bright. I turned and moved to the railing overlooking the pool. Around me, people were talking and laughing. They were relaxed and on vacation. It has a different feel when people let go.

I saw a group of single women across the pool. By themselves, or were their husbands already gambling or drinking, no way to tell. Some of them looked good in their skimpy new suits. A couple of them probably should have rethought that option. I glanced further around the pool. There was a heavyset man in a speedo and two or three other men with a little bit less on than was necessary. But, they were older, and I suspected the older you get, the less you care about what other people think.

Slipping down to the pool I tossed my tee-shirt over a lounge. I swam competitively in college and still swam regularly as a form of exercise. It was a long pool that was not particularly wide, so it was good for swimming laps, if I could keep away from all the bobbing people. Taking long, slow strokes I watched carefully around me. The water relaxed my muscles, and as I got a rhythm, I just glided back and forth, for who knows how many laps.

Some of the women from the group I'd seen earlier were sitting in adjacent lounges, and when I finally got out, I noticed them looking at me, sightseeing, I guess. It's hard not to at a pool, for anybody.

I lay in the lounge for a few minutes. The ladies next to me got up and made their way toward the exit. Noticing several lingering looks I was glad it was dark. I probably looked better than I would have otherwise. Who knows, maybe it will help some husband get lucky tonight. I laughed at myself. *That was an arrogant thought.*

Toweling off I wandered back to my cabin. Changing into comfortable clothes, I decided to take another, longer stroll to see what else I might have missed. Most of my time had been at the front of the ship, so I decided to stroll aft and see what it had to offer.

I didn't know how many people were on this ship. I suspected it held several thousand plus the crew and support staff. Lots of people were on the decks, and I heard bits of conversation while periodically stopping to look at the water. There was more shopping, more pools, and more things to do than it would ever be possible to get done on a single cruise. I guessed the cruise line tried to entice you, to keep you coming back.

One of the reasons I'd picked a cruise was an article I'd seen about a man who had spent the last fourteen years of his life on a cruise ship. His wife had died, and he didn't want to be alone, so he took a cruise and never went home. He still owned a condo in Fort Lauderdale, but he hadn't set foot in it in all that time. He was on a smaller cruise ship and said that everyone knew him, and it felt like family. He was happy, and he just stayed onboard. He said there was everything he needed. What a life!

I worked my way toward the rear of the ship. There were so many people. As I made my way to the top deck, aft of the ship, I thought it was time to sit down, have one last drink, and call it a night. The stress was melting away, and I began to feel like there wasn't much to keep me going.

Reaching the last deck, I stepped into a lounge that sat high in the night sky. It was all wood and brass, chrome and glass, very cozy and small for the size of the ship. I ordered a drink at the bar. Hearing voices from a table behind me, I looked in the mirror to see the silver-haired man and his security team. I glanced around the bar and didn't see the women. The men had their ties loose, and their collars unbuttoned and were chatting loudly about some sort of business deal. They were talking about a "buy" they wanted to make that was contingent upon an event that was to occur in the next ninety-six hours. It all seemed kind of coded. Ninety-six hours is a lifetime in business. It's actually a couple of lifetimes. It's glacial in the business world. So many things can change in that amount of time. We'd be south of Hawaii before they got a chance to act. I wondered what could have them so animated. I must have been watching a little too closely, as one of the burly ones got up from his seat and moved around to where his back was to me, blocking my view. I guess he put me in my place.

Sipping the drink, I looked casually at the other patrons in the bar, and thought about the ninety-six hours again. I took two weeks for this cruise and would need most of that to get back to Nashville for work. This was called a "slice" cruise. A passenger embarked in one city, visited a handful of ports across a significant portion of the world, ended up in a destination city, and then flew home. I understood that a traveler could circle the globe with the "slice" tours and see the world. This cruise's ultimate destination was Brisbane, Australia. From there, I would fly back to LA and on to Nashville. There was an option to spend extra days on the backside and see Brisbane, Melbourne, and Sydney. There was another "slice" cruise that originated in Sydney. I would have liked to spend some time in Australia, but two weeks was a lifetime in business, and I knew I'd need to get back. It had been tough enough to get that much time off.

Glancing at one of the monitors on the wall I saw stock tickers running and a financial news program. This must be the bar for business guys. Well, that would be me, but at the time, I was on vacation.

I wandered out to the rail to watch our wake and to catch the breeze. It was a warm and wonderful night as I watched the stars come out and shine in the heavens above. The breeze whipped my hair. It felt good to be alive. This was going to be a great adventure.

4

THE 2ND DAY

The next morning I met Jamal and Angelic for breakfast. We were going to take a scuba refresher course at one of the pools. Jamal felt like, in his words, it might be better for him to "ease into" the water.

Breakfast was enormous and tasty. I needed to be careful how much I ate, or I'd get back to work and have to listen to "fat" jokes. The ship was a floating buffet.

We got to the pool a few minutes early and took seats while we waited. Angelic was dazzling in a multi-color one piece. Jamal and I went with your basic gym shorts in a solid color. A tanned young guy in a black speedo and a slender blonde in a black bikini arrived to instruct us. There were a half dozen other people in the class.

An older man, slightly stooped in long baggy board shorts, was accompanied by a heavyset broad-shouldered woman in a box cut suit. They fussed constantly.

We managed to get the group into the diving gear and then into the water. As we swam along the bottom of the pool, I flipped over on my back and looked up at the sky.

There wasn't a cloud anywhere, just different shades of beautiful, brilliant blue.

Jamal thrashed in the water, and I rolled back to help him stand up. Fortunately, we were in the shallow end of the pool.

"I'm getting water in my mask, and I can't keep it cleared," Jamal said as he rubbed at his face.

We paddled over to the side of the pool and asked the female instructor if there were any other masks. She dug around in a dive bag for a few seconds and came out with a large rectangular glass one. It was enormous. Jamal held it to his face and inhaled. The mask stayed on. He went to slip the straps over his head. Angelic had wandered over to us.

"You look like a space alien with that thing on," she giggled at him.

"A dry space alien," he replied. He pushed out in the water and dropped below the surface. I slipped down beside him and watched for a few seconds. I gave him the ok sign, and he flashed it back, followed with thumbs up. It looked like he might not drown after all.

As we emerged from the water, we overheard the older couple standing on the pool steps, arguing about the regulator and the weight belts. Something about how much weight they each needed. The old guy seemed to need the weight where the wife didn't. She wanted them to be the same. It sounded like he didn't take much air while she took a lot. He'd be forced to come up with half a tank or more of air left when she was redlining. They were hysterical. She would berate anything and everything he said. His shoulders finally slumped, and he stopped talking as she continued to deride him. We couldn't help but laugh.

I looked at Jamal and Angelic and said, "Will that be you in a few years?"

Angelic replied, "I'd rather be divorced and alone than to live like that."

"Agreed," nodded Jamal.

WE TOWELED OFF AND HEADED FOR ONE OF THE OUTSIDE BAR and grills. There was a light breeze, and the sea and sky were the same bright blues I had seen from the pool. I couldn't tell where one stopped and the other one started.

"How long do you suppose they've been married?" Jamal asked.

"Way too long," responded Angelic.

"I wonder why they're still together." I added.

Angelic offered me a small smile and said, "Afraid of being alone, maybe."

"There is a difference between being alone and being lonely," I responded.

Jamal raised his eyebrows at me. "The voice of experience?"

"Not really," I replied. "Sometimes circumstances force you to be alone. You can be lonely or not, it's your choice."

Angelic nudged Jamal. "Leave the man alone." She smiled brightly again.

"If you're alone, it's only because you choose to be."

"You're a smart woman," I replied, looking at Angelic and then, looking at Jamal, "and you're a lucky man."

At that moment, a short, dark-haired young woman in a fringe thong walked by. She flashed me a smile and I couldn't help but stare. Angelic winked at her, and she winked back but kept walking.

"Is that your type?" she asked me.

"I hope so," said Jamal.

"I don't know, I didn't really get a good look," I answered.

"I thought your eyes were going to jump out of your head," she said, grinning. "I haven't seen a man look at a woman like that since the first time Jamal saw me."

Jamal looked at her hard. "What're you talking about?"

"You know it's true, you couldn't even say hello. You were so tongue-tied. It was one of the things I found endearing about you," she said as she draped an arm across his shoulder.

"Well, maybe," replied Jamal while taking her arm in his hand.

I rolled my eyes at both of them.

We ordered some lunch and talked about what to do for the rest of the day. Angelic and Jamal were in agreement with me. It was way too nice to do anything indoors. We needed to be out in the sun, to be having fun. That was what this trip was about.

We sat at the bar on tiki chairs in the shade for almost two hours, just laughing, talking, people watching. We speculated on what we wanted to see in Hawaii, and Tahiti and Fiji. We talked about how nice it would be to have more time, to really enjoy the sun and sand and sea, to really relax.

5

THE WORKOUT

I said to them, "When you guys need me to wander off, you let me know, I don't want to intrude."

Angelic winked at me.

Jamal let out a, "Dude, what you talking about?" followed with a fist bump.

"I think I'll take a walk and hit the gym," I said. "I've got formal dinner tonight. What about you guys?"

"We got a little private thing booked, and formal dinner is tomorrow night," replied Jamal.

"Alright then, text me later if you want to get a drink or get together," I said. Getting up, I strolled down the dock, and waved at them as I slipped away.

Walking slowly around the deck toward my room, I confirmed in my mind that I didn't want to monopolize all their time. They were so nice, but I was sure they needed some time alone. A good workout, that's what they needed, and I could use one too. Doubting that it would be the same kind of workout or that I would have near as much fun, I'd take what I could get.

Arriving at the room I changed into some workout gear. I

started for the gym and picked up my shoulder bag. It's a funny thing about that bag. I have all kinds of stuff. There's a full shaving kit, a small Maglite, a towel of my own, sunglasses. I just like to have my things with me. You never know what you might need.

I thought I'd get some strength training, a little cardio, and then swim. Maybe a hot tub or steam after the workout and before getting ready for dinner. I hated to bring dress clothes on the trip, but I didn't want to miss that element of the cruise. So, I scheduled the dinner early to get it over with. Wear it once and push those formal clothes to the back of the closet.

I went to the largest of the gyms and entered through the glass doors. It was crowded. Maybe that wasn't a good idea. I wandered back to the free weights, and there wasn't much activity. Most people looked to be in classes. There were spinning, functional fitness, yoga, martial arts, tai chi, and aerobics classes, along with lots of weight machines. People were bouncing around. There was music and banks of televisions. I passed on a headset because I could watch TV at home.

It was basically cable TV, I noticed, as I climbed on an Elliptical to warm up. People were flipping through channels. There was pretty much anything you wanted to see. Out of the corner of my eye, I caught an old black and white TV series intro that made me smile. I'd watched the reruns as a kid. The tune to the opening credits ran through my head. They were pulling out of Honolulu harbor. A place I'd be in another couple of days.

Looking around the gym there were lots of shorts, yoga pants, and crop tops, but after being around the pool and all those bikinis, people seemed almost overdressed.

I did a couple sets of squats, deadlifts, curls, and bench

presses then rode for several minutes on the Elliptical again. I was winded, but I felt good, strong, and ready for dinner.

While I was finishing my cool down, I noticed an older man in an expensive Panama hat. He had on shorts, boat shoes, a silk shirt, and he walked with a cane that had a glass or quartz cut handle. He seemed to be strolling through taking in the sights. There was no sign of him working out. He looked totally casual and entirely at ease for an old guy. He had a silver goatee and a twinkle in his eye as he surveyed the surroundings. I had to admire his style.

Going back to the pool where we'd taken the scuba class, I slid into the water for a few laps. I was stroking along slowly, not keeping up with the lap count, and on one of the turns, I saw the short brunette with the fringe thong. Not wanting to be obvious, I thought I'd catch her eye on the next lap. I made a sharp flip turn and broke the surface to look for her. But, she was gone. I guess I missed my window.

Getting out of the pool, I went back to my cabin, and began to clean up for dinner.

6

THE FORMAL DINNER

I wore a white jacket, black slacks, and black canvas slip-ons. Yeah, I know, the shoes weren't formal, but I figured nobody would see them, and they were really black and blended in with the slacks. Entering the main dining room, I identified myself, and was led to the captain's table. It was one of the benefits of the high dollar cabin I had reserved, dinner with the captain.

There was already an assortment of people around the table. They were mostly older, wealthy-looking, and well-dressed, which made me feel bad about my shoes. I was seated between an older gentleman and his wife on one side and a middle-aged woman and her husband on the other. We made small talk for a few moments.

I noticed the captain's chair, and seven others around it, were still empty. In a few minutes, I saw why. The captain, in full uniform, which honestly was quite elegant, but unlike any service uniform I had ever seen, entered. He looked more like a doorman or a theater usher, although he was otherwise quite dignified. Beside him were the older silvered-haired man and his entourage of six. The old guy was in formal wear. The men with him were in suits. The women, like the older man, had dressed for dinner. They were in long silver-white dresses that draped in the back and plunged in the front. They were in full makeup, hair perfect, wearing copious quantities of expensive-looking jewelry. They were on display. It was quite an entrance. They all sat down at the head of the table as one. The captain introduced himself and nodded to everyone else at the table.

Dinner was served. Throughout the meal, the silver-haired man spoke only to the captain. His security didn't talk to anyone. The women chatted among themselves. Several of the other women attempted to engage the good captain in conversation but were cut off by the silver-haired man to whom the captain seemed unusually attentive. All in all, it was a good meal, as to the food, but not very enjoyable as to the company. I was grateful when it was over and made a note to myself to studiously avoid Mr. Aloof and his sidekicks if I came into contact with them again.

I left the dinner at the first opportunity and took to the deck for a stroll. Rounding a corner, I saw a woman standing on the rail. It was her again, the woman from the pool. Her waist-length hair was in a long braid. She wore a formal gown that was largely backless and cinched into a small waist, revealing wide and curvaceous hips.

She glanced over her shoulder as if she felt a presence. Our gazes met and she smiled but took a step across the deck and headed back into the bar.

I walked on, and passing the bar, I saw her engaged with a group of people. It just wasn't my night, and I strolled back to my room.

7

THE 3RD DAY

I woke the next morning to the familiar sway of the ship moving beneath me. Out on my private deck I was greeted by a gentle breeze and another brilliant, blue, cloudless sky. We had two days until we arrived in Honolulu. Going back inside I retrieved my shoulder bag and pulled out a small hand-held telescope to search the horizon. What was I looking for? I didn't know, other sea traffic, a few fish, maybe some dolphins. There was a good view, all blue, through the scope. Just for fun, I spun it around toward the pool. Up close and personal. Some of those folks really shouldn't be in those swimsuits. They were going to get burned. As we sailed closer and closer to the tropics, it would get hotter and hotter and brighter and brighter and people were going to get burned a whole lot quicker. We'll see at dinner. There will be some bright red out tonight!

I could already imagine the claims of, "Oh, it doesn't hurt," as I pulled my industrial sunscreen out of the bag and slathered up. I get dark pretty easily, but everybody burns, it's just how quick!

I shot Jamal a text and told him I was headed for

breakfast. He pinged me back a few minutes later and said they'd meet me there. I smiled. It was nice to have company.

They both looked sleepy-eyed as they strolled up and sat down. I couldn't help but grin at them.

"I trust you had a pleasant evening?"

Jamal grinned a really big grin.

Angelic just rolled her eyes and said, "I'm hungry."

We each knocked back a quick omelet and decided how to spend the day.

"We could sun by the pool," said Angelic.

"Dee and I could hit the gym, and you could shop," replied Jamal.

They both looked at me. "We could always play shuffleboard."

They both groaned.

"It doesn't matter, a little pool time, a little shopping, check the scuba gear, check the sights, have a beer, we're on vacation, and do we really need a plan?" I offered.

They both smiled and nodded.

Angelic threw her hair back and put her sunglasses on. "Let's get to it."

Jamal and I followed.

Angelic stopped at the first boutique she spotted. Jamal and I looked across the way and saw a dive shop. We pointed at that, and Angelic pointed at the boutique. We went our separate ways.

We entered the shop and Jamal's eyes got big. They had a tremendous selection.

"You're really into it now," I said.

"Now that I know my mask isn't going to flood and drown me, yeah, I'm into it."

He grabbed a handful of things and asked, "Is this good, what about this, what's the best?"

"The gear we used in the pool wasn't bad, it was in good

shape. You might want to make a few dives and see what you like and don't like and then narrow your choices a bit."

He looked at me and said, "My wife is going to be buying stuff, so I need to come back with something."

I waved to him and said, "Follow me." I led him over to the dive knives. "I left mine in my dive bag, but I've wanted another one for a while anyway." There were a dozen or more, and we worked our way through them. We tried the feel, the fit, and the weight, and examined the blade configuration. I settled on a fairly traditional model with a 6-inch blade and a sheath.

"What do you use the knife for?" Jamal asked.

"I mostly probe with mine. I wear gloves, and I like to turn things over and explore areas, I use the blade for that. If you get caught in any kind of line or undergrowth, you can cut it away. You can also use a smaller knife topside on the boat. It just depends on what use you think you might have, and what you're comfortable with."

He tried a few more and settled on a folding knife in a case.

Walking across the store, we looked at wet suits, spear guns, and lamps. We turned to look at a rack of tanks, and there was Angelic, with several bags in each hand. I looked at my watch. It had been nearly two hours.

"Let's get a drink," she said. "I need to drop these bags in the room and go to the pool for a little R&R."

We sat in the little bar from the day before and started talking about the trip.

"You know we got Tahiti, Fiji, Tonga, and Vanuatu that I can think of," said Jamal.

"We got Hawaii first, babe," replied Angelic. "I want to see Diamond Head and Waikiki Beach."

"Pearl Harbor," replied Jamal.

'The North Shore," I threw in, "Maui, the big island, Kauai, there's a lot to see. I think we're only there for one full day. The meaty part of the trip is Honolulu to Brisbane through the South Pacific."

"Man, there ain't enough time for all this," replied Jamal.

"That's why they call it a slice tour. You get a big slice in a short time, got to be quick. They hope you'll come back later and take more time, more tours, spend more money," I said, grinning at him.

Angelic sighed, "We'd better figure out what we want to see. I bet the excursions overlap one another totally. She went to her phone and pulled up the data. "Yeah, we need to make some decisions."

Jamal pulled out his phone and asked, "How much time are we going to have in the islands?"

"We start in Tahiti or French Polynesia and move west toward Brisbane. There are stops in Tonga, Fiji, and I don't recall where else. There are bunches of islands. It's one long chain from Tahiti to Brisbane," I replied.

"Are you just going to dive?" Angelic asked.

"I haven't decided," I replied. "I'd like to get out in the sun, see the beaches and some local sites, maybe surf a little or parasail. "

"You like that crazy stuff." She grinned. "I don't know if Jamal should be around you. But I'm game." She winked at me.

Jamal replied, "you ain't seen nothing yet." He slapped me on the shoulder and turned to Angelic. "Me and my boy get rolling, nothing gonna stop us."

She raised her eyebrows at us. "I'm going to the pool."

8

AFTERNOON OF THE 3RD DAY

We went with Angelic to the pool. All that speculating and salivating caused Jamal and me to think that we needed to rest up, why not poolside. Angelic was in a white thong, and she wasn't really all that shy, bouncing back and forth in the seat between Jamal and me. I had a spectacular view. The ocean was lovely, too!

We lay in the sun for a while, and I warned them about sunburn. They both said they could feel it. We moved into the shade and sat on an elevated deck with a view over the pool and out to sea.

I saw the old man with the hat and cane stroll by taking in the sights. There was also the heavyset woman with her browbeat husband. And then, there was the dark-haired woman, all the way across the pool. She had on a blue bikini that wasn't quite the same shade as the sky or the ocean, and it stood out. Couldn't miss her. Angelic saw me watching and smiled. The woman got up and headed for the pool. I watched her walk across the pool deck. She moved smoothly.

Angelic turned to Jamal and me. "You guys want something to drink?"

"Surprise us," said Jamal. Off she went, flouncing away!

It was several minutes later before Angelic returned. She had a couple of tall, cold beers for Jamal and me, and a fruity drink for herself.

"We thought you had gotten lost," said Jamal.

"There was a long line," she whispered almost wickedly.

Jamal raised his eyebrows, and Angelic punched him and grinned at me.

We sat in the shade and enjoyed the breeze and the drinks.

I asked them, "Are you looking forward to the formal dinner tonight?"

Jamal shrugged his shoulders.

Angelic, on the other hand, lit up when she said, "I have a killer dress."

I thought to myself, *if she thinks its killer, it must be fantastic. It's a shame I went last night. I guess I could dress up again and slide in long enough to check them out. It might be fun.*

We sat for the rest of the afternoon, taking in the sights, resting, enjoying the breeze, people watching. The pool had thinned out considerably by the time we broke for the day to get ready for dinner.

9

THE 2ND FORMAL DINNER

"I'd like to see you guys cleaned up. I think I'll slide back into the formal dinner and see if I can catch a seat."

Jamal grinned. "You're a glutton for punishment."

I looked at Jamal. "Maybe so, but I got nothing else to do but watch you squirm," I said, and turning to Angelic, continued with, "and watch you shine." She beamed back at me.

I got to the room and pulled my formal clothes out of the closet. Fortunately, I brought a second shirt, because I couldn't make up my mind what to wear, so I'd wear that. I dressed and headed to meet them.

They were coming out the door of their cabin as I walked up. Jamal had on a fitted three-piece that must have cost a fortune. It draped him like a glove. Angelic was breathtaking in an off the shoulder shiny red gown. She had on killer high heels and jewelry. They were a stunning couple.

I looked down at my own clothes and turned to them. "Good thing I'm not sitting with y'all. If anyone asks, just tell them you don't know me."

Angelic laughed. "You look good, and you look comfortable. Jamal just likes to put it on."

"He's not the only one," I replied. He grinned, and she gave me a playful look, like who, me?

We strolled to the dining room, and they turned for the captain's table. I made my way to the back and found a seat.

I sat next to an attractive middle-aged blonde in a silver dress. She smiled as I sat down. There were two other couples and a nervous-looking little man in an ill-fitting suit.

I wondered sometimes why I provided so many detailed clothing and related descriptions. I was an accountant. Details were my business. I couldn't turn them off!

The couples were the Jameses and the Skagens. The little man was Willard, he didn't say if it was his first name or his last. The blonde was Holly Smithson.

Everyone jumped in and started discussing how much fun they were having and how they were enjoying the ship and their cabins. The James's were interested in the on-shore excursions and had a long list planned for across the South Pacific. The Skagen's were interested in water sports, excursions and shopping.

One of Willard's few comments was that he wanted to see the Pearl Harbor Memorial. He looked like he might have been ex-military in some fashion. He didn't appear to be a warrior, not that I knew anything about it, but you never can tell.

Ms. Smithson was interested in sightseeing, shopping, and her tan. It was quite dark for her blonde hair and light blue eyes, which were the color of the sea we had been on for the past day. The silver dress had a plunging neckline and a high side slit that she didn't seem modest about. I guess what happens at sea, stays at sea. As far as I could see, without staring, she had a smooth, even tan all over. I couldn't help but wonder if she had tan lines. If not, it wouldn't be from the ship, maybe a private pool or a tanning bed of her own. The tan looked natural.

The dinner was as good as it had been the night before. We sat around afterward. We talked about the upcoming events and what everyone had planned.

The couples finally began to leave, and I noticed that Willard had slipped off without as much as a nod. I guess I had been paying more attention to Ms. Smithson than I realized.

Holly waved over one of the waiters and ordered us an after-dinner drink. It was some kind of dark sweet thing that she seemed to enjoy. I thought it was a little on the sticky side.

"So, this is your first solo cruise. How do you like it so far?" she asked.

"I've had a good time, met some interesting people." This brought another bright smile to her face. "And I think I will enjoy it enough to do it again someday."

She moved closer to me and leaned forward, revealing cleavage with no indication of a tan line.

"On the excursions the ship staff recommends you partner up with someone to help keep an eye on where you are, the time, and getting back to the ship. If you go ashore in Tahiti or Fiji, perhaps we might go together." She had turned while speaking and pressed her legs up against mine. She put her hand on my knee.

I took her hand in mine and stroked her fingers. I smiled at her. Her eyes were an even softer blue than they had been earlier.

"I'm flattered that you would ask. You are a beautiful woman," I said. Then I kissed her fingers. I heard her sigh and felt her press a little more firmly against my legs. She was still leaning forward. It was quite the view.

"I'm not very far removed from a bad situation, I don't

really think I'd be very good company right now. I was mostly planning to scuba and spend time in the water."

She took both my hands in hers and smiled. "I'm sorry to hear that. I actually believe you. I don't do this a lot, but I don't get turned down very often when I do."

"I'll probably regret it later, but not right now."

"We have another week, maybe you'll feel better," she said.

She had my attention, and I was glad the suit was black, so things weren't so obvious. "Could I get a number where I could reach you?"

"Absolutely, or we could talk some more if you like?"

"I think I'd better go now." I stood, and she quickly jumped to her feet, hugged me, and kissed me on the cheek. She smelled even better up close, and she felt great, soft but firm, with lots of curvature.

I left the dining room thinking how much of an idiot I was. I didn't know how I would respond to her and I wasn't ready for that right now.

10

THE WALK AFTER

I decided to walk the decks and take in the night. It was pleasantly dark, and there was deck lighting and noise from the pools and bars. During the stroll, I let the evening replay through my mind, forgetting all about Jamal and Angelic. Holly might have made an excellent fourth to the party. Remembering them, I suspected Jamal and Angelic were already back in their cabin, while I was out walking the deck alone. Stopping at the rail I looked out at sea. There were some distant lights, and I wished I had my scope. I thought about going to the room to see if I could catch the lights before they disappeared. I turned.

Jamal and Angelic were looking just as sharp as they had hours before. I wondered how they did that. Jamal threw up a hand.

"How you doing, wait, don't tell us, we saw you, we know, where did that fine young lady go?"

I looked at Angelic. "I didn't take her up on it." Angelic looked at me, thoughtfully.

"I don't know you that well, but it seems something is wrong, what gives?" she asked.

I stood there for a moment, exhaled, and smiled softly.

"I was married for five years, up until last year. We were professionals, independent careers, no kids yet, but starting to talk about it. She was coming home from the gym and was t-boned on a cross street. Died instantly but…. she was pregnant." I looked away.

Angelic touched my shoulder and then took me in her arms. Jamal stood behind with his hand on my back.

"That's terrible, we are so sorry, I didn't mean to pry," she said.

"That's okay. I was ready to get it out. The dinner tonight really brought it back. There was desire, but there was doubt. I don't know how I would have functioned. I didn't want to know badly enough to ruin Ms. Smithson's evening."

"Did you tell her?" asked Jamal.

"No, I just said I was coming off a bad experience, and she seemed to be okay with that."

"I'll say it was bad," he replied. "Let's grab a seat and have a drink, we don't have to talk about that, let's just take it easy."

I nodded and followed them around the deck.

11

LAST DAY TO HONOLULU

Waking the next morning, there was boat traffic. I went to the patio and saw another cruise ship off our starboard. It was the same cruise line. I heard a sound, and saw a motor launch that was traveling between the ships. Given how far at sea we were, Honolulu was not scheduled until evening, I wondered what was happening.

I grabbed the scope and drew a bead on the launch. There was a handful of crew, nothing that looked unusual, and no passengers. Maybe some shared information, or a cup of sugar, who knows.

I went back inside and cleaned up. Coming out, the other ship was gone. Couldn't have been too important.

There was a knock on the door. It was Jamal and Angelic.

"Let's do something different for breakfast, I'm on omelet overload," said Angelic.

"What are you thinking?"

"There is an open-air grill on the next deck, shish kebab, island-style, food from the tropics, let's check it out," said Jamal. He had his arms moving to and fro for open-air and was swaying when he said "island style." It sounded like it might be fun.

We headed for the deck, arrived, and grabbed a table under a straw roof. We sat down to grilled pineapple, fish, mango, kiwi, and papaya, on skewers.

"I could get used to this," mumbled Jamal while licking his lips and his fingers and waving for another one. Angelic was dainty and clean in her eating, but she wasn't letting any time pass wolfing it down. Neither was I.

"We need to do that again," I said as we finished and rose to leave.

WE WERE READY FOR A CHANGE. THIS WAS OUR FOURTH DAY on the ship. We were starting to get excited as we neared our first port.

"What are we going to see?" Jamal asked.

"You guys can decide. I lived here as a child, I've seen a lot of it. What do you think you might like, and I can tell you what I know? There are lots of things to see, or we could try and catch a chopper ride and look at it from the air. That's a good way to see a lot quickly and get an idea of something specific. There's not a lot of time."

"An overview might be good," offered Angelic.

"We gonna do a Magnum PI?" asked Jamal.

"We can, if you want," I replied.

He mimicked, holding a chopper stick in his hands and started dancing around the deck.

I suggested, "Let's start in Oahu and look around the island, then maybe Maui, or if we have enough time, perhaps the big island, see the volcanoes and the lava fields. "

"What can we see on Oahu?" asked Angelic.

"We can do Diamond Head and Hanauma Bay, Chinaman's hat, Waikiki Beach, Pearl City, the Arizona memorial, Hickam Field, the north shore, the Pali highway, valley of the temples, the Hawaiian culture center, both of the Magnum houses, acres of pineapple … what do you want to see?" I asked.

"All of it," she said with a wide smile.

Jamal chipped in, "I'm good with that!"

"Ok." I pulled out my phone to browse for island chopper services.

Turned out, there were several to choose from, most had itineraries that reflected what we wanted to see. That left us with price and access. Sometimes I can't stop being an accountant. Oahu was 112 miles around. Most of the trips were two or three hours, depending on the exact number of locations and the number of stops along the way.

"If we mostly nonstop around Oahu in the morning, can we get to the big island, and back in time to catch the ship?" asked Angelic.

"If we make arrangements, start early, take the shorter of the Oahu tours, we should be able to get to the Big Island, see a chunk of it and get back in time," I replied. "The ship docks later today in Honolulu, and we have all day tomorrow. We don't leave port until sometime early the following morning."

"That's a plan," noted Jamal.

I was excited and knew that they would enjoy the islands, particularly the beauty of the big island. Being there was like you were alone in the world or on another planet. I couldn't wait.

Angelic paused for a moment. "There was the strangest thing at our table at the formal dinner last night. There was this old guy with silver hair, and he had a party of six with him. There were three skinny runway models, all glammed out, and three burly guys that looked like steroid boys. I mean, they were bigger than Jamal. The old guy dominated the whole conversation, took every bit of the captain's time, and wouldn't speak to anyone else. The thugs just glared at people, and the women were in their own world. The captain seemed oblivious."

"Maybe he was afraid, or intimidated," I said.

Jamal rolled his eyes. "I don't know, but it was strange."

"That guy and his posse were at my table the night before, it was the same exact situation. Who do you suppose he is?" I asked.

"I couldn't really hear, we were too far away, but man, it was rude. I've seen a lot of arrogance in the corporate world, but that guy sets the bar. And those idiots with him, why would you have them along on a cruise? Nobody at the table seemed to know him," explained Jamal. "It was more like he wanted to draw attention to himself. It was weird."

"How did everyone else at the table react?" I asked.

"They ignored him, and after a few attempts to speak to the captain, they ignored him too, and the thugs and the women. We talked among ourselves. It was a nice group," replied Angelic. "We did meet another couple, Mike and Keno Williams. They were fun and fascinating. She's from Hawaii and is part Japanese and part Hawaiian. He's a contractor from St. Louis, where they live now. She wanted him to see her home. "

"Should we invite them along tomorrow?" I asked.

Angelic piped up, "They're going to see some of her family. She owns a salon and wants to visit a couple in the Waikiki area. He's tagging along. She is cute as can be. And he's not bad looking," she said, patting Jamal's arm, "not quite as muscular as the Jam, but close."

"The Jam," I said and laughed. "You call him the Jam."

Jamal made a face. "I call her Angel sometimes, and she repays me by calling me `The Jam.'"

I tried to stifle another laugh and almost choked. Jamal slapped me on the back and nearly knocked me over.

"I'm sorry, man, I didn't mean to laugh. You don't have to hit me so hard."

He looked at me stoically. "I wouldn't want you to choke." Then he grinned.

"This is Mike's first trip to the island and his first cruise as well," said Angelic. "Keno said she hadn't been home in almost ten years."

"One day won't be very long to visit," I noted.

"Yeah," agreed Angelic, "she wasn't thrilled with that, but they both want to see the South Pacific, especially Tahiti. I think she has family there as well."

"Was he from St Louis?" I asked.

"Yes, originally. He played football for the University of Missouri. Keno was a cheerleader. His family was in construction, and he went into their business after college," she replied.

"No pro ball?" I asked.

Jamal jumped in, "Blew up a knee in his senior year. He wanted to play for St. Louis but never got the chance. He was all-conference in his junior year. "

"So maybe he would have had a chance," I replied.

"Maybe," replied Jamal, more curtly than I would have expected.

I looked at him. His face fixed.

Angelic jumped in, "Jam was an all-conference wide receiver at the University of Georgia as a junior and a senior, but he didn't stick."

I looked at him, and asked, "What happened?"

Jamal paused. "I was drafted by a team that was six deep in receivers, two of them were all-pro, I had no chance. I went to the coaching staff before camp was half over and asked to be traded. They said no way. I just couldn't do it. By the end of camp, it didn't look like I was even going to make the scout team. I thought to myself, I don't need this. NFL has always stood for "not for long" anyway. I hung it up and went to work. My college team was tight. It was fun. It was a game. Pro football is just a business."

He paused again, and then asked me, "You play a sport?"

"I swam freestyle for the University of Tennessee."

He fixed me with a curious look, then said, "And?"

"And, I swam for four years, and then it was over."

"You didn't try to go pro?" he asked.

"There is no pro in swimming, only the Olympics and endorsements," I replied. "In pro ball, any pro ball, many are called, but few are chosen."

He laughed at me. Angelic smiled at both of us.

"You're just a couple of has-beens," she noted.

"How about a might-have-been and a never-was," I replied.

Jamal threw me a fist bump.

12

LAST NIGHT BEFORE HONOLULU

I suggested we get some exercise since we'd be sitting around all of the following day, and we'd been sitting for the last couple of days.

We went to the pool and swam laps. While we were drying off, Angelic turned to me and said, "I meant to tell you, when I was in the line getting our drinks yesterday, I ran into and talked to that cute little brunette with all the curves."

I looked at her blankly.

She said, "You know the one, you about fell out of your chair watching her walk by." I didn't respond.

"You know you did," she said. "Anyway, we were talking, and I mentioned being with my husband and a friend, and she described you. I asked her how she knew. She said she had seen you swimming laps. Anyway, her name is Gina. Sorry I didn't get the last name. We were interrupted, and she had to go. I was going to invite her over."

Jamal jumped in, "You should have followed up with the blonde. This whole trip ain't gonna be nothing but missed opportunities for you, brother."

I replied, "Jam on it, Jam," and he laughed.

I LET JAMAL TAKE US TO THE GYM, AND HE PUT ANGELIC AND me through one of his corporate workouts. Man, I didn't envy his clients. They ought to be fit or dead.

We rolled out of the gym and headed to the cabins to clean up. We decided to eat at one of the open-air grills and enjoy the late afternoon sun. I brought along my scope to check for Honolulu, other cruise ships, or water traffic we might see.

We had grilled fish and vegetables. That was one thing I could say for the cruise. The food had been excellent, no matter what you ordered, or which restaurant you ordered it from.

It started to get darker, and I could see light on the horizon. It looked like we were going to arrive as scheduled. We had our tour reservations for tomorrow, and we talked excitedly about the day.

While we were sitting there, the older gentleman with the cane strolled past. Jamal waved and asked him to come over and join us.

He sat down gingerly, noting that he was a little old and his joints got stiff quickly. He introduced himself as Tom Jones (seriously). We all looked at him with raised eyebrows. "I'm not Tom, yes-I have a very big, Jones, the singer," he said, "I'm just Tom Jones," and he winked.

Angelic pointed a finger at him. "Are you sure?" she asked.

"What's new pussy cat, whoa, whoa," he belted out, almost on key. "See, I told you. You're sure now, aren't you?"

Jamal and I doubled over laughing at Angelic, who was standing there with her mouth open and her finger still pointing. With that, Tom tipped his hat with his cane handle and strolled away.

13

———

TOURING HAWAII

We ate dinner that night in a different outdoor grill. Angelic texted Mike and Keno, and they joined us. I liked them immediately.

We talked about the next day's plans. Keno shared a lot about the islands and how much they had changed over the years she had been on the mainland. She was anxious to see the changes for herself.

Mike told stories about the construction business and some of his rowdy clients. Jamal jumped in and shared a few of his stories. I just listened, nodded, and laughed. It was a good evening, and I felt like I had made new friends and was comfortable in a group for the first time in a long time. I was still alone, but happy. Periodically, I looked around for the curvy brunette, Gina, I think Angelic had said. I even looked for Holly Smithson, the older blonde. But it's a big ship with a lot of people, and I didn't see either of them.

THE NEXT MORNING WE WERE JAMMED. GOT UP EARLY, LEFT the ship, and met our pilot and the chopper. We were scheduled to circle Oahu and then head for the big island. Depending on time, we'd see what we'd see.

The ship was harbored off the port of Honolulu, and we started west toward Pearl City and the military. The pilot took us low altitude in places, and we had great views.

As we approached the Arizona, the outline of the ship was visible in the water below the floating memorial. I told Jamal and Angelic that when I was a child, the bow chain and the very tip of the bow were still above the water. But the ship had settled in the years since and continued to sink. I added that there was still a scum of fuel oil on the water after all these years. They nodded solemnly and Jamal noted that the memorial was an impressive and intimidating sight.

From there, we flew up the west coast into pineapple fields, and development as far as you could see. We came around to the North Shore.

Jamal asked, "Dude, why the big waves?"

"It's a winter phenomenon, as the currents come down from the north. They produce the big waves the surfers crave."

"Do you surf?"

"Badly," I replied. "It's been a few years, but I still try, when there are waves, and I can get to them. There is nothing quite like it. You'd enjoy it."

"Do you think we could try it at one of the stops?" he asked.

"I saw surfing in one of the brochures, so yes, if you'd like, it would be fun." I motioned to Angelic and said, "You'd like it too."

"Can't I just watch from the beach and show off my thong?"

I raised my eyes and smiled. "I'm for that."

She smiled back.

Jamal jumped in, "You get out there with us and see what you can do!"

She laughed and tapped him on the arm. "If you say so, baby," she cooed and winked at us.

We circled to the east toward Chinaman's Hat. From there, we turned inland and crossed the Valley of the Temples and the Pali Highway. We sat down on an overlook that let us gaze across the island and out to sea. We walked to the rail overlooking the highway.

Jamal had an expensive Panama hat on his head. He put a hand up to secure it.

"Take the Pali test," I pressed him.

"What?" he asked.

I pointed to other people standing on the overlook who were throwing their caps out over the edge where the wind would rush up, catch the cap, and hurl it back on the overlook and beyond the point where the people were standing. Small boys were racing back and forth, flinging their caps as fast as they could and running again, trying to catch them as the wind returned them from below.

Jamal looked dubious. "This is an expensive hat," he said. "I'm not about to lose it!"

I reached in my pocket and pulled out a hundred dollar bill. "Try it. If your hat doesn't come back, this is yours. You have to catch it, though. I can't guarantee someone else won't run off with it."

Angelic was giving him the eye. "Well, come on, you big sissy."

Jamal walked up to the edge slowly and took off his hat. He stood there a second or two and pondered. Just when I thought he wasn't going to do it, he fired the hat over the edge and into the air. The Panama dropped from sight for a moment and then came whipping back over his head and landed several feet behind him. He ran back and grabbed it, examining it.

He looked up at us, and a big grin came over his face. "Can I do it again?" he asked gleefully.

Angelic waved at him, and he ran forward and sent the hat flying even further. The hat stayed gone a second or two longer this time, and just as his face began to stiffen, the hat came flying back over the top. He tracked back and caught it with one hand in a smooth, graceful motion. I could see him in that second gliding across the field, into the end zone, ball in hand. That was definitely the NFL's loss. He grinned broadly, in his element.

The pilot called to us, and we re-boarded the helicopter. We flew toward Diamond Head and Hanauma Bay. The view on the ground of those two is impressive, but from the air, it's almost unbelievable. You can see down into the extinct volcano and see the texture of the mountainside clearly. As we circled over Hanauma Bay, you could see where the side had blown out and allowed the sea to enter and extinguish the lava flow.

I told them, "When I was a kid, you could still snorkel in the bay. It was beautiful. As Hawaii got more tourists and more residents, the bay got trashed up, and the legislature prohibited any further activity. It's too bad, but that was probably the only way to protect and preserve the bay."

"Will we get to snorkel somewhere you think?" asked Jamal.

"Absolutely. I have to think Tahiti and Fiji, and some of the other stops are going to be fabulous. As you can see here on Oahu, the colors are so much more intense. The blues are bluer, the greens are greener, the pale colors are brighter, and there is richness in the color and the depth of field that you just don't get in the Caribbean or on the mainland. The Caribbean has a lot of colors, but they're softer."

. . .

THE PILOT PULLED THE CHOPPER UP FROM THE BAY AND looked back at us while giving the finger swirl. We were headed for the big island. Moments later, there was nothing but blue seas and blue skies as far as we could see.

The pilot came over the intercom, "We'll travel for about an hour before coming into Kona."

We clipped along, being lazy and watched the wind and sun on the water. The pilot handed us a set of binoculars, and I pulled out my telescope. We scrolled along the horizon. Jamal saw a large, white luxury cruiser off the starboard. He punched me and nodded to the boat.

"Isn't that our silver-haired friend and his bodyguards on the rear deck? I believe the ladies are on the front deck."

I drew the scope around and focused on the boat. It was sixty feet or more in length, white and silver with blue trim, and multiple decks, an expensive-looking luxury yacht. Sure enough, it was our guy and his entourage.

"What do you suppose he's doing?" asked Jamal.

"Touring, I guess, same as us."

"That's touring in style."

"Probably not a whole lot more than chartering a helicopter for a day," I replied.

"If the dude can travel like that, what's he doing on a cruise ship?"

"Looks like they're talking business with someone on the boat," I answered. I turned my scope to the front deck. "Looks like the ladies are sunbathing."

"Man, they're skinny. Not wearing much either," replied Jamal.

"Looks like sunglasses, to me."

Jamal turned and looked at me and then at Angelic, who was lying back in the seat. "Yeah, white ones."

I went on the intercom, "Could we fly around that yacht?"

The pilot nodded and changed course.

We looped around the ship. The men saw us and stood up shouting. The women saw us and waved. Jamal and I waved back.

The ship came on the radio and demanded we withdraw immediately.

The pilot responded in a friendly tone, "On our way, just admiring your ship. Have a nice day." He dipped the rotors and peeled away quickly.

The pilot came over the intercom, "Look back at the guy on the roof deck of the ship."

We did. He had some type of weapon on his shoulder.

"What was that?" I asked.

"Surface to air rocket, those guys are serious. Do you know them?"

"Not by name," I replied. "We've seen them on the cruise ship. What would they be doing out here?"

The pilot shook his head. "These waters are full of dealers, of all kinds, criminals, pirates. No way to know, and you don't want to."

"What do you suppose they were really doing?" asked Jamal.

"Who knows where evil goes," I said and shrugged my shoulders.

He grinned, and Angelic, who was watching us, laughed.

THE PILOT CAME OVER THE INTERCOM. "KONA IS ONLY A FEW minutes away. We'll do a quick run around the north shore to see the homes, stop in Hilo for late lunch, and then hit the south side for the lava fields, black sand beaches, and volcanoes."

Angelic perked up in her seat, and Jamal rubbed his hands together.

We circled Kona and flew north. In a few minutes, we stared at large tropical homes nestled up in bays, on points, and behind sea walls. There were large sea cruisers like we'd seen earlier, and seaplanes.

Jamal looked at me and asked, "I wonder who these people are? I mean it's beautiful but awfully remote, where do they work, do they even work?"

"Must be online, or by seaplane to a connector," I replied.

The island was beautiful, the houses sparse, but magnificent to look at.

"I'm starting to get hungry," said Angelic.

I nodded at her, as did Jamal.

I guess the pilot had been listening as well.

"We'll be in Hilo shortly and land for lunch. There's a nice grill right on the water just off the LZ."

We landed a few minutes later and were glad to get out and stretch our legs. There was a light breeze, the sun was warm, and the colors of the sky and sea so bright it nearly blinded us. The pilot waved us toward the grill.

"The quicker you eat, the more we can see of the island."

After a quick fresh fish and a cold adult beverage, we walked back to the chopper. The pilot was sitting and eating a sandwich. We laughed at him.

"No fresh fish?" Angelic asked.

He grinned while chewing. "Too expensive for me, PB&J is good!"

We lifted off and started for the lava fields. They were unbelievable. There had been eruptions the year before and widespread flow across the island. The lava trails ran through what had once been housing developments and meandered across the island like great big, black gnarly fingers. As we slipped beyond the lava, the black sand of the beaches came upon us. Angelic's eyes grew wide as she marveled at the vast, empty, windswept shore. We circled back for the volcanoes, and the pilot took us awfully close for an active volcano. Inside, the lava bubbled and glowed and churned in a frenzy. As we pulled back in the air and headed for the shore, the black sand seemed unrelated to the hot frenzied mass we had seen inside the volcano.

I looked at Angelic and Jamal and said, "Hard to believe that's the before," as I pointed to the volcano, and then said, "that's the after," as I pointed to the sand.

"I can see why few people live on this part of the island," noted Jamal, "just too dangerous. I remember seeing videos of some of the inhabitants running from the lava flows. You couldn't run fast enough!"

I nodded to him. "It's a beautiful beach to visit, but not a place to live, don't stay too long."

Angelic nodded.

We circled the southern portion of the island, and the pilot came over the intercom, "Are you ready to return to Oahu?"

Angelic came on the intercom, "Yes, but can we go back a different route where we might see some of the other islands?"

The pilot nodded. "It'll take us a little longer, but we should have time. I'll call out what we're crossing as we go."

The pilot skipped along the curve of the islands and called out each one as we crossed it. He noted the name, the primary activity on the island, and threw in a fun fact or two. It didn't seem long before we touched down in Oahu.

We thanked him and tipped him generously. He gave each of us a cap with a "Hang loose Hawaii" logo. I put the three of them in my bag to carry. Suddenly, quite weary, we started back to the ship.

WE WERE RIDING QUIETLY WHEN ANGELIC SPOKE, "How about a nice quiet outdoor dinner and an early evening?"

I looked at Jamal, raised my eyebrows, and then looked at Angelic. She took a playful swing at me. "It's not like that, I'm tired. You and Jam only got one thing on your tiny little minds."

Jamal huffed at her. "Ain't nothing tiny about my mind, or anything else, girl, and you know it's true!"

I think she might have blushed, and he and I burst out laughing at her.

"Well, at least you dream big," she replied as she smiled and batted her eyes at us.

"Do we want to clean up or just go sit, drink, and eat?" asked Jamal.

"I'm okay either way," I replied.

"Okay by me," Angelic responded.

We found a grill facing the sunset and took a table in the shade. We ordered three really tall cold beers and sat back.

"I don't know if I'm up to another eight days of this," murmured Angelic.

Jamal looked at her. "Girl, we're just getting started!"

She looked at me. "This is where his job gives him an advantage. I get tired from helping people all day."

"I help people all day too," he replied, looking hurt, but in a playful manner.

"It's not the same," she said, sighing. She looked exhausted.

"Let's just chill for a bit, finish this drink, get a bite to eat, and call it a night," I said, looking at Jamal. "I think she needs some rest, and it's not going to slow down." I elbowed him. "We got a lot to do yet!"

We sipped on our beers and watched the sun go down. We ordered a couple of seafood salads and some dessert. It was good.

Angelic looked like she was going to nod off.

I turned to Jamal. "See you guys in the morning?"

He nodded, and so did Angelic.

"I'm excited," she said. "I just need some rest right now."

I grinned at her. "Some days, we all do."

I left them and went back to the room. Showering I put on some clean clothes and went out on my patio, sat and watched the sea and the shore in the distance. I thought to myself, *I'll take a short stroll, and then go to bed.*

I walked across an outer deck, not paying much attention, just enjoying the softness of the air and the smell of the sea. The ship didn't visibly rock, but I could feel it in my feet and knees after a day of being onshore. It was nice, I adjusted quickly and comfortably. I might take a liking to this cruise ship thing.

Stopping in one of the outer bars I ordered a beer. Taking a sip I saw Holly Smithson across the room. She had on a white summer dress and was sitting on a stool. The dress was slit on the side and revealed a long expanse of tanned legs. I caught her eye, and she smiled, then looked a little wistful. In a moment, I saw why. A large man, taller than me, and broader in the shoulders but running toward fat, came back to her with a drink in his hand. He offered it to her while taking a long look up and down her figure. She turned toward him with a bright smile. I suddenly felt very alone as I watched their ritualistic mating dance begin.

14

THE DAY OF THE DEPARTURE

Awakening early the next morning I was reminded of something my mother told me as a child when we lived in Hawaii. "Red sky at night, sailors delight; red sky at morning, sailors take warning." The sky outside my cabin was blood red. The sea was still as a pond. We were no longer in port, but we weren't moving. The ship sat dead still.

I lay in bed for a few moments and there was still no movement. Getting up I went out on my patio. The sun was coming up, and the air was calm and silent. It was a little eerie. There were no other ships around and no activity in the water. I scanned the horizon with my scope and saw nothing.

The ship sat there for an hour, and we slowly began to move again. I thought maybe there was a maintenance issue or a crewman fell asleep at the wheel. Regardless of what it was, the ship continued to crawl along at a slower pace than we had been traveling. Going inside, I cleaned up, and got ready for breakfast.

I met Jamal and Angelic at the outdoor grill. Mike and Keno were sitting alongside them. We had more of the grilled fruit and eggs. As we finished, Angelic said to me, "We're going to take a class on Asian and Island cuisine this morning. Would you like to join us?"

I didn't think so. I looked at Jamal and Mike, who shrugged their shoulders. I didn't want to be rude, so I said, "I think I'll pass and get some exercise, but you guys have fun, and maybe I'll see you for lunch. You can fill me in on what you learned."

Angelic smiled. "I think the class lasts into the early afternoon, but I'll text you if we get out for lunch."

I didn't want to be the fifth wheel in their group. It was bad enough being the third leg with Jamal and Angelic. Leaving the group, I thought about the diving I wanted to do once we reached the South Pacific. I wondered when we'd get to Tahiti and Bora Bora. Jamal and, especially Angelic, would really enjoy both places.

Wandering the deck, I noticed again how slowly the ship was moving. I went back to my cabin and sat on the patio, in the shade. It was getting warmer the closer we got to the equator. Scanning the horizon with my scope I continued to be amazed at how little ocean activity or sea life was visible.

I dozed off for a time, and when I awoke, the ship was again sitting perfectly still in the water. I got up, moved over to the rail, and heard the PA engage.

"Good news! The ship is well ahead of schedule, and the captain has decided to drift for a few hours. Everyone relax and enjoy the facilities, and we will resume later this afternoon."

I didn't think much about it, but in the back of my mind, it didn't really make sense. Here we were, the first day out of Honolulu, headed for Tahiti, with about 2,750 miles to travel on a tight schedule, to begin with, and we were going to drift for a few hours.

Putting my shorts and shoes on I started for the gym.

When I got there it wasn't very busy, most everyone seemed to be on deck or at the pools. I was doing cardio when I noticed the silver-haired man and his entourage over in the heavy-weight area. They were all sweated up and maxing out the big bars—deadlifts, squats, presses, they were going at it. They were strong, no question.

Again, I noted how no one was around them, and I wondered if they created an atmosphere that didn't engage people or if they forcibly kept people away. It seemed odd for a group like that to be on a cruise, which, by definition, is a very crowded social activity.

Wrapping up my ride I decided against any strength training. I didn't want any issues with the goon squad. Slipping back into the locker room I tried the steam, sauna, and whirlpool. Then I showered. By that time I was hungry again. Something about being at sea, or the salt air, or being alone, was making me hungry. I wondered about the class and whether the others would be available.

Then the PA came on again.

"We have had a minor inconvenience and need to relocate a few passengers from this ship to our sister ship for a couple hours while we make repairs."

Repairs, move people, what's going on?

After getting dressed and tugging my bag over my shoulder, I made my way to the deck. Looking out over the rail I saw there were already several motor launches in the water. They were headed toward another ocean liner harbored across from us. I must've missed a few things while in the gym.

I heard Jamal say, "Yo, Dee, over here." He was waving at me. He and Angelic, Mike and Keno, were all standing in a line to board a launch.

"They took us from the class and led us here," Jamal said.

"What's going on?"

"The instructor didn't know for sure."

Mike and Keno nodded but didn't say anything or look too happy. Angelic was craning her head in every direction, trying to see what was going on.

"What do you suppose it is?" she said to me.

"I heard repairs, on the PA. Something mechanical, I guess."

"Why would we need to get off the ship?" asked Jamal.

"Maybe it has something to do with the weight, although they'd have to move a lot of us to make any difference. Maybe it's access to certain areas of the ship, "I replied.

"Yeah," said Keno. "It looks like they're just taking us at random."

Mike nodded. "There doesn't seem to be a strategy to it."

I slipped in line with them, and we worked our way slowly toward the loading area. There was lots of discussion about what could be going on. There were as many theories as there were people.

We'd been in line for several minutes. It was midday and fortunately we were under one of the canopies, as it was growing hotter by the second. Angelic saw a crewman come on deck and waved him down.

"Can you tell us what is happening?" she asked.

We all closed in around him. He looked at us briefly and tried to smile.

"It's just a little mechanical issue that shouldn't take long. The HVAC units on the starboard side staterooms have gone out. It's going to warm up rapidly if they don't get them fixed. Moving folks over to the other ship, distributing the weight, helps a bit and provides better access." He paused. "I really must be going," he stammered and hurried away.

"Why wouldn't they just move us around the ship if they wanted weight distribution?" asked Mike. "That doesn't make any sense, better access to the units I can see."

Jamal and Keno nodded.

I looked at Angelic.

She motioned us in close and whispered, "I'm not saying this is true, but it might be some medical thing and they don't want panic."

That made everyone in our group pay attention.

"What could it be?" asked Keno.

"Some type of virus, contamination by touch, or maybe airborne, hard to say," replied Angelic.

She went on, "I haven't noticed anyone looking sick or any unusual activity. I also haven't heard anyone complaining about the heat, although there is lots of sunburn."

We continued moving forward in line. As we reached the loading area, there were crewmen on each side helping passengers aboard the launch.

Angelic, not to be deterred, asked the crewman assisting us.

"What is happening?"

"Just a little maintenance, it helps to lighten the ship and create some workspace." He fixed her with a broad grin. "Not to worry, miss, it's nothing, probably an hour to get over to the other ship, an hour on board there, and an hour back. Think of it as a three-hour tour, to our sister ship. Have a drink, enjoy the view, and the chance to do something different that not many passengers get to do." He smiled again and assisted her onto the motor launch.

The PA boomed, "Welcome aboard the motor launch Eagle."

The crewman loaded the rest of us aft on the launch. As we were about filled to capacity and ready to disembark, the helmsman swung the boat around to the foredeck, and our favorite point of discussion, the silver-haired man and his entourage, were escorted onboard. They clustered together on the front of the launch a few feet from the nearest passengers. The women weren't with them.

We pulled away from the ship, and for the first few minutes, everyone was headed to the sea and sky, feeling the wind and the spray. It was fun. But, like most things, our attention span didn't last long, and people were soon playing on their phones and trying to stay in the shade.

We didn't move far or fast. I doubted we'd make it to the other ship in an hour. We weren't far apart, but none of the launches seemed to be moving. The offloading on the sister ship seemed to be taking a long time. There were two dozen or more of the motor launches on the water, with more being loaded.

The sun was high in the sky, and it was *hot*. The breeze flapped the flags high up on the two ships while the banner on our motor launch hung limp and still.

I pulled my telescope, at the risk of being nosy, and looked out to sea, then slowly around to the other motor launches and the sister ship.

We sat on the launch, and those passengers not in the shade, slowly baked. There was going to be a lot of sunburn this evening.

Jamal turned to me after sitting quietly for the first several minutes. "What do you think is going on?"

"Don't know, but I'd guess they don't do this very often and haven't practiced much. Everybody looks confused, or lost, or unconcerned."

"Looks like a cluster to me," said Mike. Angelique smiled and Keno giggled.

"That's his favorite expression," she squealed.

"I think he's right," responded Angelic. Jamal and I nodded in agreement.

We moved in a slow circle. Seventy-five minutes later, we

weren't halfway. Everyone in the sun had squirmed under the canopy, and we were packed tight. People were complaining loudly. The crew did not respond beyond saying, "Everybody be calm, we're moving as fast as we can."

People were getting thirsty and the crew handed out a few bottles of water. They were also complaining about needing to use the bathroom.

Angelic was getting testy as well. "I hate wasting my time, when it's not my choice," she complained.

Mike nodded at her. Jamal rubbed her shoulders. Keno and I looked at each other. I took another glance through the telescope and people were being slowly unloaded on the sister ship. So much for three hours, it looked like we might be out here a lot longer. It was beginning to feel like forever!

The PA came on again, "We have been advised there was a medical emergency in the offloading of a passenger, which is why we are sitting. If everyone can be patient for a few more minutes, we should get back underway."

15

THE WAVE

Another thirty minutes and we were halfway to the ship. We were at the outermost point of the circle of motor launches. I could see to the horizon in one direction with both ships and all the motor launches behind me. It was a vast, empty, open ocean. But then, I thought I saw some movement. I grabbed the telescope and drew down on the horizon. It took me a second to figure it out. What it was, was a giant wall of water. It was coming right at us. I rose and made my way to one of the crewmen and pointed to the wave, explained what I saw, and asked if he saw it, and what we should do.

He looked at me funny because he clearly didn't see the wave. He said, "Don't worry, it will never reach us. What you are describing is a "rogue wave." They occur in nature, random large waves that ripple across otherwise calm seas."

I looked at him. I looked at the wave. "It's heading this way."

"It'll divert, don't worry," he said and waved me back toward my seat.

I looked at him as I moved to my group and my seat. He

turned on a handset and started to talk. He looked back in the direction I had shown him, a frown across his face.

When I got back to my seat I had my group lean in close. "I'd get in my seat and strap in tight. I think there's a chance it might get bumpy or wavy soon."

They looked at me, uncertain and doubtful. "Just trust me," I said. Angelic and Jamal looked at one another and then at me and then buckled up. Mike and Keno looked at them and then did the same.

"I'm probably just overreacting, but give it a minute, humor me!"

Several minutes passed and I saw an opening in the crowd. I pulled out the scope and looked again. I could see the wave clearly now, heading toward us. I motioned to Jamal and then Mike and showed it to each of them. Their eyes got big.

"People are going to see it in a few minutes without the aid of a scope, better get ready."

"Maybe it will swerve," said Mike.

"I hope so," I replied and Jamal nodded. He had placed his hand on Angelic's shoulder and Mike had taken Keno's hand.

Another couple minutes passed. Some of the people on the outer edge of the boat noticed the wave and murmured amongst themselves about it. The news passed quickly through the motor launch. In another minute everyone was staring at the oncoming wave.

I turned quickly at the sound.

The PA crackled, "Everyone please take a seat whether you are in the sun or not. We may have a little wave turbulence in a couple of minutes. It won't last long, a big up and down, like a rollercoaster at an amusement park, a thrill ride. Get strapped in and get a firm grip on your personal belongings. It'll be over soon."

I noticed that the crewman cinched up his life jacket. We all had them on but loosened them as we had gotten hot while we sat in the sun.

Everyone was milling about and the PA crackled again, "Please get in your seats, strap in, and make sure your life jackets are secure. The wave will be here in a minute."

The crewman was watching the wave over his shoulder and maneuvering the launch to try and glide up the crest and down the backside. If he timed the wave properly, the whole thing would feel like a thrill ride. But if not, did you ever see *The Perfect Storm?* I did!

The boat started to rise and I sensed the collective intake of breath from everyone on board. We started smoothly and just as it seemed like we might cross the wave as planned, it lurched to the right and slung the launch in a hard pivot.

Out of the corner of my eye, I saw a couple of boys, thrill-seekers, who stood up and held on to the canopy poles. I guessed they were trying to maximize the ride, searching for a little extra adrenalin rush.

When the boat lurched hard, as the wave shifted, all three of them were slung into the sea. I lost sight for a moment and then saw all three bob to the surface, their brightly colored life preservers glowing against the blue water. One of the crewmen screamed into the radio and the other came across the PA, "Please sit down and hold on."

The boat continued to skid across the wave, pushed further from the two cruise ships.

I looked at the people around me. There were a lot of fearful eyes and firm, set faces. This wasn't like any thrill ride we'd been on before.

The launch was caught in the bow of the wave, neither rising nor falling. It was light enough to be pushed along and not plunged under the wave. Given the circumstances, that was a good thing. We would've been swamped if the wave broke around us.

The helmsman tried to make adjustments to climb over the wave. He got little purchase at the angle we sat. The launch was pushed further and further away from the cruise ships. The boys in the life jackets were left far behind.

Angelic looked over at me. "What's going to happen?"

Around us, people were shouting, screaming, and thrashing in their seats.

"Stay calm," I said, "the helmsman seems to be keeping us in place. We won't get hurt if we sit in the bow of the wave. At some point, it will shift again, like when we started climbing the face. We could be shot out to safety, or we could be swamped. No way to know. If we start to swamp, you'll want to get out of those straps as quickly as you can. It'll be total chaos. If it flips, you'll be flung from the boat or trapped underwater. You'll have to get free from the straps and back to the surface. I'll take my chances jumping clear if it comes to it!"

The boat turned and the wave moved, as it spit the launch out the side of the wave tube. It looked like we would glide free and the wave would move on, but then it broke over the stern, and flooded the rear quarter of the launch. The water washed quickly across the deck and overboard.

Just like that, we were out of it. The thrill ride was over.

I LOOKED BACK AT THE CREWMEN AND THEY WERE SOAKED, but hanging onto the stern. All the rear passengers seemed to be in place. But then I noticed the engine had gone quiet.

The PA crackled, "Wasn't that something! Everybody okay? A little wet perhaps, but what a story you'll have to tell."

I looked to the horizon. I couldn't see the cruise ships. I couldn't even see them with the scope.

Jamal asked, "What do you think happens now?"

I shook my head. "I suppose we motor back to the ship. I don't know how far that wave pushed us but we're out of sight."

Mike said, "Do you suppose they can track us?"

"I would think these launches have transponders or some type of signal tracking."

People were milling around now, moving back into the shade and out of the sun. There was some mumbling about getting back to the ship and about the three boys that went over the side.

Angelic and Keno were surveying the crowd.

"There are some burned people here and with no water there's going to be dehydration, too!" Angelic noted.

"How long to get back?" asked Keno.

"No ideas, since we can't even see the ship," I noted, looking back at the crewmen. One was on the radio and scanning the horizon.

The PA crackled again, "Folks, we are having a little issue with the engine, the wave that broke on us appears to have flooded the engine compartment. We are working on it, and we have contacted the ship. They estimate that we are only a couple of miles from them and they will have another launch, with food and water and towels, here for us shortly. They are going to pick up our jumpers on the way." There was a small cheer from the crowd. "We sincerely apologize and assure you that this will be over shortly. You'll be back on the ship soon, having dinner and laughing about it."

"We're not laughing right now!" yelled a large woman from the crowd.

She was right. There were a lot of sunburned and dehydrated people, with no restrooms and no more patience.

I looked around the launch carefully for the first time. We were busy talking and watching the process while we were waiting in the boarding line. I hadn't paid any attention to who was on the launch with us.

I spoke to my group, "It's seven miles to the horizon, that's when things drop out of sight. We're at least that far away. It might take a few minutes." They nodded or looked at me blankly.

I scanned the crowd. I saw Holly Smithson and the big man, from the bar, next to her. They were back near the helmsman and had gotten soaked in the wave. They looked like drowned rats. Her hair was in straggles down her face and her clothes dripping. His comb-over was out of place, and he was severely sunburned.

I knew the silver-haired man and his entourage were on board. They hadn't made any noise or drawn attention to themselves. They sat quietly in the front of the launch. Not far from them was the old guy with the cane, Tom Jones, still looking dapper and whistling to himself, unconcerned. Near him were the heavyset lady, the one who had called out, from the scuba class at the pool, and her skinny husband. She looked angry. He looked depressed.

It was not a happy crowd. Time passed. More time passed. The crewmen tried to fire the engine, but it didn't respond. We appeared to be drifting with the current.

It had grown late in the afternoon, and a strange quiet had fallen over the crowd. It was as if everyone sensed that something wasn't quite right.

THEN I HEARD IT, A FAINT RUMBLE OF THUNDER IN THE distance. The sky was blue, and the sea was calm. But there was something out there. Now it was a matter of time.

The sky darkened. A cloudbank had formed and blocked

out the sun. People were able to spread out on the decks again and move back to their seats.

The PA came on, "The ship says they are headed our way. It shouldn't be long now."

Jamal looked at me and asked, "You believe them?"

"I hope so."

"It does look like it could storm," threw out Mike as he looked to the horizon.

"It could, or it could pass us by, or dissipate. Hopefully the launch will be here soon," I answered.

The sky grew darker, and a small breeze picked up. The waves formed a light chop. We drifted faster. People moved back under the canopies and closer together. Everyone buckled in and adjusted their life vests.

"I don't think they're going to get here," said Angelic.

Keno nodded. "Something is not right."

"We don't know what kind of storm it is, if any," I said. "It could be wind, it could be light rain, maybe a few waves, we don't know."

"But we do know that it's going to be dark soon," replied Mike.

I looked at him and nodded. I pulled my scope and scanned the horizon again. I couldn't see anything but an approaching storm.

I held the scope across my leg. "The storm is coming. I can see it on the horizon." We were in the back third of the launch, well under the canopy, in as good a place as any. If we got swamped, we should get out. If we got flipped, it might be tougher.

People were milling around now. Nothing came from the PA. The crewmen were watching the sky.

Lightning crackled, and after a long pause, the thunder rumbled. The storm was here.

16
———

THE STORM

Darkness fell, and the waves grew stronger. We were pushed across the water at an increasing speed. The motor launch began to rock, and the waves slashed across the gunwales. People began to scream and to clutch frantically at their life vests and their neighbors. The wind whipped and spun the launch, the thunder rumbled, and the lightning crashed. Then the rains came, in heavy massive sheets. The boat slowly climbed the face of a wave, whipped wildly at the crest, and rolled rapidly over the backside, down into the pit of the wave trough. It rose and fell, pushed along in a frenzy of motion. The lightning flashed on and off like a wall switch gone mad.

People's faces were illuminated for a few moments, and then went dark. Each time it occurred, I realized there were fewer passengers remaining aboard. The boat spun, tipped, got swamped, and recovered. The waves crashed on the deck and receded away, taking more captives every time the lightning returned.

Seconds felt like hours, and hours felt like days. On

through the night, and into the next morning, we were tossed and sprayed, windblown and bounced across the water like a rubber ball. Hour after hour, we got pushed along, twelve hours in the storm. It felt like forever!

We drifted through the late morning, until noon when the sky cleared, and the wind dropped, and the sea was once again calm and blue, and half the boat's passengers were gone.

THERE WERE, ORIGINALLY, APPROXIMATELY FIFTY OF US ON board, plus the two crewmen. We lost three on the rogue wave. Now there were nineteen of us left. We lost thirty people in the sea, including both crewmen.

I looked around the boat. The back couple of rows on the stern were empty. They must have taken a lot of direct wave hits. The crewmen and the back three rows of passengers were gone. I saw Holly Smithson and the big man from the bar in the next row. I saw the heavyset woman and her skinny husband still arguing between themselves. I saw a handful of others that I did not know. All of them were wet and disheveled. Our group looked the same. Jamal's Panama was missing, but Mike still had his ball cap low over his eyes. Angelic and Keno looked wet and tired.

I turned to the bow of the launch. There were several empty rows. That section must also have taken a lot of waves. I saw the silver-haired man and this three bodyguards. Standing next to them, still in his Panama hat and with his cane in hand, stood Tom Jones. And then I got a surprise.

Standing alone to the other side of the bow was the dark-haired girl Angelic had spoken to at the bar. I caught her eyes. She didn't smile, just kind of nodded, but her eyes sparkled. I nodded and turned to my group.

I pulled out the scope and looked over Jamal's shoulder,

where I saw nothing but open water. There wasn't a cloud in the sky. With less than half the passengers remaining, we had plenty of shade. People didn't move much or talk. I think we were all in shock. Sure, there was relief as well. We were all glad to be alive, but what was our future?

"You think that transponder or signal will work from here?" Mike asked.

"I don't know, I guess it depends on what tracking range they thought they might need."

"How far do you think we traveled in the storm?" asked Jamal.

I shook my head at him. "No way to know."

Angelic stood up. "I'm going to check with everyone and see if they're okay," she said.

"I'll help you," chimed in Keno.

The ladies worked their way around the boat, greeting the passengers and inquiring about each of them. I saw people smile and chat for a moment. No one seemed to be hurt, just wet, and tired. With the sun out and a light breeze rustling under the canopy, we were all drying out.

We drifted for another hour, and the sun was high in the sky. There was no sign of any ship, and we hadn't seen or heard any planes. I hoped that we might be in one of the shipping lanes, or there might be air traffic that could spot us. I scanned the horizon again with my scope and saw nothing but a vast expanse of open water.

Not long after we got out of the storm, people started making calls on their cell phones. No one was having any luck, as we were apparently in a low coverage or dead zone. Soon they were complaining about their dead or dying phones.

"Jamal, is there anyone you could text that might contact the cruise line for us?"

He nodded and quickly went to work. The texts appeared to go. No response came back to him.

Another hour passed, and it was the middle of the afternoon. The ladies had finished up their rounds and were back with us.

The boat drifted steadily. I pulled out the scope and checked the horizon in the direction we were headed. I looked for a long time. Jamal finally tapped me on the shoulder.

"What's up?" A quizzical look was on his face.

"I think there might be something out there."

Jamal arched his eyebrows. Mike was watching us. I waved them both closer.

"I see something on the horizon. We appear to be drifting toward it. I can't tell what it is yet."

People were beginning to mill around the boat. I kept the scope out of sight.

Forty-five minutes later, I snuck another peek. This time I could tell. It was an island. It looked to be good sized. If the current held up, we were headed toward it. It was still a long way.

Over the next hour, we continued to drift in that direction. The island grew larger in the scope. I could actually see the outline and the bluffs. It was a tall island, a good size landmass. Jamal and Mike had looked around the boat for paddles or anything that we might steer with. They had found nothing. We kept drifting toward the island.

In another hour, the other passengers caught on to the sight of the coast. There was shouting and applause.

"Oh, thank you, thank you, Lord, for delivering us to your salvation!" shouted out the heavyset woman with the skinny husband. Nobody else said anything.

The three bodyguards were firmly stationed at the front

of the boat watching the island while the silver-haired man sat in the shade. They murmured among themselves.

We drifted closer. I saw the beach, the shoreline, and cliffs. There was a natural harbor straight in front of us.

We were almost there.

17

LAND HO

Another hour and the island loomed before us. Everyone was excited and jabbering. The current continued to push us toward the harbor. I hoped that it would hold the course. There was a reef and a channel to the inner water of the harbor. If the current didn't pull us through, we could have problems. It might smash us into the reef, or bounce us out of the current, or back to sea.

I spoke to Jamal and Mike, "If we don't clear the reef, we'll need to swim for it. I'll take my chances on an island, compared to floating around on a non-motorized boat with no sails, food, or water. The canopies are keeping us in the shade. Otherwise, we'd be having more problems with dehydration."

"What about the others?" asked Mike.

Concern lined their faces. I asked, "When you were looking for paddles, did you see an anchor or rope or any kind of line that might be attached to it?"

Jamal shook his head and said, "I think there's a reel of line, and an anchor is probably at the end of it, back by the engine compartment."

"If the three of us and a couple of the others got in the water, with the line, we might direct the boat through the reef and pull it to shore. Otherwise, I doubt that all of these people could swim from the reef to the beach. We'll lose more to drowning," I replied.

Angelic spoke, "Are you guys strong enough to pull us in?"

"If we get everyone in the water that we can, lighten the boat as much as possible, and don't get a cross-current, we might make it."

"The cross-current could really be difficult," noted Mike.

I nodded and said to him and the others, "If we bounce off the reef and get caught in a cross-current, it could be almost impossible. If the boat gets damaged or smashed and capsizes, we could be stranded. The currents are steady right now. We should be able to navigate the boat. Everyone is in a life vest, if we could get them inside the reef, they would float to shore eventually. It would be nice to save the boat. It might be helpful if we can get it to shore. I'd rather not abandon it if we can keep from it."

"We should try to get everyone organized," said Keno.

They looked at me. "Okay, I'll give it a shot."

I stood on one of the seats and got above the group.

"Hey everybody," I called and waved my arms. "There appears to be a reef around the harbor ahead. If the current doesn't lead us to the opening, we may bounce off the reef. If so, we need to consider abandoning ship and swimming for the shore. We could try to navigate the boat through the channel with the line from the anchor. As many strong swimmers as we have could go overboard, lighten the load, and direct the boat onto the beach. It would be nice to keep the boat intact, if possible. We may need it again." I stood there for a minute and waited.

The heavyset woman from the pool called out, "That sounds like a good plan, and I second the motion!"

There was a group of young guys, four of them, standing close together, one of them called out, "We swim, and we can pull."

That would be at least seven of us in the water. That would be a good start. I looked to the silver-haired man and his group, still standing in the bow, arms crossed, shoulder to shoulder, saying nothing. That's a lot of weight, those guys had to be 200 plus pounds apiece, that's another 800 pounds of weight in the water and pulling, that could make a difference.

The skinny husband and the big guy from the bar were standing next to the young guys who had volunteered. They spoke up, "We'll help."

That was two more and another four hundred pounds in the water and off the boat. We might just make it.

I didn't wait any longer. "Okay, let's get the anchor line and see if we can rig it."

We scrambled for the next few minutes trying to get something improvised. Basically, it looked like we were going to have to get in the water, drop the line, collect it as it came out, and then try to direct the boat through the opening in the reef. Not an easy task as we'd end up pulling the boat in stern first. We needed some way to get the line free from the anchor and attached to the bow of the boat.

We were drifting slower and appeared to be heading directly for the channel.

I organized teams to get in the water. We'd drop the anchor and then try to redirect as necessary. We'd try to pull the line manually and reattach to the bow.

Our backup plan was to go over the sides and try to direct the boat, bow first, through the channel.

I slid the scope out, from the back of the boat, as everyone watched the island grow closer, and followed the reef around. We were still headed straight for the channel.

As we got closer, all the volunteers lined up on each side of the boat to jump in the water and push toward the channel. The silver-haired man and his bodyguards had not agreed to help and had moved to the mid-section of the boat, deeper in the shade.

We glided with the current, drifting a little to the right, which didn't hurt us, and then just as we came up to the channel opening, the current swung us back hard to the left, and the boat bounced off the reef with a thud. I looked back to the sound and didn't see any apparent damage.

Then we bounced back into the middle of the channel and continued to drift toward the beach. There was a collective sigh of relief and a cheer from the guys lining the side rails. We drifted for a few seconds and began to slow and finally stopped. I guessed this was where we got in and pushed.

We sat for another minute, and the breeze picked up slightly, and we began to move toward the shore. The water didn't look deep, but that's always deceiving. I nodded at Jamal and Mike.

"Let's see if we can push it into the shore."

I looked over at the other side to the young guys and nodded. Seven of us went over the sides, three on one, four on the other.

The water was about shoulder height. We got traction in the sand and started pushing, gaining speed as we progressed. As the water got shallower, we picked up the pace, and as it continued to drop, we lifted the boat and tried to leverage it as far ashore as possible. We hit the sand with a thud and kept pushing for several more feet. We were firmly ashore. We leaned against the boat and slipped down into the water to rest.

Up above, I could hear Angelic, Keno, and most of the others shouting and clapping. The Eagle had landed.

PART II

THE 2ND HOUR

18

THE ISLAND

The first person off the boat and onto the island, without getting in a drop of water, was the silver-haired man. He stepped ashore like a conquering hero, or an early explorer discovering the new world. He had an arrogance that radiated from him, as if he owned the island and expected servants to run forth with palm fronds and flowers. His bodyguards were the next three off the boat. They stepped onto the sand and formed a protective circle around him.

Everyone else disembarked. Some stood motionless, getting their land legs back. Others ran down the beach screaming and waving their arms. I sat in the water with Mike and Jamal.

Finally, we stood up, trudged to shore, and sat in the sand.

"We're going to need those canopies for shade," I said to them.

"It's going to get hot here quick," replied Mike. Jamal nodded his agreement.

We rose from the sand and walked over to the group. Angelic and Keno pointed excitedly at the beach and the peaks that were inland. Standing on the shore, it looked like a big island.

There were calls from down the beach, from the young guys that had jumped into the water with us.

"Hey, down here, we found it," they yelled.

We jogged down the beach where, over a dune, stood the four young guys in a small stream of water. It appeared from inland, ran across the beach, and into the ocean. They were in the stream, splashing and throwing water in the air. Two of them jumped in as we crested the dune.

"Freshwater!" one of them shouted.

Jamal turned, looked at me and spoke. "Unbelievable!"

"Lucky," said Mike.

"Grateful," was the best I could add.

We walked over as the rest of the group made its way to the stream.

You could see relief in everyone's face as they made their way to the water's edge and drank.

It had been almost twenty-four hours since we left the ship. Was it really no longer than that? We had been sunburned, stolen by a rogue wave, smashed by a storm, and left adrift for hours with no communication. We'd been busy!

People cupped water in their hands or stuck their faces in the stream. There was a fast current, which indicated there should be a steady flow of water for us. It was clear and cold.

I motioned to Jamal and Mike.

"Let's follow it inland and see what's there."

Angelic saw us and called out, "Shouldn't we search the island to see if there are people here?"

"We thought we'd follow the stream a little way and see if it leads to anything," replied Jamal.

I noted the silver-haired man and his crew watching us closely. Mike seemed to notice it too.

He spoke. "I'll stay here, call out or come and get me if you need anything."

Jamal and I started up the banks of the stream.

Several of the younger men were already wandering further down the beach exploring. Most of the group was sitting by the water, just resting and drinking. I waved to Angelic.

"Why don't we see if we can move the group back closer to the tree line and some shade?"

She grinned. "Keno and I were just about to suggest that. We'll take care of it."

Jamal and I were twenty yards into the trees and underbrush when we came upon a large pool. It was a natural watering hole. It would have great access to the beach and provide plenty of water. We couldn't have been any more fortunate.

"Let's follow it out the backside and see if we can locate the source," I said to Jamal.

He nodded, and we moved on. There was a smaller stream feeding in that looked like it came down from the highlands above, probably the source. The water pooled in the pond, and when it overflowed, ran down to the beach where we first discovered it.

We followed the stream another hundred yards as it climbed gradually up the slope of the cliff, as the island rose out of the sea. We broke into a clearing and looked back at the beach. We weren't that high up the cliff face, but we could see the open ocean and the shoreline. Our group was not visible through the trees. It wasn't a jungle, but it was thick tropical foliage. There were lots of palm trees and underbrush.

Hopefully, we'd be able to exist on fish, coconuts, and freshwater until somebody found us. We could explore the island and see if there might be a town, a village, a settlement, a fisherman, anything that would help us. The island looked too big to be uninhabited.

"We could find people this afternoon, and it would all be over," I said to Jamal.

"That would be great," he replied. "It's going to get hot, and if we get very far off the beach, it's going to get muggy and buggy."

"Yeah, summer is coming to this part of the world."

He nodded toward the beach, and said, "You want to start back, tell them what we found?"

19

GETTING ACQUAINTED

We walked back to the beach and found the group huddled under the trees. Mike, Keno, and Angelic were standing at the rear of the group. The silver-haired man was standing in front and began speaking as we walked up.

"My name is Antoine Debaucher, and I am CEO and COB of Global Unlimited Network Systems formerly United Amalgamated Logistics. These gentlemen," he pointed to the three men who were standing beside him, "are my assistants. I manage several thousand employees and multiple locations around the world. I could suggest several things for us to do, and make what I'm sure will be a short stay more pleasant. I will be happy to manage this, and my assistants can execute the details while we await our rescue."

I looked at Mike, he shook his head.

The heavyset woman, and the man from the bar, both nodded and shouted, "That would be great."

The silver-haired man smiled.

My group looked at me. "Let's see what he suggests. "

I wasn't interested in him appointing himself king, but I wanted to hear his ideas.

"I think we should organize a search party, now that we have water, and try to determine if there is anyone else on the island. Some of the rest of the group can gather up coconuts, and a third group can see about catching some fish. I think we might take shelter right along the tree line so that we can see anyone approaching, and they can see us," he concluded.

None of it sounded like bad ideas. I nodded to the group. "Let's give it a shot."

Antoine looked at the group for another moment. "Who has a cell phone?"

Everyone in the group appeared to have one and pulled them out. "Does anyone have any reception?" he asked.

Most shook their heads, and several called out, "Mine's dead or no signal." It appeared that over half of the phones were already out of commission. Antoine nodded and put his phone away. I noticed that while he pulled his phone out of his pocket, he never checked the screen.

Earlier that morning, while we had been drifting, I noticed several people had tried to make calls. I didn't see anyone succeed, and no one mentioned getting a call to go through. I felt like we were too far out of the shipping lanes for consistent coverage or too remote for a steady signal. That made me think we had drifted a long way out of cruise ship traffic.

This was a sizeable island with water and a beautiful beach, so maybe casual sailors and fishermen frequented it. Hopefully we'd see someone, or somebody would sail into the harbor and spot us.

My thoughts were brought back to the present as the four young guys stepped forward, and one of them said, "We'll catch fish," to Antoine.

Antoine's face was frozen for just a second, then he smiled and nodded. He turned to the older husband and wife, the blonde and the big man, and the balance of the group, other than us.

"Let's take a look at some shelter," he said as he grouped them and prepared to walk the beach.

He looked at our group and said, "Would you see about gathering some coconuts?" Then he turned back and led the others away.

Jamal looked at me and then broke into the old Harry Nielson song, "Put the lime in the coconut, and call the doctor, wake him up."

"Say doctor, doctor," chipped in Mike.

"Call me in the morning," chimed in Angelic and Keno.

As I started inland for the trees, I sang out, "I said doctor, is there nothing I can take to relieve this belly ache, oh doctor."

They followed me along while they laughed and continued to sing.

COCONUTS ARE FROM A SPECIFIC TYPE OF PALM, MEANING that not all palms have coconuts. Our good fortune continued as we shortly discovered a grove of the trees. There were several with coconuts hanging and a large quantity of the fruit lying on the ground. The ladies started rounding them up.

I stopped everyone for a second to say, "The ones on the ground are older or riper, watch to see how soft or mushy the shell is. If you pick it up and tap on it, you should get a hollow sound if it's ripe. Gather up about two dozen. We'll use those for the meat. Jamal, Mike, and I will try to get a few out of the trees for some coconut water."

They looked at me like I was from outer space, except Keno, who grinned.

Angelic put her hands on her hips. "I get my produce at

the grocery. How do you know all this?" then she smiled at the others and pointed at me, "you lived in Hawaii as a kid!"

"My mother took me shopping and showed me around the island, so I'd know what was going on. I guess she thought it might be helpful someday. Looks like it is," I said, and grinned back at all of them.

"How are we going to get these open?" asked Angelic.

Keno jumped in, "Without a knife or a machete, we'll have to split them on the rocks," the others looked at her, "I'm half Hawaiian, we know these things," she smiled and laughed.

We split up, and the ladies started gathering the fruit on the ground.

Jamal looked at me and said, "You think we're climbing those trees?"

"Well, since we don't have a monkey or a picker, we're going to have to if we want fresh, young coconuts." Jamal and Mike looked skeptical.

"Okay," I said. "Look for a shorter tree that's growing at an angle."

We searched the area and examined several trees. I finally found one that looked climbable.

"I haven't done this since I was a kid," I said as I studied the tree and prepared to make my climb. "Try to catch me if I fall." They both shrugged. "Okay, I'll just try to hit the sand." I started up the tree.

Move your hands, move your feet, try to use the angle of the tree. Edge your way up and hold on. Climbing is not that difficult. It's not that far up, and the bark is scaly enough to hold on. The angle helps with not having to use so much body strength to maintain a position. I had done this before, but still, I was slow. I was halfway when Jamal and Mike started clapping. I looked down at them and considered giving the middle finger universal sign of support, but decided it might be wiser to hold on. Angelic and Keno had wandered over and were watching too.

"I'm going to sell tickets next time," I called out.

"Well worth it, if you fall," replied Jamal. Angelic punched him in the shoulder.

Keno stepped closer, waved at me, and called, "You can drop them to me when you're ready."

"You got a lot of faith in him," Mike said to her.

"He knows what he's doing," replied Keno. Mike stepped closer to help her.

I was near the top. My hands were a little scuffed, but I was holding on tight. I eased into position and thought to myself, *I should have brought the diving knife.* I hadn't wanted to take it out in front of anyone. I did have a small pocket knife, and I hoped that I'd be able to initiate a cut and then work some of the riper fruit off the tree. It might take a while.

That's what happened. I held on with one hand, worked out the knife, initiated a couple of cuts, and waggled the fruit back and forth until it gave way. I dropped a cluster to Keno and Mike. There were five of them.

I worked my way down the tree. It's actually harder than climbing up. When I was ten feet from the ground, I jumped, and rolled in the sand when I landed. I brushed myself off as Keno and Mike handed out the fruit for each of us to carry.

We walked back to the beach. Out in the sea, the young guys were laughing, splashing, and slinging water on each other. I didn't see how they could catch any fish.

Antoine and the other group were on the beach in the shade of a line of palms. We started toward them carrying the fruit.

Keno was watching the tree line for sharp rocks, or a boulder, or wedge that we might use to split the fruit. So far, she hadn't seen anything.

As we approached the group, I noticed there was a tide

line several feet further back in the trees. Antoine was closer to the beach on a relatively flat area that did look good for shelter, as long as the tide didn't come in that far.

I suspected what I saw was a storm line, and the daily tide, in and out, was down the beach where you could see the debris. Still, I didn't think I'd set up a shelter in that spot.

Antoine was talking when we approached with the fruit. He smiled when he saw us. His three assistants took the fruit and piled it under the trees.

"This seems like an excellent spot to build. We have a good vantage point, we can see and be seen. The ground's flat, materials are readily available nearby, and close to the source for food and water."

I really couldn't argue with him other than the storm line. I raised a hand, and he nodded.

"What about the tide line back there?" I pointed to the trees inland of us.

"That's a random occurrence," he said with a quick glance then turned back to the crowd.

"Like the rogue wave that washed us away."

He frowned at me and continued, "We'll break into pairs and start salvaging material to produce a little shelter."

"What about searching the island?" I asked.

"We want to get food, water, and shelter first. There's obviously no one nearby," he replied, looking over to his assistants and then at me. I felt them, rather than saw them, look at me.

A couple of his assistants pulled four or five-inch blade knives from their pockets. The kind of knife that has a clip, and you can hook it to your pants. I saw one thumb push the blade, while I heard several others click out, and into position. They started to work on the coconuts.

Antoine pointed from one group to another as he said,

"You look for long sticks or small saplings, you look for vines, and you look for palm fronds, as many as you can find."

He looked out to the beach where the young men were clowning around in the water. He motioned to one of the assistants who went over to him. I could not hear what he whispered in the assistant's ear, who then turned and strode down to the beach.

Antoine looked at us and pointed to the cache of fruit under the tree. "That was good," he noted while smiling rather unenthusiastically. "Can you gather about that many more?" he said as he turned away.

We took a couple of steps inland and stopped to watch the scene on the beach.

The assistant had gathered the young men around him and appeared to be quizzing them. One of the group stepped forward and followed behind as the assistant turned back toward the beach and Antoine. The young man did not look happy. The others were standing in the water, watching their leader walk away. They were still and silent, all signs of a good time gone.

The two men walked up the beach toward Antoine, who waited patiently in the shade of the trees.

"Just what are you gentlemen doing?" he asked, in a rather icy tone.

"We were fishing," said the young man, looking directly at Antoine. There was a moment of silence as they looked at one another, eye to eye. Even from several yards away, I could see Antoine's gaze bore in on the young man, "the executive look." I'd seen it before in business. Antoine bored into the young man who finally looked down at the sand.

"And how were you doing?" purred Antoine.

"Not very well." The young man did not look up. "We have no rods, no line, no nets. The fish are very fast."

"And you were making lots of noise," noted Antoine, "scaring them."

"We don't even have a knife on us. "

"How did you propose to catch the fish?"

"We don't really have a plan."

"I suggest you get one," replied Antoine. "Perhaps you could fabricate some netting."

The young man gave him a blank stare.

"Weave a net and cast it upon the waters, you know, like a fisherman."

"Okay."

"Your time would be better spent developing a methodology for catching food rather than playing in the water, like small children," hissed Antoine.

The young man looked crestfallen but with an underlying tone of annoyance.

Antoine must have left the HR functions to one of his other managers.

I motioned to my group, and we started to move. The young man walked back to his friends. Antoine's gaze drifted around the area, as if he were surveying the work and progress of his minions.

WE FOUND ANOTHER GROUP OF TREES NOT FAR FROM THE shelter site and began to gather fruit. We watched the young men walk from the beach, inland, then stop and pull vines from the ground and surrounding underbrush. We heard a clamor, and the stick and frond group was approaching Antoine, who was sitting in the shade, surveying his domain. His assistants stood idly nearby. The group dropped what they had gathered and were sent back for more. The assistants sorted the items in a pile as they were brought in. We brought the second load of fruit and placed it under the trees and were again sent back for more. On this trip, we passed the young men sitting in the sand and attempting to string together some of the vines. They did not appear to know how to braid or weave. We spent the rest of the afternoon gathering fruit. By the time we stopped, there was a significant pile of food and materials.

Antoine gathered everyone together and suggested that we take a break and get some water at the pool Jamal and I located. His assistants cut up some of the coconut and passed it out.

We sat by the pool and watched the ocean through the trees. Angelic and Keno looked tired. Mike stared at the sky. Jamal seemed subdued. I looked around.

Antoine stared at me, gaze fixed on the gym bag slung over my shoulder. I'd barely thought about its presence until then. He motioned to one of his assistants with a gesture at my bag.

I got up to get some water and another piece of coconut. One of the assistants, who handed out the fruit, gave me a hard look. I ignored him and stooped to get some water. When I stood, Antoine was beside me with another of the assistants at his shoulder.

"What's in the bag?" Antoine pointed to my shoulder.

I looked at him, and the assistant, who was standing arms crossed, to one side.

"Dirty gym clothes," I replied and grinned at him. "Want to take a look?" I put a hand on the strap.

Antoine turned in disgust. Jamal wandered up beside me and stared at Antoine while he spoke.

"No, I don't want to see that."

I stepped away with Jamal, as Antoine turned to his assistant and whispered something.

I knew Antoine would want to see what was in the bag and would take it away from me. We'd seen a pile of cell phones that he or his assistants must have confiscated from the others. He had not yet asked us for our phones. I suspected I'd better do something if I wanted to keep the bag and not have it forcibly taken from me.

Jamal sat next to Angelic and started talking. Mike and Keno were also huddled close together. I looked over at Gina, the dark-haired girl. I hadn't seen her during the day as she had been working with the material-gathering group. She was in profile and looking out to sea.

I slipped around the back of the pool and stood for a moment, watching everyone relax. Antoine was preoccupied talking to his assistants. Everyone else was resting, talking, or dozing. *Maybe I could scout the island, try to find some useful information,* I thought to myself. *Perhaps there was somebody on the other side, and we could get out of there.* I didn't like the way this was going. I needed to buy some time. I looked back at the group and saw Gina looking at me. I smiled at her, and her features brightened. I nodded. My decision made, I slipped back into the undergrowth and started inland on the island.

I climbed the slope of the cliff for a few minutes and saw a ledge that ran out and around the island. Taking that path I paralleled the water, thirty feet above the beach. It was late afternoon, and I was tired. There wasn't a trail, but by staying close to the bluff line, I managed to avoid much of the underbrush. Still in sight of the ocean and the beach, I reached the tip of the island in less than an hour. Pulling out the scope, and looking back up the beach, I could see Antoine and the others down by the water. Antoine was talking to a couple of his assistants and pointing in my direction.

Putting the scope away and walking to the edge of the bluff line, I saw around the tip of the island. Below me, the tide came in and pounded on the rocks. I looked for a way down to the beach. The far side of the island looked like bluff line as far as I could see. It was forty feet to the beach below. A few yards around the point of the island, I saw a stream that led to a waterfall. It tumbled over the rock cliff and pooled on a split of ground about fifteen feet below me and twenty-five feet above the beach. The breeze kicked spray in my face, and I realized this was the windward side of the island. That made sense as we landed on what would be the leeward side, in the harbor. There's not likely to be anything on this side, with the bluff line, and the wind.

It was going to be dark soon, the tide was coming in, and I knew it wasn't a good time to try to traverse the island. There was water and coconuts within reach. I could sleep on the bluff and keep an eye out for Antoine or his men. Scouting the island would come in the morning.

20

HOME AWAY FROM HOME

As it grew darker, I surveyed the bluff and found a sandy spot where I could sleep. Scooping some of the sand I shaped the space so that my head and shoulders were higher than my back and legs. I faced the harbor, so there was a view of the sunlight as it faded across the water and melted into the sky. Lying down on the customized sand bed I listened to the sound of the surf and watched the moon and stars come out. It was peaceful and comfortable enough. The sound of the surf grew louder, as I was about to nod off, and I realized what was happening. Crawling out of my makeshift bed I walked to the edge of the bluff that rounded to the windward side. The tide was in and not more than twenty feet below me. When I first arrived at the spot and looked, it was forty feet to the beach below. That was low tide. Now it's high tide. If the windward side was all bluff line, I'd have to be careful about picking my times to go down to the beach. Or, I'd have to stay on the bluff line and fight the vegetation.

Awake now, with something to think about, I crawled

back into the sand bed and got comfortable. I picked up my shoulder bag, and under the bright night sky, went through its contents.

It was my gym bag, and yes, I did have dirty clothes in it. I had just come from the gym when we were boarded on the motor launch. But, there were a number of other things.

Pulling out the telescope I took one last look around. The sea was still flowing, the stars twinkling, a light breeze blowing, but the roar of the surf was subsiding.

I laid the scope down and pulled out the gym shorts, tee-shirt, socks, and shoes I wore when I worked out. It would be nice to have a second set of clothes if we were here for a few days. I laid them aside. I pulled out the three caps from the helicopter ride. I'd need to give Jamal his as he'd lost his Panama during the storm. I'd give Angelic hers too. I dug deeper.

There was a small flashlight with the scope. I hadn't thought about it until I saw the light clipped to the inner liner of the main pocket of the bag. Wrapped up in plastic at the bottom of the pocket was the scuba knife I'd just bought. It could be a lifesaver. The only other item in the main pocket was the toilet kit. I pulled that out and opened it. There was a small pair of scissors, a penknife, fingernail clippers, razor, shaving cream, toothbrush, toothpaste, dental floss, shampoo, mouthwash, sunscreen, a comb, and a small brush. All of it was travel size, but it was all new, purchased for the cruise. All that could be handy.

The bag had two smaller outer pockets, and I thought to check them. Unzipping the first one, it was empty. I flipped the bag over and unzipped the second. Sticking my hand inside, I felt something and peered into the bag pocket.

I'd gone to an outdoor cookout on Radnor Lake the month before and forgotten to unload a couple of things. I pulled out a short-bladed ceramic paring knife in a sheath, a one-strike firelighter, and an empty water bottle. Just call me Batman. None of them weighed much, and I hadn't realized they were still in the bag.

Looking at the items, it wasn't that I minded sharing with the group. It was being told by someone to do it. All they had to do was ask, not take. Most people are charitable when you get right down to it. In a group, though, they can get greedy. I'd have to see how long we were stranded here, and what I could do to help out.

With those thoughts in mind, I lay back and looked up at the stars. The breeze was still light, bringing with it the smell of the ocean. Palm leaves swayed overhead and I heard the sea as the night deepened. It wasn't bad. Like the guy on the motor launch said, think of it as an adventure.

I woke to the early morning light and the sound of the new tide. I recalled it was twelve and a half hours between high tides, and they moved about an hour each day, so they revolved across time.

I was thirsty and walked to the stream and got water. There were coconuts, and I grabbed a couple for breakfast. Crawling back in the sand pit I slept for a few more hours.

When I woke again, the ocean was only a faint murmur. Low tide would be about six and a quarter hours from the high tide. I got up and looked over the bluff. What a surprise. The tide was forty yards or more out on the beach. There was plenty of room to walk. It would be a good time to skirt the island quickly.

I filled the water bottle and cut one of the coconuts with the dive knife. It was handy for a knife its size. The paring knife or my pocket knife would have been difficult to use. I ate quickly and looked for a way down to the shore.

If I doubled back slightly on the leeward side, I could

make my way from the bluff line to the beach. I slipped the bag over my shoulder and took a quick look with the scope up the beach and toward the boat. I didn't see anything in either direction. With a general sense of caution, I walked down to the beach and quickly around to the windward side.

21

NICE DAY FOR A STROLL

Once I got windward, I relaxed. There was a stiff breeze, and the sand was rockier and debris-filled. But the sand was firm enough to walk on, and I made good time. Checking my watch I set out. I soon saw water on the horizon, so the island wasn't going to go on forever. I knew I'd feel better when the far end of the island was in sight.

Looking up to the point, to the overlook, where I had slept the night before, I saw the waterfall below it. That'd make a great shower. I was going to have to figure out how to get down there.

There were shells, crustaceans, sea life, sea weed, all of it marine as far as I could tell. Had there been driftwood or trash, perhaps there was life on this island aside from us, but there was none. I walked on trying to keep a steady pace as I surveyed the beauty of the island.

The breeze brought the strong smell of water and salt from the ocean. It whipped my hair and fluttered my shirt. I stopped to unbutton it as my pace, and the climbing sun, warmed me.

The air was full of light, in so many different tones, that

when they all came together, it glowed in a warm golden aura. The color was rich and thick around me. There were intense light blues of the sky, deep blues of the sea beyond, greens of the water around me, of the undergrowth and the bluff line, and the mountains beyond. That's all you could call them, was mountains. It wasn't so obvious from the leeward side. They sat back and away, crowding the windward side. But they were tall, at least from down on the beach. There were brilliant reds and yellows scattered among the foliage on the sides of the mountains. Everything was clean and bright like it was brand new, and we were the only people in the world. On the bluff that morning, the ground had been dry. It felt firm under my feet. After the grey of the storm and the slash of the wind, it felt good to be alive.

I maintained a quick pace for three-quarters of an hour, then stopped, caught my breath, and moved closer to the bluff line for shade. I sipped slowly on the water wanting to conserve it. Perhaps I'd discover more, perhaps not. I glanced out to the sea and noted that the tide was further in than it had been when I started. The clock was ticking, and the tides turning on me. I walked closer to the tide line, pulled out my scope, and looked. There it was, the tip of the island. I guesstimated it would take me another half hour to reach it. That would mean about eighty minutes of brisk walking. The distance on the windward side would be in the neighborhood of four miles.

With my destination in sight, I slowed my pace and took my time. It was late morning, and I stopped and cut up the coconut. I liked coconut, but I was growing tired of it. I'd have to determine the best way to fish. I still had a half bottle of water.

Reaching the tip of the island I rounded the corner to the leeward side. What a view, the island running back to my left, the open ocean before me, midway between, the reef and the change of color in the water, the beach, the sand, the sun shining directly on me. It was hot. I thought about it and realized we were moving into the South Pacific summer. Winter in the northern hemisphere is summer in the southern. Late October would be spring in this part of the world.

I had sunscreen in my bag, but I was sweating so heavily there was no reason to apply it. It wouldn't last. Through my scope, I spotted the beach and boat. The distance couldn't be more than two miles. I figured it would take me forty minutes to get back to that spot. Based on that calculation, I was approximately a mile below the group on the bluff where I had slept, plus the two miles it would take to get back, which made the island approximately four miles on the windward side, and three miles on the leeward side. Not a big island, but plenty of room. Why was nobody here? I'd think recreational sailors might seek it out unless the island was just too far off the charts.

Walking down the beach, I kept an eye on movement and an ear on sound. I didn't see or hear anything in the first twenty minutes. When I felt close enough, I searched for a way to get inland to approach the group on my own terms.

I wandered about twenty yards inland and found an area with palms and undergrowth. I could move quickly along through here until I saw or heard someone.

WALKING ANOTHER TEN MINUTES I ESTIMATED THEIR CAMP to be no more than a half-mile away. My progress through the undergrowth had been slower than when I was on the beach.

I knew you could hear a loud voice up to 600 feet, which would be just over a tenth of a mile. Moving closer, I'd walk a little way, stop and listen, walk again. The process was killing my time, but it allowed me to recover from the hike. I crossed another stream and stopped to fill my water bottle. That raised a question. I had my bag and my water bottle, and all the other stuff. I didn't want those things seized.

Moving deeper inland I eased along in the underbrush. I could walk all the way back to the bluff, where I camped, and leave my stuff, or stash it somewhere and recover it later. The question would be how I would be received. If Antoine asked me what I had done with the bag, what would I say? What if they tried to restrain me from leaving? Having already decided I'd rather be alone on the island, I didn't mind helping them out, but I didn't want to be mandated.

Finding an observation point, I pulled out the scope and saw the boat on the beach directly in front of me. I could hear the water upstream of the pool, where we had all gathered.

I pressed on and crossed the stream that feeds the pool. Continuing for a hundred yards I saw a recess on the cliff face. It was just big enough for my bag and looked dry and secure. I set the bag in the recess and covered it with some downed palm fronds.

Hiking back across the stream I went a hundred yards beyond. At that point, I turned and walked down to the beach and then along the sand and tree line toward the group.

It wasn't but a minute and I heard voices. I couldn't tell what they were saying, but I could hear other sounds, like movement and work.

Arriving at the flat spot Antoine had picked, I could see the group constructing huts.

Jamal saw me first. He ran over and grabbed my shoulder. "You okay?"

"I'm good, went for a walk and got lost. I've been all the way around the island."

Antoine saw us, as did the others. Everyone stopped what they were doing.

I grinned at them. "I went for a walk, got turned around, and ended up circling the island."

"I saw you through the trees, coming up from the far end of the island," said Gina, pointing in the direction from which I had come, as if to confirm my story.

Antoine stood with hands-on-hips. His three stooges eased in towards him. He and his boys were dry and alert while everyone else looked damp and tired.

"We're attempting to build some shelter," said Antoine. "Our young men are casting their nets," he continued, pointing down to the water. "We're going to grow weary of water and coconut."

"Well, I'm afraid there isn't much else on the island. There were no piers or docks. In fact, the far side of the island is all bluff line and windward."

"Are you content then?" he asked.

I nodded.

"Good, let's get back to work. I'm told you harvested the young coconuts. The milk in them was quite tasty. Perhaps you could gather some more," he said.

"Happy to!"

"William will go with you," he said, nodding to one of his assistants.

Jamal looked at me and grinned. He spoke softly, "You didn't miss nothing."

As William approached, Jamal turned and rejoined his workgroup, which looked to be Mike and several of the other men.

"Let's go, Bill," I called out.

"It's William to you," he snarled.

I turned to go.

"Wait," he called out.

I stopped, and he walked up beside me. "Now, we can go."

I searched for several minutes, wandering through the palms and getting a feel for where everyone was and what they were doing.

"Stop wasting time," William said.

Without stopping, I replied, "I'm looking for the right tree. It takes a little time."

He grumbled.

Ahead, I spotted a tree with a large coconut cluster. It was a little taller than the one from the day before, but the slope was right.

"This one will work."

"What are you going to do?" he asked, in a suspicious tone.

"I'm going to climb the tree and throw the coconuts down to you, so don't let them hit you."

He scowled.

"You got a knife, Billy?"

He stepped right into my face. "My name is William, are we going to have a problem with that?"

"Not if you have a knife, William."

"What for?"

"It's easier if you can cut the stalk. Otherwise, you have to waggle the fruit back and forth until it breaks, waste a lot of time," I answered.

He nodded, reached in his pocket, and handed me a switch action knife with a five-inch blade.

"Very nice."

"I want it back."

"No worries," I said and I pocketed the knife and started up the tree.

He watched from the ground, shaking his head.

It took me a few minutes to get to the top. Once near the

fruit, I wrapped my legs securely and fished out his knife. It opened and locked with a reassuring click. I began cutting the stalks and waggling the fruit. The knife was sharp, and it made quick work.

As the coconuts turned loose, I dropped them to William. After just a few, he hollered at me, "Slow down, I can't catch them and stack them."

Fortunately for me, the angle was comfortable enough that I could hold on, but just the same, I thought I'd have a little fun with him.

"You better hurry, I can't hang up here all day." To my surprise, he moved a little faster.

I cut a dozen, put the knife away, and made my way down. William was walking the fruit back to the group. By the time I got down, he had carried most of it away. I dismounted the tree and tossed him the knife.

"Thanks, that made it a lot easier."

He nodded and started back to the group with the last of the fruit.

Over his shoulder, he called out, "Come on, let's go!"

Under my breath, I said, sure thing Willie!

22

—————

GROUP DYNAMICS

We spent the rest of the afternoon gathering fruit. I'd locate a tree, climb, cut the fruit, throw it down to William, and dismount. Then we'd repeat.

After we'd collected a couple dozen coconuts, I said to him, "How many do we need? They'll spoil if we cut too many."

"Antoine says he wants three dozen, we get three dozen."

"Why so many?"

"Doesn't matter."

I looked at him for a second. "You always do what Antoine tells you? You don't ask why?"

"Get back to work," he said sharply.

I guess that was my answer.

We gathered another dozen coconuts and walked back to the camp. Everyone was clustered by the pool, sipping water and resting. I sat in the sand next to Mike and Jamal. Angelic and Keno were cutting coconut and handing it out to the others. I noticed there were a half dozen gallon water jugs scattered among the group, which made drinking easier.

"Oh, Great Food Gatherer," said Jamal and gave me a fist bump. Mike nodded.

"Where did the jugs come from?" I said, pointing to the plastic containers.

Jamal replied, "Antoine's assistants found them in a storage bin on the motor launch. By the way, Antoine said no one should go around the boat so that they don't get hurt. His assistants searched it and have been guarding it since then."

"What could they have found?" I asked. "I didn't see much of anything."

"We didn't see them bring anything ashore, but they've stayed close since they searched it," replied Mike.

We sat in silence for a moment.

"What have you guys been up to otherwise?" I asked.

Mike pulled his ball cap off and wiped his forehead. "We have been building huts, you know, like Gilligan's Island." He laughed. "They're about halfway out of the ground. First big puff of wind will blow them away."

"You not offer any construction advice?"

"Antoine seems to have an idea of what he is doing. He must have a construction background, although there's not much you can do with sticks, vines, and palm fronds."

I looked at them both. Exhaustion lined their eyes.

Jamal saw me looking. "Antoine gives the instructions, his assistants manage it, and the rest of us do the work. It's getting old. I'm getting tired of it. We need to get off this rock soon."

"How is everyone taking it?"

"There's some tension," replied Mike. "Jamal and I are doing most of the shelter work. The others are older and do what they can. Gina has been really helpful and energetic. Tom Jones doesn't have much energy, but he keeps us entertained."

"How're the young guys doing with the fishing?"

They both shook their heads. "They haven't caught anything," replied Jamal.

"Their nets keep breaking," added Mike.

"Antoine isn't thrilled with them," followed up Jamal.

Through the trees, I saw down to the beach where the young guys were casting nets. I looked up at the sun, it was late afternoon. "It's not a good time for fishing, is it?" I asked.

Mike grinned, as did Jamal. "No," said Mike.

"Antoine has them so jacked up, they keep going at it," added Jamal.

"I think they're getting pretty frustrated," said Mike.

We sat and rested.

The group of young men came up from the beach carrying their nets, but otherwise empty-handed. They slumped by the pool and got water to drink. They looked tired, weary, and frustrated. I nodded to them, and they looked at me and glazed out.

"I see you weren't successful," Antoine noted. He stood above them as he approached with his arms crossed. Two of his assistants flanked his sides.

The young man who had spoken to him earlier jumped to his feet. "We're tired of this bullshit! We're not fishermen. Catch the damn fish yourself!" he spat out. His fists were clenching and unclenching at his sides.

"You're not doing your part. That is unacceptable," Antoine said as he leaned over the young man. It looked to me like Antoine was trying to provoke him. It worked.

The young man sputtered and stepped up to Antoine with his fists raised. One of the assistants stepped in and drove a fist into the boy's stomach, sending him stumbling back. He doubled up and staggered. Two of the other boys jumped to their feet and were at once face-to-face with the other two assistants.

Mike and Jamal were both leaning forward.

"Gentlemen," cooed Antoine, "violence is not necessary, we all just need to do our part so that we all prosper."

"And just what are you and these goons doing to help?" the young man on the ground gasped out as he tried to catch his breath.

Antoine took a step closer to the young man and tented his fingers while looking down at him. "We are planning and managing the operation, a necessary and integral function."

"Bullshit! You think you're some kind of king," he said and flung sand in Antoine's direction.

The closest assistant to Antoine took a quick step forward and kicked the boy in the chest, hurling him back into the sand. The largest of the other young men shoved the assistant nearest to him to try and go to his friend. He caught a hard right under the chin, from the assistant he shoved, that knocked him to his knees.

The entire group was watching and drawing closer.

Antoine raised his hands above his head. "Stop!" he called. "This is not necessary. We all must work together, do our part, and get along. Everyone must give their best effort so that we all succeed. Don't you want off this island? This is the only way! I will lead you from this place."

Nobody spoke. The two young men on the ground were recovering their composure while their friends watched in silence.

Since the huts weren't finished, we slept on the beach near the tree line. People mostly slept in their workgroups, separated by a few feet of sand. Jamal, Mike, Angelic, Keno, and I were in one area. The rest of the hut crew was together a few feet away. Antoine and his guys were further up in the trees. The group of young men was several feet away and down the beach. The boat lay at rest in the sand beyond them.

Daylight came early, as did the night. We were all tired, and it only took a few minutes for people to start drifting off to sleep. We customized the sand to make a mattress, more like a foxhole, to fit our individual shapes.

It was beautiful when you lay down, like we were only a few feet from the stars and the water. We had the sounds of the surf, and the smell of the ocean and jungle, to lull us to sleep.

I nodded off quickly and slept for several hours. I woke and rolled to my side to the reflective face of my watch. It was a little after one am and very quiet. The tide was out as even the water wasn't making any sound. I could feel something in the air. I lay still and silent and listened to the breathing of the group of people along the shore. I didn't think anyone was awake. I rolled to my back and stretched my neck while looking toward Antoine's group. I could see no movement and heard only a slight collective breath.

I rolled back toward the beach and the ocean. That's when I caught a glimpse of motion and heard, rather than saw, movement. The group of young guys was slowly easing out of their beds.

I didn't move. From my vantage point, I could see two of them start down the beach toward the boat, while the other two moved in my direction. The two coming toward me might not have been able to catch fish, but they were stealthy. They slipped past my group and continued toward Antoine and his assistants. I tilted my head and shifted my eyes without moving my body to follow their trail.

I had no idea what they could be doing, although I was beginning to sense a plan. There was no way for them to overpower the assistants, so they must want something else. What could that be? Food and water, portable water in jugs?

I saw the food and water stacked in a pile, a few feet from Antoine's group, as we had prepared for bed. I guessed Antoine felt so comfortable that no one was standing watch over the food or the boat.

The supplies were to the side of the sleeping men. The young guys eased around and approached the food and water. One of them held his arms out, and the other stacked a large pile of coconuts into them. He had long arms, and I guessed they must have taken about half of what was there. The fully loaded young man started toward the boat. The other young man grabbed the six water jugs, three in each hand, and made his way back to the boat.

I watched them glide across the sand. I rolled my head back to check Antoine and his group. They were all sleeping.

I watched the two young guys with the provisions reach the boat, which the other two had apparently been working on, sliding it toward the water. They handed over the supplies, and all four began pushing.

I rolled lightly out of the sand and walked slowly toward them. I waved my arms above my head in a slow, signaling motion. When I saw one of them see me, I stopped.

I held my arms still, upright, palms out. Then I took a few steps toward them. No one made a sound.

As I got closer to them, the leader stopped pushing and turned to meet me. I stopped a few feet from the group and spoke softly.

"Midnight cruise?" I smiled.

They did not respond.

"Look, guys, that's not much food or water. You have no way to navigate the launch. You'll most likely die out there."

The leader finally spoke, "It's better than dying here!"

"Here, you got plenty of food, water, and shelter. Someone will find us. If you get out of the lagoon and through the reef, you'll most likely drift in circles and die of dehydration."

"We'll find another island," said the leader.

"You know, I walked this island, and I saw nothing but water. There's nothing close by. There are four of you, and there are six jugs of water and some coconuts. That won't last long," I said.

"We're not staying here and putting up with that asshole," replied the leader. "All that bitching about fish, I don't even like fish."

"And those thugs," whispered one of the others softly, "I think they broke my ribs."

"We'll take our chances," replied the leader.

I made one last attempt, "Look, he may be over the top—"

I was interrupted by one of the others, "He's a self-absorbed, narcissistic moron with a God complex."

"Maybe so," I replied, "but much of what he's had us do —gathering food and water, building shelter— needed to be done. You just have to humor him for a few days. I think he's generally harmless."

"Can't do it, we're out of here," the leader said as he resumed pushing. "We have our phones. We'll make contact with the authorities and tell them you are out here. We'll be okay."

"Alright, good luck," I said. "What are your names, so I can notify authorities when we are rescued?"

"It doesn't matter," replied the leader. "You're not going to be rescued. You're the ones who are going to die."

They began pushing the boat again.

I turned and walked back to my sand bed. I settled in and watched them as they maneuvered the boat into the water. There was low tide, so they were able to push far into the lagoon and point toward the opening in the reef. It took them a couple tries. When I heard the launch bang off the reef, I knew we were going to have trouble.

One of Antoine's men jumped up and shouted, "They're stealing the boat!" He ran toward the beach. The others stumbled and started after him. Antoine merely stood up, crossed his arms, and watched. As his assistants got near the beach, yelling and waving their arms, everyone in the group woke up and stared.

Jamal tapped me on the shoulder. I pointed toward the reef, where the young men were trying frantically to get the launch realigned to the channel so they could escape.

"No shit," he murmured.

The thugs, as the boy leader had called them, were running into the water, and I suddenly heard a sound ring out. Several of the women in the group gasped.

One of Antoine's men had a gun.

23

THE MORNING AFTER

I thought I heard a bullet strike the launch. At that moment, the young guys caught the current in the channel and slipped the boat through the reef and into the open sea. They were pushing and swimming hard. The current caught the launch a few feet beyond the opening and pulled them out to sea. The thugs stopped, and I heard one more shot. I thought I heard an impact, a hollow sound like a thump, but I couldn't be sure.

Antoine called from his spot under the trees, "Everyone go back to bed, there's nothing to see here, it's over."

The thugs made their way back ashore and walked to where Antoine stood. Everyone settled back into the sand. There was muttering, a sense of shock and awe in the air, an invisible barrier that had been crossed. People were upset, confused, and afraid.

"Go to sleep, we'll talk about this in the morning," called out Antoine.

The rest of the night passed uneventfully, in a fitful sleep.

As the sun came up, people milled about and chatted

among themselves. Jamal, Mike, Angelic, Keno, and I were huddled together, talking quietly.

"Why do you think they did it?" asked Angelic.

"They didn't like Antoine and his thugs," replied Keno.

"Can't really blame them," added Mike.

Jamal looked at me with questioning eyes.

"I think Keno's right. They were tired of being humiliated, and they saw themselves as young, strong, smart, and invincible," I replied.

"Despite Antoine's thugs kicking the shit out of them," threw in Jamal.

"Despite that," I confirmed.

"Will they make it?" asked Angelic.

"I doubt it, they didn't have much water or food or any way to navigate or propel the launch. Unless they are very lucky, they'll drift around in circles and die. "

I didn't think it wise to share that I had watched them launch. Now that we knew Antoine's guys could be truly dangerous, the less someone knew or said about the theft and escape, the less they might get hurt.

Antoine let the groups talk for a few minutes. Then he stood and, flanked by his assistants, began to work the crowd. They parted in waves as the four men moved about the beach, making contact with each group.

"What happened last night was unfortunate. Those young men made a grave error. By not following my guidance, my leadership, they will most likely die. Our strength lies in working together for the common benefit. It is the only way," he said. The speech had started in a slow, almost soft tone, but as he continued, it rose in volume and timbre until he was near thundering.

I looked around the group. There was relief in some faces, anticipation in some, and fear in others. Antoine was getting out of hand with his leadership. Hopefully, we would be found and get off this rock. *It can't be soon enough*, I thought.

"Let's get some fruit and water and get back to work. It would be nice to sleep in the huts tonight," he concluded.

We ate what was left of the coconut and drank water from the pool. Antoine split everyone back into their workgroups. Jamal and Mike nodded and headed for the huts. Antoine asked Angelic, Keno, Gina, and a few of the other women if any of them sewed, knitted, wove, or braided. Most of them nodded. Antoine pointed to the pile of vines that the young men had gathered.

"Would you see if you can form some sort of net or netting, about 8' by 8'?" he asked them.

The heavyset woman with the skinny husband spoke up, "I've done some macramé, sweetie, and we'll take care of it." She stepped into the center of the group. "Ladies, let's get at it. I'll show you what to do."

William broke away from Antoine's group and started toward me. I knew my job. After yesterday and the frequency of climbing, my arms, shoulders, and legs were sore and scraped. But, if you want to eat, you got to gather the food. Until the ladies finished the netting and we proved we could actually catch fish, it was going to be coconut, chunky style or milk, take your pick.

I nodded at William, and we started off through the trees. I didn't think he was the one with the gun. But, it didn't mean he didn't have one. The good news was they hadn't used the guns or even made us aware of them until the theft and escape. The boat wasn't really an asset at this point. There wasn't anything we could do with it. We might have pulled some of the canopy material off for the huts. That would have been helpful. We actually could have slept on the boat, but the benches would have been hard. I preferred the sand. I wondered why Antoine and his assistants had spent so much time around it the day before.

William didn't have much to say. He just pointed toward the trees, and said, "Let's go."

"Good morning to you too!" I smiled at him.

"Just do your job," he hissed and brushed at my shoulder to turn me.

I let it pass and turned to the trees. I thought to myself, *Antoine is chewing on these guys. William either doesn't like the beach or he's just always cranky. Either way, I'm getting tired of it.*

We spent the next couple of hours gathering fruit and stacking it at the base of the trees. I would climb, cut, waggle, and toss the fruit to William. He would catch, mostly, and stack. He kept us at a steady pace. We stopped once for water as it grew hotter. He wasn't talkative, but he did seem to relax. He had gotten to where he let me keep the knife between trees. We had circled further and further from the campsite.

After I climbed a half dozen trees and we had collected several dozen coconuts, I realized what I was going to do. It was near mid-day, and I figured we would stop to cut fruit for lunch.

Calling down to William I said, "Hey, maybe we should start carrying some of these back to camp. It's about lunchtime. People are going to be hungry. We ate the last coconut we had this morning."

He turned his head toward the camp and bent to gather as much of the fruit from the ground as he could carry. Then he turned and started walking toward the camp.

I climbed down the tree. Halfway, I stopped and watched as he trudged back to camp. He was sweating profusely and never looked back.

I dropped from the tree, rolled in the sand, and disappeared into the jungle, his knife in my pocket.

24

ON MY OWN

I made my way into the jungle and started up the base of the mountain. I traveled parallel to the beach and toward Antoine's camp. Stopping every few feet I listened for any sounds. I finally came to the stream that ran down the mountain and fed the pool we drank from each morning. From there, I located the outcropping where I left my bag. It was still there, everything intact. Shouldering it I started toward the point at the end of the island.

It wasn't that I minded helping out. Most of what Antoine was doing made sense for the group. What I didn't like was that he seemed to be setting up a hierarchy with himself and his thugs in charge. Yes, they were participating, but not working. The process of working together, as he talked about it, involved everyone working, not just talking or directing. Yet, they still benefitted and weren't afraid to use force to do it. The second thing I didn't like was that he didn't seem to actively be doing anything about getting off the island. I had a couple of ideas.

Staying higher on the cliff until I was halfway to the

point, I made my way back to the water, but kept at a slow pace and listened for any sounds of people or pursuit.

The day grew hotter as I grew weary. That was another thing Antoine and I disagreed on. It was scorching in the late morning and early afternoon. The sun was bright. Several people in the group were sunburned already, and it was going to get worse if they didn't get in the shade and rest. There should be more frequent water breaks and rest periods. He wasn't very aware of or attentive to the people's physical conditions, needs, or personality. It was a top-down management system. You see them all the time in business and government. They work, but never well. The people are treated as disposable resources.

I didn't like leaving Jamal, Angelic, Mike, and Keno, but I thought I could help them more by trying to get us off this rock.

I REACHED THE POINT OF THE ISLAND AND STOPPED TO LOOK at the ocean and catch my breath. Pulling the water bottle from my bag I filled it from the stream. The sand where I had slept was in the sun, so I decided to move into the tree line and stay in the shade. Cutting one of the coconuts I had stashed I ate it while I watched the tide slowly recede. Leaning against a tree I rested and tried to think about how best to help the group.

There was still no signal on my cell phone, so I shut it off to save the battery. I wanted to get to higher ground on the island to see if there was any reception. Also, I wanted to test the signal at different times of day to see if there might be a satellite passing. If we were far out of the shipping lanes, there might only be an occasional opportunity for coverage, when a satellite orbited the area. Perhaps I might also see something from higher up. Maybe there were nearby islands.

I needed to go to the top of the mountain and take a look. First, I would need to get a few supplies together.

I planned for what I needed. The clifftop looked a long way, possibly a couple of hours, depending upon the climb. By following the stream up the cliff, I could stay hydrated until I got familiar with the terrain. The island seemed to have plenty of coconut palms, but I would carry some fruit in my bag. I wouldn't mind some fish. I didn't care for sushi, so I'd need to cook it. Smoke rising from a fire could pose a problem, but while watching the ladies with the vines and netting, it gave me some ideas. I might need a net of my own, or I could try spearfishing with a sapling and one of the knives. A hut probably wasn't necessary because there was enough shade from the trees and I needed to stay mobile. That meant keeping all my gear together or carrying the bag most of the time. That could be a problem, if Antoine sent his assistants after me, or if I encountered them by chance. I wasn't sure how he would react. He hadn't seemed to be visibly upset by the young men stealing the boat, but I bet he wouldn't like defection from his group.

Gathering a few vines I sat in the shade, and began to braid, and then weave them into shapes. The breeze coming over the cliff line from the beach below was pleasant. It cooled the sweat on my skin and relaxed my mind. I dozed for a time and some of the tension drained away.

I could see the beach in the direction of Antoine's camp. I pulled out the scope, which I had brought initially for whale watching or sightseeing, and looked up the beach. I saw nothing but small waves, the tide undulating, in and out. It appeared I was alone in the world.

My time was spent weaving or braiding, then I'd stop to listen and survey the beach through my scope, then repeat. By the time I was through, it was late afternoon. There would be several more hours of daylight. I could try to spear a fish. A fire might work after dark, the smell could be an issue, depending on which way the wind blew. If I built a fire to the windward side the smoke and smell would dissipate in that direction, so I still had options.

I took another look at the beach, and I spotted one of Antoine's assistants. The one who, I think, had shot at the motor launch. He strolled down the beach, his head scanning in all directions as he moved slowly along. He was looking for something, probably me.

I watched him stroll, and he continued in my direction. Dropping into a crouch I followed him through the scope. I doubted he could see me. He was still that far away. I didn't want the sun to reflect off the scope, and as he got closer, I put it away and could see him unaided.

He stayed on the beach, and while glancing up occasionally, he didn't seem to pay much attention beyond the tree line along the shore. I watched him as he continued below me and reached the tip of the island. The bluff line rose fifty yards or so beforehand. I was up high. He was down low. There was a smooth rock point with a few outcroppings right on the tip of the island where you would round to the windward side. I thought I could ease out behind one of the outcroppings and watch him continue on the windward side.

I worked my way there and revolved around this one outcropping, as he moved further along the windward side. He was now below the bluff line. As I rotated around the outcropping, I noticed two things. One, the tide was coming in and would soon be at his feet. Two, there was an opening on one side of the outcropping.

25

THE CAVE

I returned to the tree line and dug in my bag. Finding what I was after I went back to the outcropping and looked down at the beach. The walking man was headed further around the windward side. The tide continued to rise.

I slipped into the opening of the outcropping and clicked on the camp light. The light was small and fit in the palm of my hand. There was a shaft and a lens that sat at the top, angled at ninety degrees. I could stand it on the base, direct the light beam, and had both hands free if I needed it.

The opening was three feet deep and then took a turn. I eased around the corner and shined the light into the darkness. When my eyes adjusted, it was dusky rather than dark. I could stand upright with no problem. Slipping around the turn I started down a gently sloping grade. I traveled twelve or fifteen feet, and the passage opened into a small room about twenty by twenty. There was sunlight near the middle, which illuminated the cave, and I shut off my flashlight. The space was empty, with a sand floor and the skylight. I traveled around each side of the cavern, examining the walls. They were smooth but had a texture like they had once been under high stress or heat. Then I understood. This was a lava tube from when the island was formed or from a subsequent eruption. Either way, this would make a great base of operations.

I finished my examination of the walls and noticed the floor dipped a little in the far corner. I could follow the pattern in the rock, so I suspected the tunnel had once continued downward but over time had become filled with sand. There was no way to know how far down it might have led, probably all the way to the ocean. I liked the cave.

Stepping back into the sunlight I blinked and recalled the walking man. I could no longer see him unaided, and when I checked with the scope, he was not in sight. The tide was pounding the rocks below.

From the entrance of the cave, I estimated where the opening for the skylight was located. I started from the outcropping and traced my way to the top of the rock where I thought the cave lay.

There was a small depression. It seemed like the perimeter of the depression had collapsed inward while the center was still in place. The light streamed in around the edges. That would account for the diffused quality of the light in the cave and cause smoke to dissipate if I were to light a fire. That and darkness would make a good cover. Only the smell of the smoke might give me away. I thought it was worth the risk.

I liked the idea of having multiple locations to camp. I didn't want to stay in one place and make it easy for one of Antoine's assistants to find me. I could set up on the bluff line, work there in the day, and sleep in the cave at night. I had the sand bed already laid out on the bluff. I could sleep in it occasionally.

I went to work around my site on the bluff. That seemed the most obvious, so I would make it appear to be where I lived. I gathered more vines for braiding and weaving and laid them at the foot of the tree line. I fashioned a bench seat in the sand with a view toward the water. I gathered a few sticks and piled them on the other side of the trees. I sat in the seat for a few minutes and surveyed the site. There were a couple different ways to approach the outcropping, and I'd want to rotate and use them all to keep trail wear down. The question was, where should I start first?

26

THE CLIMB

I wanted to see the surrounding area, and it made the most sense to begin at the top. Looking up at the cliff's peak I decided that was my destination. Cutting into a couple coconuts I ate while resting and recovering some of my strength. I would sleep in the cave and start out early in the morning.

I sat in my bench seat and watched the beach, windward and leeward. There were no signs of activity. Tossing aside the vines I had been braiding, I approached the cave from a lower angle. Going inside, I picked out the best spot for shaping a bed. There was a lot of room and plenty of choices.

Getting the bed shaped I settled in as the light began to fade. There was a slight breeze filtering into the cave, and if I listened carefully I could hear the tide. It was comfortable. I set the alarm on my watch and fell asleep immediately.

I woke to the soft dinging of my alarm. It was 5am, and light was filtering through the opening. I wanted to be at the top of the peak before the full heat of the day. Grabbing my bag, I started out of the cave, but stood at the opening for a moment and listened. All I heard was the tide. Stepping outside, I studied the bluff campsite for a moment. It was undisturbed.

I gathered a couple of coconuts and reminded myself I needed to start fishing. Heading for the stream I filled my canteen, and followed the flow up the cliff.

At times, I had to separate from the stream and work my way around rock bluffs, small waterfalls, or dense vegetation, but I could always hear the sound. I ascended the cliff face. The angle was steep in places but flattened out comfortably in others.

An hour into the trip, I was two-thirds of the way up the cliff. I stumbled upon a flat space, stopped, and turned to the ocean. There was still a half-hour, at my current rate, to get to the top. The sea spread out before me, light blue in the lagoon and deep blue beyond, all the way to the sky, there was only water. It was breathtaking. I realized my hiking had brought me around the island, closer to the original landing point and Antoine's camp. It dawned on me that the water was all from the same source and filtered out around the island. I was high enough on the cliff that I couldn't see or hear anything from Antoine's group.

I pulled out the scope and took a look along the beach line. There was movement, but I couldn't be sure who it was or what they were doing. I started up the cliff again. A half an hour and a hard climb later, I was at the top. It spread out in a flat plateau. There were palms and foliage and a great breeze. Walking the perimeter, there was only ocean in every direction.

It had gotten really hot on the trip up. It was the climb, as I had been mostly in the shade. There were a few occasions when I'd broken into the sunlight, and it had been hot and bright. I sat under a group of palms, sipped some water, and cut one of the coconuts.

I rested for a few minutes and thought about what to do next. Pulling out the Satellite phone, I checked for a signal. There was nothing. It was late morning, and I told myself I should check the phone every hour to see if I got any signal from an orbiting satellite, then I shut off the phone.

What else might I do? I had all day if I wanted to check the phone signal. I glanced across the sky, took out the scope, and studied the horizon. There was nothing I could see, but maybe someday there would be. I wanted to be prepared.

WHEN I WAS A KID, I SAW A MOVIE WHERE A GUY WAS STUCK on a deserted island, and he spelled out "Help" with coconuts. I didn't want to waste coconuts, and I wanted to make a more prominent sign. So, I decided on palm fronds. Tying them together and arranging them in place in ten or twelve-foot letters, I'd stake the letters down and use a few coconuts to help anchor them and add visibility. I'd set up a fire pit on each end of the sign and light it, if I saw, or heard anything.

Gathering fallen fronds and vines, I selected greener ones although I knew they wouldn't stay green long. Contrast was needed against the sand. Maybe I could use brown, dead leaves and vines and stake them against greenery. That would make them visible from a distance.

I walked the clifftop again. There was a green space, with only a little foliage, which I could clear. The downed foliage would help me as a fire starter. Going to work I got the area cleared. It took an hour. I sat and drank the last of my water and ate another coconut. Walking to the stream, I refilled my canteen and came back to my resting point near the edge of the cliff. I sat under some palms in the shade and looked out to sea. It was unchanged as if no time had passed, or maybe an eternity had passed, and it remained the same.

I powered up the Satellite phone again, and there was still no signal. Shutting it off, I put it away.

Laying palm fronds in the cleared space I saw there was enough room to create fifteen-foot letters that would be visible and unobstructed. I didn't know how high in the air the message could be seen, or how far out the fire could be seen, but it created a possibility that we didn't have otherwise. Hopefully the island might be a destination for casual sailors, but I was disappointed that, so far, I'd seen nothing.

Braiding a couple strands of the vine to give it more strength and longevity I tied off the palm fronds. My watch chimed again, and I stopped long enough to check the Satellite phone. There was no signal. I reset the watch. I had worn my diving watch on the cruise under the assumption I'd be diving. It was an older self-winding model for which I was grateful. It had no battery to die, and it was waterproof, so I never took it off. The dial was luminous, so I could see it in the cave. This wasn't the vacation I had planned or hoped for, but it was shaping up to an unexpected and unique adventure.

I tied off more fronds then gathered more coconuts. My watch alarmed, and again I checked. Nothing had changed. It was the middle of the afternoon, and the sun was hot. I decided to take a break. It was apparent to me that it would continue to get hotter during the day. That meant the best time to work would be early morning and late afternoon, early evening. It would be too easy to get sunburned and dehydrated, working during the heat of the day.

Facing the leeward side of the island I saw portions of that beach were visible in both directions. The foliage kept me from seeing the middle beach where we had landed, but I could see the lagoon. I saw no signs of activity. Sitting on a rock, I caught the breeze and watched the sea and sky. I braided some of the cord to stay busy, but napped periodically and checked the phone as the day progressed. The only thing that changed was the amount of light and the color in the sky. It was peaceful, unless you thought about being secluded on a deserted island, half a world from home, with only water and coconuts.

Late in the afternoon, I moved to the other side of the cliff and watched the windward shore. The tide crashed far below. Gathering downed foliage and old fronds, I built the fire piles at each end of the sign. There was the possibility that the fire would flicker, and ash would land on the fronds and ignite them. It might make a better signal. I considered lighting the sign on fire if there was an excellent opportunity for it to be seen.

After finishing the fire piles, I scouted the cliff top for the best place to camp. There was a spot on the leeward side under a grove of palms. The sand was soft enough for me to scoop out a bed. I continued checking the phone with no results. Eating another coconut, I settled in my new bed for the evening.

My plan was to check the phone every hour through the night to see if there was a signal. The sun set and it was stunningly beautiful. The sky deepened, and dusk descended on me. As the sky grew dark and the stars came out, they seemed even brighter than they had from my beach camp at the tip of the island. It was almost like I was in space itself, or maybe heaven. They were so close and shone so bright, it felt like I could reach out and pull them from the sky.

I checked the phone each hour throughout the night. There was never a trace of a signal. The island must be remote. I thought, and feared, *we might be here for a long time.*

. . .

I laid back and looked at the night sky. I thought about my friends in Antoine's camp and how fortunate I felt to have met them. Then I thought about my two best friends from college, Mason Bennett and Michael (Ike, the Iceman) Mann. The three of us roomed together at the University of Tennessee-Knoxville.

I swam, Ike played tennis, and Mason was a wrestler and a fencer who went on to learn several different martial arts. He was a one-man army. Mason works for the CIA. He can't tell me what he does, or he'd have to kill me. He tells me with a grin. Mike was on the pro tennis tour, once ranked as high as #8 in the world. Now he coaches and reps for some of the big tennis companies. Dee, Mace, and Ike, we were brothers for life. I missed them. I missed them all.

I woke with the sun as light spread across the mountain top. There were a few hours left to check the phone before I started back to my beach camp. Circling the cliff, I looked for what might be the best trail. By that, I meant fastest, least likely to be seen, and easiest to hike. What were the possibilities? I felt I could hike it on a canteen of water, so I didn't need to stay as close to the stream. I wanted to travel back and forth from my beach camp on the tip of the island. What would be the fastest, easiest, and most direct way? I studied several approaches through the morning as the time passed on testing the phone. By late morning I was done. There was no signal.

27

A NEW WAY TO GO

I started down the cliff and stayed near the stream for the first few minutes. Then I veered to the left, toward my campsite at the tip of the island. It looked quicker and more direct if I could travel the distance uninterrupted. I passed the first forty-five minutes without any problems. The sun was more visible, and it was rockier than the upward ascent had been. There were multiple views of the ocean, and I caught a stronger breeze. Noting that the hike that far had only taken about thirty percent of my water, I felt good about having a supply to reach the beach camp.

At a small crest, I stopped to check the time and scan the beach and skyline. I noticed that the cliff veered in two directions. One side ran toward the windward, and the other continued toward the beach. The windward branch didn't appear to travel far before it ended. I decided to hike out to the point and check the view.

Not long onto the slope and I could see far down the windward side to the shoreline. All quiet, no sign of anyone or anything. As I turned back, I saw a dip in the rock face that caught my attention. Hiking along the line of the cliff, I arrived at a depression in the rock face. It was an oddity of the rock formation, but I noticed the foliage disappear around what should have been the end of the trail. I thought, *why not?* So I followed the curvature of the rock.

The trail didn't end. There wasn't a wall. There was a cut out in the cliff that led into a small canyon with a flat floor about the size of two football fields. I stepped into the canyon.

It was made up of three sheer walls and the opening through which I had entered. It appeared that the canyon was located halfway between the beach and the clifftop. I decided to explore. Maybe I would find something interesting.

I took a few steps into the canyon and immediately stumbled upon a path which made me both elated and concerned. It seemed like a really odd place to find a path on what I thought was a deserted island. I felt in the bag for my dive knife but did not remove it.

I eased along the overgrown path. Advancing a few yards, I stepped into a clearing.

To the right was a pavilion with a small stream beside it. But what was most impressive lay directly in front of me. There stood a cluster of coconut palms, half a dozen rows of pineapples, and a large group of other plants that looked like tropical fruit.

Now I was both hopeful and worried. Who would this camp belong to, old hippies, dopers, preppers, pirates? How about friendly natives?

Taking a few cautious steps inward, I tried to decide whether or not to call out. I didn't want to get shot, so I thought I'd better announce myself.

"Hello, anyone here?"

"Hello?" I stepped closer to the pavilion.

There was no reply, other than the echo of my words off

the canyon walls.

I reached the pavilion, stopped, and took a hard look, trying to harness my excitement and anticipation. The pavilion was twenty feet wide and forty feet long. It looked like a concrete pad with four by four supports holding up a wood frame roof, covered with palm fronds. It was like a picnic pavilion in a national park. Except that it had woven side walls or covers which began a couple of feet above the pad and stopped several feet short of the roof. It was like a sunscreen or a wind buffer. As I studied the pavilion, I saw the side walls were torn in several places. A nearby downed palm may have caused the damage. I stood and looked at the site for a long time until I absorbed that sense of emptiness that surrounds a place when no one is there. Could this be abandoned? I stepped closer.

At the edge of the pavilion, I could see into the shadows. I stepped onto the pad. It looked like an area that was once a dining room. There were tables and chairs scattered about, some over-turned, some upright. There was no evidence of food or recent usage. I walked further inside and came upon two sets of bunks, two on each side of the walkway. They were bare mattresses with no bedding. I sensed that whoever had been here had packed up and left, for however long, and not come back.

I passed the beds and stepped into an area that looked like a workshop. There was a long table with a few tools and building supplies stacked on it. There was a manual grinding wheel in a corner. The kind you pump with your foot, and it turns the wheel. It was probably for some of the tools for cultivating the plants.

Beyond the workshop, there was a full wall with a door, and I realized the back portion of the pavilion was a room. I walked to the door and knocked. There was no reply. I knocked again, still no answer. I tried the doorknob. It was locked. I listened. All I could hear was the breeze and the stream outside the pavilion.

Backing away from the door I started toward the front of the pavilion. Stepping into the sunlight, I glanced about the area then walked to where the palm had uprooted and damaged the woven walls. Absent that, the place would be intact.

I wandered toward the coconut palms and the pineapple field. As I walked the rows, I saw mangos, papaya, bananas, kiwi, and some other fruits I didn't recognize. Whoever had been here was well stocked. I entered the pineapple rows, and at the far end, as I turned , I saw it. There was an old machete wedged into one of the pineapple stalks.

Grabbing it with both hands I tugged. It took a couple of tries as the plant had grown around the blade. Had whoever lived here been gone that long? With the blade free, I held it aloft and thought of the grinding wheel in the workshop. The blade and the wheel went together. I started toward the pavilion and noticed where the stream flowed across the field. Someone had constructed a dam and made a small pond. I assumed they gathered their drinking water. Just beyond the drinking water, I saw another crop. It was a small stand of marijuana. It wasn't enough to be a product. It was more like a personal stash, recreational use. I scanned the rest of the valley floor. Could there be a larger patch anywhere? I didn't see it. Whoever had been here was well thought out and well equipped. Why would they have left?

I returned to the pavilion and rechecked it. There was nothing written, no books or magazines, no sign of whom it might have been. I sharpened the machete as best I could by knocking off the rust.

Deciding to take some fruit I scanned the eating area and the workshop looking for a bag or a box, but couldn't find one.

I crossed to the stream and filled my canteen. Returning to the field I cut off a couple of pineapples and wrapped them in the towel from my bag. Carrying the machete in one hand, I would need to fabricate a sling when I got back to the beach camp.

Walking out of the valley I looked for any signs or markings of its identity. There was nothing. I could call it "Shangri-La" or "Little Hawaii," or I could just call it "The Cliff Camp."

I walked down the trail, turning periodically to memorize how I had gotten to the camp. Once I left the valley and was off the bluff line, it was impossible to see the entrance.

Reaching the split in the trail I looked up at the peak and down to the beach. It was halfway between. I took my new machete and cut an "X" in the closest palm tree, visualized my distance from each point, and my distance from the windward side. Hopefully, I could find it again.

I resumed the hike down the slope, and after a few minutes, I broke into an open area where I could see the beach and cliff face that marked the tip of the island. It appeared that the trip back wouldn't be as long or as difficult as going up had been, and I should be able to find the canyon again.

I actually bounced down the last of the cliff face as I made my way to the bluff. I was that excited. Now, there would be more to eat than coconuts and fish. I couldn't help but wonder why the camp was abandoned. There had been no trace of any activity or life. The camp looked like it had been deserted.

Arriving at the bluff I was hot and sweaty from the exertion and the sun. I smelled myself. I hadn't thought about it before then. I'd been on the island for several days, and I'd been busy, in and out of the water several times, caked with sweat and dried saltwater. I needed a shower.

28

TAKING CARE OF BUSINESS

I walked to the bluff line, where the stream cascaded over the rocks and fell to the landing above the beach. There didn't seem to be a way down to it. The rocks were almost inverted and cut away underneath the ledge, so there was no way to climb down or back. I'd have to work on access. In the meantime, I needed to clean up. The stream ran across rock a few feet before it plunged over the bluff face. It wasn't very deep, but I could sit down to take a bath and rinse out my clothes. It wasn't going to be very comfortable, but it would get me cleaner.

Reaching in my bag I pulled out my toiletries, my gym clothes, and the towel with the two pineapples. They all smelled awful. The clothes had been sweaty after my workout in the gym, and the towel had gotten soiled from the pineapples. Plus, most of it had been shut up in the bag for days. Who knows, the smell might've knocked Antoine out had he stuck his head in there.

I shook the pineapples out and laid them aside. The towel would clean up. Stacking the gym clothes I thought to pause and check the beach to see if there was any activity. I'd hate to have been mid-bath and one of Antoine's thugs come calling. I left the fruit and clothes where they were and walked toward the leeward side.

Surveying the camp, everything was just as I had left it. I approached the cave from a low angle and made my way to the entrance. There were no tracks or evidence of activity. Inside, the sand bed was undisturbed. I went back to the rock face and walked along the bluff toward Antoine's camp. Finding a soft spot between some palms, I lay down to rest and observe. I scanned the beach and the tree line with the scope, not seeing anyone. Looking back into the foliage, there still wasn't anything to see. I was going to have to get closer to determine what progress had been made and how everyone was doing. But first, I was going to take a bath.

After walking back to the stream I slipped out of my shoes and then my clothes. The water was cold. Actually, it was cool, which was suitable for drinking, but chilly for bathing. I had filled my canteen closer to my camp, above where I had entered to bathe, and I thought to myself, *you're going to have to keep the upstream, downstream thing in mind when you enter the water.*

I rinsed and soaked myself once I adjusted to the temperature. Then, rinsing all my clothes I wrung them out, leaving the gym shorts to wear after I dried. Slipping them and my shoes back on, I gathered up all the other items. Walking back to camp and into the shade of the palms I noted there was work to do to set up camp. I had to assume we'd be there a while, and I wanted to make things more comfortable.

Stringing braided vines between two palms that were close to the bluff line and in the sun, I knotted a couple of the vines together and was able to get the length needed to circle the trees and tie them off. I had a clothesline. Hanging all the wet clothes on it, I went back to the stream to rinse out the towel.

I hung the towel on the line and retired to the shade, sat on the ground, and rested. Cutting into one of the pineapples, I bit into a chunk and was reminded how much better than a coconut a good, ripe, fresh pineapple can be. I drank some water and thought over what was needed for the camp.

It didn't take long for the items to dry in the heat. There was a lot of humidity as well, and I came back to the realization that we were in the tropics, inside 20 degrees of latitude. It was going to be sticky, as well as hot, in the tropical summer.

I put on the walking shorts, rinsed out the dry-fit, and hung them on the line. I didn't mind being shirtless in the shade, but I didn't want to spend much time in the direct sun. I needed to work on getting a tan. Running a hand across my chin, I realized I hadn't shaved in several days and felt the start of a beard. I hadn't seen my reflection since we'd been on the boat, not even looking at myself when I'd been in the water. With no one else around, it hardly mattered.

STAYING IN THE SHADE, I GATHERED MORE VINES. I NEEDED quite a few for all the items that were occurring to me, a way to get down to the falls and back, a net for fishing, a hammock for napping in the heat of the day, and a hat with a full brim rather than the ball cap I had been wearing. I also thought about a vest that could be worn open over my chest and back. There might be some other things, but those would be a good start.

While I braided, I considered how large a net I might need for fishing. I could use a spear , but that would be one fish at a time. A net would make more sense if I could estimate the size and how to handle it. With a pile of braids, I could weave them and create a net. With small openings, I could trap some fish, select a few, and throw the others back. I think it would be more effective than using a spear.

Working through the afternoon and into the early evening, I had a large net started by the time I quit. I thought about a fire. There was the "one strike match" in my bag. But, there wasn't a reason at this point. I had no fish and didn't think smoked pineapple would be that good.

I had grown stiff from sitting. A camp chair would be good, along with everything else, but I really needed to get a little exercise, to stretch.

I STASHED EVERYTHING IN THE CAVE, TOOK MY SCOPE, AND walked up the beach toward Antoine's camp.

It was getting dark, and I worked my way along the top of the beach near the tree line. I hadn't traveled far when I looked up the beach and saw a flame. Antoine and the group had a big bonfire on the beach. Good for them. Maybe they figured out how to fish. At least they had discovered fire. That would make it easier for me to have one as well.

I slid forward in the sand, confident they couldn't see me with an unaided eye. It wasn't cold but the group huddled around the fire as the day died down and the temperatures cooled.

Jamal and Angelic sat side by side, as did Mike and Keno. Gina, Tom Jones, and several others, stood further away and caught up in conversation. Antoine stood to one side, looking out to sea. His guards were at his shoulder. They looked tired and a little disheveled. The same as I felt earlier. At least they could see each other and report on what they saw. I had made a choice to leave, it was on me. Being alone wasn't going to be that much fun.

Jamal looked down the beach in my direction, but I was positive he couldn't see me. He looked my way for a long time, a blank expression on his face.

He finally turned away, and as it got darker, I could no longer see the group clearly. I walked back to the cave and sat on the bench seat by the tree line for the next hour. I listened to the tide and felt the breeze on my skin. It was black dark by the time I made my way to the cave and went to bed.

29

A BRAND NEW DAY

I woke early the next morning as the light filtered into the cave. Sleeping with the light, rising and retiring, made a lot of sense when you were living with nature. It had a logical rhythm that I was now a part of. It was the same rhythm as working early in the morning and working late in the afternoon and staying out of the heat and sun as much as possible. All those things were very different from how I spent my day or my time in the music industry. I'd had to adjust. I didn't mind it. It made me think of an old Otis Redding tune, and while I don't sing professionally, I am from Nashville, and everybody sings. I looked around the cave, and while I knew there was no dock, down on the bay, I was sitting in the morning sun, wasting time. I sang it with feeling.

I had to admit, I felt better! It was just Otis and me getting the day underway.

Standing at the cave entrance I checked the camp but could see nothing different from the night before. Perhaps I overestimated my value to Antoine or his curiosity about me and my bag. I felt like it wasn't so much me, as the threat to his authority, the disruption I might cause. But then again, I may have overestimated his concerns, and he had simply gone back to work. Either way, I needed to get to work.

Wanting to finish the netting first and try my hand at casting for fish, I ate the last pineapple and added a little coconut. Needing to harvest more fruit meant I'd need a bag or a sack of some kind with a strap for carrying. I also wanted a cover and strap for the machete so it wouldn't have to be carried open-handed.

I made good headway on the fishnet the day before, so I thought to finish that first. To gather additional vines, I strapped the dive knife to my leg, used it to cut, and collected the vines over my arm. I was going to need a belt for my shorts or go to the dry-fit, as the shorts I was wearing were beginning to slip down my waist and hips. I'd lost a few pounds. When I got home, I could write a book on the coconut, pineapple, and water diet.

Sitting on the bench seat overlooking the sea and in the shade, as the sun heated up, I worked on the vines.

I braided for a couple of hours until my stomach rumbled. Finishing up the net, I watched the water and thought I could fish as the tide came in, and perhaps net something. I could cast the net or use a drift technique. That technique might work for me. I'd have to figure how and where to set the net, a way to anchor it, and how to keep the net unfurled during the tide. It would take more work. But first, I stopped and got more coconuts.

Eating the coconut I thought about the netting. I'd need to tie off the net to keep it upright and extended, which meant a rope through the top and some way to anchor it. There would need to be some weights. I could braid in rock at the bottom to keep the net extended. But, keeping it in place might be difficult. I had the net and a length of vine to serve as rope, but was going to need more. One day back and I already decided to return to the cliff camp where I could further explore and gather more food.

When the tide was out, I noticed there were several large rocks scattered along the exposed beach. Perhaps I could string the net between them. With it weighted at the bottom, the net would act as a sieve between the rocks when the tide came in. I'd just have to test it, and also try spearfishing. Maybe I'd get lucky.

I worked on weaving two bags to carry food, and anything useful I found at the cliff camp. I wanted the finished bags to be approximately two feet wide and three feet deep. Cutting a couple of small bamboo stalks from a grove nearby, I tied three vines to one end and braided them together. The length should've been approximately six feet. I braided until holding the stick out, even with the top of my head, the bottom of the braid reached the ground. I then tied that end off on the other stick. It was approximately six feet. Hanging one of the sticks on a nearby palm that was still in the shade, I let it drape to the ground. The palm acted as a stabilizer. I wanted to be able to stand for a while or sit while I worked and not be in one place for too long. That way, I could move around with or away from the sun.

I cross braided the vines between the sticks. When I finished, I tied off a couple on each end of the stick and made a sling to carry the bag. With two bags, I'd have one for each shoulder to distribute the weight of anything I carried. Working all day, I got one of the bags completed and the other underway.

As it grew dark, and my back and fingers ached from the braiding, I stopped to gather more coconuts. Feeling less hungry, I guessed a limited diet could do that to you. I didn't feel the passage of time, or despair, or even fear. I'd done things to keep myself busy, but I missed my friends. I missed my deceased wife and the child we might have had. There I'd said it, for the first time since she was killed. I was alone. I'd learned my lesson, it left a scar.

There is a difference between being lonely and being alone.

30

BACK TO THE CLIFF

In the morning, I took another bath. The water felt cold when you felt hot. It was cramped and reminded me that I needed to figure a way down to the waterfall. But, that would have to wait.

I started for the cliff camp with my woven shoulder bags, my gym bag, and my machete in hand. Climbing the trail quicker than I thought, I saw the ridgeline from below as I approached it. The mark was still on the palm, and there was no evidence of activity on the path. Whoever had been there, must have been gone for good.

Making my way along the ridge, I dropped around the outcropping into the valley. It was unbelievable how hidden the entrance was from the trail.

Approaching cautiously, I grew closer to the camp. There was no activity. The breeze was blowing, and all seemed at peace.

Whoever built the camp had picked a great spot, and I wondered how they had found it. Were they like me, and stumbled upon it? At the valley opening, you could look down the windward side of the island and see nothing but blue water and blue sky.

As I got closer, I called out, "Hello, anybody home?" Again, all I got was the echo.

Everything seemed as I had left it.

Walking into the field I gathered a couple of pineapples and some of the other fruit. I loaded both bags. Already beginning to think I might stay for a few days, rather than carry all that produce around, I was a long way from being able to fish.

It had gotten hot, and finishing up, I went over to the small dam to fill my canteen. I bent over the water and something moved, causing me to startle.

I set the canteen down to get a closer look. There was more movement, which I soon realized was fish. The pool was stocked. That must've been its purpose. It wasn't irrigation, or bathing, or filling a canteen. You did all that in the stream at the pavilion. These folks had thought of everything. I studied the pool and realized just how full it was. It was overstocked.

I didn't know if it was Friday or not, looking at my watch, it wasn't. But I'm having fish.

Setting the bags down and walking over to a small grove of bamboo, I cut a shoulder-high shaft and carried it back to the pond. I took my diving knife and tied it to the bamboo shaft with some of the braided vine I brought with me. When finished, it made an excellent spear. Now, could I hit anything with it?

The overstocked nature of the pond helped. After a stab or two, I got the technique and soon had several fish on the rocks beside me. I cleaned them as best I could and left them on the rocks to dry.

Gathering some downed palm fronds and other debris I went over to the picnic area. There was a fire ring.

I set up the kindling, took out my "One strike," and lite it. Fire!

Retrieving the fish I held them over the flame on my knife. It wasn't very pretty cooking, but I got it done. Let me be clear, I don't care for sushi!

It was good. I wasn't sure what kind of fish it was, but there were a bunch of them in the pond.

Some fruit and water for dessert and I felt the best I had since we landed. Sitting in the shade, I napped.

Just before I fell asleep, I thought to myself, a*ll that effort braiding the fishnet, if I'd just looked the first time!*

LATER, I GOT UP, GATHERED MY STUFF, AND HIKED TO THE pavilion. Setting my gear on the table in the lounge area, I righted one of the chairs and sat.

Looking back into the pavilion, I studied what I could see. There might be something useful back there now that I had an idea of what the camp offered. A skillet would be nice, some utensils, maybe a rod and some fishing line. I was going to take time and look around, while it was still daylight.

Stepping into the pavilion, I looked for any sort of cabinet or shelf. There wasn't anything in the lounge area, but between two of the beds was a small dresser I hadn't noticed before. I sat on the bed and opened the drawers.

The top two were empty, and I figured I was out of luck, but there were a few things in the bottom two drawers. There was a whetstone and a can of 3 in 1 oil, some fishing line, a fork, and a pack of Kleenex. No papers or books or notes. Just a spare drawer with stuff someone thought they might need someday, but not enough to take it with them. As I stood, my foot nudged something and I took a quick step back. I looked down. It was the blade of a shovel. I reached and pulled it from under the bed, glancing to see if there was anything else. I thought to look up to the underside of the mattress. I saw through the springs. There was nothing.

I decided I should check under the other three mattresses. Looking at the floor when I bent down to get the shovel, I hadn't seen anything else, but the mattresses were half folded. The other half was sitting on top of the springs. I went to the second bed and raised the mattress, nothing. I went to the third bed and raised it, nothing. Thinking it was a waste of time, I still decided to check under the last mattress. I raised it and was rewarded with a small black box wedged in the springs. Pushing the mattress aside I worked the box out with both hands. It was a small plastic case, and I had an idea what might be in it. Popping the latches I opened the box. There was a Glock 9mm model 17 and a clip. I picked it up and looked it over. The gun was older and worn, and I couldn't find any markings, so I assumed it was a first-generation. There was no ammunition in the box. There wasn't room other than in the clip, which was empty. The old gunnies tell you, it puts too much pressure on the spring to leave it loaded all the time. I looked again, but no sign of ammunition. Holding the gun up I slid the clip into place. Well, it looked good, and I could bluff somebody if I had to, but I'd need to be careful. Ejecting the clip I put it and the frame back in the box. I closed the box and sat for a moment.

I was puzzled about the camp. I'd seen no other indication of guns or weapons of any kind other than the machete, which seemed to be for use in the fields. It must have been a band of old hippies, or new agers, maybe. Where would they have gone? A hidden gun like this, quite old and well worn, somebody had it for a long time and had used it. Maybe it was a backup or an insurance policy.

Leaning the shovel against the wall I moved on into the

pavilion, until I came upon the wall with the locked door. Maybe I could pick the lock with my fork?

I tried the knob again. I turned it slowly to the left and it stopped. Then to the right, and it gave, and then just a little further. It clicked and popped open. *Must've been in a hurry last time and made another mistake.* The door swung open, and it was a surprise.

Stacks and stacks and stacks of boxes, crates really, were the first thing I saw. I stepped inside. It was an "Aha" moment. This was a supply room. Why hadn't I thought of that before? I made an assumption and thought it was a meeting room or a bedroom, if I had even thought of it at all.

31

THE GOODS

As my gaze moved across the boxes, I noticed a doored cabinet on the interior wall. I stepped across, released the hinge, and swung the door open. Nice!

There was a Remington 870 20 gauge and a Mossberg Maverick 20 gauge. They weren't heavyweight shotguns, but they'd get the job done, and the recoil was more manageable for people. There were a couple of boxes of shells on the floor of the cabinet, but no nine-millimeter for the Glock.

It made me wonder again who these folks were. Why would they leave so much equipment behind? Either they had plenty, or they didn't care, or they planned to come back. That made me nervous. They looked more like preppers now than hippies. They could be out scouring somewhere. Surely I would have seen or heard them traveling around the island. Worse, they could have seen or heard me and investigated. That meant they probably had a boat and they're out on it, on other islands, or a supply run.

I stepped back, thinking about it. Looking again, I realized there were more items. Specifically, there was a compound bow and a quiver of arrows. Were they playing

Robin Hood or Rambo? There were no explosives on the arrows, only hunting tips. What were they hunting?

Next to that were four ocean-fishing rods and reels. Those would be useful. Lying on the floor of the cabinet under the rods was a machete cover and sling. I grabbed it. Alright, that's one less thing I'd have to make. Next was a small box of fishing tackle. That was everything in the cabinet.

Turning to the stacked boxes to see what was inside, I expected it would be canned food. A couple of boxes were open, and I grabbed them only to see utensils, assorted kitchen paraphernalia, several canteens, and a couple of grills that would lie across a fire pit. I kept looking and realized that all the remaining boxes were the same. They were boxes of chewing gum. It was the kind of gum that comes in little plastic containers about three inches wide and four inches tall. All the boxes were marked "cinnamon".

I stepped around each row of the remaining boxes and checked. They were all the same. That made no sense. Why would anyone have that much chewing gum? I slit open one of the boxes and looked inside. There were forty-eight little containers, four rows of six, two rows deep. I pulled one of the containers out and looked at it. I held it up to the light, but the plastic was opaque, and I couldn't see through it anyway, because of the label. I stood there looking when I realized that the wrapper at the top was gone. The container wasn't sealed. The top would pop right up. I opened it and looked inside. That's a lot of chewing gum.

Closing the top, I grabbed another container, and put them in the pocket of my shorts. I shut the open box of chewing gum and closed the cabinet. I took the Remington, because it had a sling, and the boxes of shells. Closing the door to the room behind me, I made my way to the front of the pavilion. Setting everything on the table, I began to organize.

Then I remembered the rods and reels and went back for them. The reel was loaded with line, so I grabbed the small tackle box from the shelf floor, and then grabbed a small metal grill, a spatula, and a medium-size plastic container for cooking. I could hardly carry it all.

I thought about climbing to the clifftop to see if I could spot anything, and check on my "help" signal.

Before leaving I went back to the pond, speared a couple fish and stored them in the plastic container.

I loaded the bags over one shoulder and put the machete on top of them. I hung the Remington from the other shoulder. I'm ready. I'm on safari!

Walking toward the entrance, I got nervous. I didn't know much about guns. I'd been to the range a few times with friends and shot some targets with pistols. I'd taken a Metro Nashville law enforcement course on home protection and the basic use of shotguns, but I was no kind of gunman. I could probably keep from shooting myself, but more than that, I couldn't guarantee.

Taking a few steps, I realized it was getting late so I pushed ahead.

32

MO BUSINESS

Reaching the fork in the trail I pushed up the slope toward the cliff top. I guessed familiarity did save time. Laboring with my new stuff and carrying it up the mountain meant I'd have to carry it down the mountain, but I wanted a look around. I made it to the top of the cliff as darkness was falling.

Setting everything near the help sign, I built a small fire. I didn't think anyone below could see it, and I didn't care at that point.

While I cleaned the fish and got ready to cook dinner, it dawned on me what a vacation this had become. There I was on a seemingly deserted island, alone, with another group of castaways at the bottom of the cliff. I'd found a deserted camp, for which I was eternally grateful, and I'd been running around like a chicken in the barnyard for the last couple of days. I mean, this was supposed to be paradise. I should have been enjoying it.

Actually, I had been. So many things had happened since leaving Antoine's camp, it seemed like forever. I needed to go back to the camp and check on them.

Laying the grill across the fire, I cooked the fish. I cut open a pineapple and a mango for sides. Next time I'd put them on a skewer. As I finished, I looked up to the sky. It was a rich dark blue, and it wrapped around the clifftop. It was a room without a roof. The stars twinkled, and the sound of the surf drifted up from the sea. It was beautiful. I crawled into my sandpit and got comfortable, asleep in no time.

THE NEXT MORNING I WOKE WITH THE SUN. AFTER MY HIKE the previous day, I was covered in sweat and grime. I slipped into the stream and rinsed off. I was going to have to wear the dry-fit full time or figure out something else to do for clothing. It was hot all the time. Any movement caused me to break into a heavy sweat.

Taking my scope I circled the cliff top, looking in every direction. There was nothing but open ocean, blue water, and blue sky.

I went back to the fire pit and my gear. Cutting up fruit, I ate slowly and tried the phone again, but still no reception. My signal was beginning to fade. I lay against one of the palms and tried to plan out the day.

In an hour, I walked the cliff top again, checking on the horizon. If I saw a ship, I didn't know whether I'd be excited or afraid. It could be anyone. All I could do was hope for the best. Staying on top until early afternoon I decided it was time to go back to the beach camp. I'd leave my supplies in the cave, and then slip over and locate someone from Antoine's group.

BY THE TIME I REACHED THE BEACH CAMP, I WAS DRIPPING sweat from the sun and the weight of my gear. Stashing it in the cave, I refilled my water bottle, ate some coconut, and started for Antoine's.

I'd just begun when I caught a glimpse of white through the trees. On the beach was a woman walking toward my end of the island. I pulled out the scope to get a closer look. It was Gina. Her hair was loose and blowing in the breeze. She had on a white tee shirt that came down to her upper thighs. I didn't remember seeing her in it when I was in camp with them. Maybe she had a bag full of stuff too. I could see her clearly, strolling casually, looking lost in thought. She glanced at the trees occasionally but focused mainly on the ocean. She had a towel in one hand.

Moving closer I stopped at the top of the rise that ran from the beach and led into my camp. As she neared, she glanced my way again, but I don't think she saw me.

She stopped, turned, dropped the towel, and waded into the water. She drove under a small wave and resurfaced in a few moments, hair and shirt dripping. She pushed her hair out of her face as she headed back to shore.

That's the nice thing about a scope. It takes you up close and personal. I could see the softness in her face and the depth in her eyes. She was magnificent to look at. The tee-shirt clung to her every curve. They were amazing curves, full breasts, tiny waist, round hips and butt. Barbie never had it so good. Gina wasn't tall, but she had strong, shapely, short legs.

Let me go back to the tee shirt for a minute. When they get wet, they cling, but they also become transparent. It was like that. Under the scope, I could see every line of her skin as if she were naked and rising out of the sea.

Gina walked up the beach, picked up the towel and wiped the dripping water from her face, then wrung out her hair and brushed her legs. Unless that shirt was dry-fit, I didn't see how she was going to return to camp without being exposed.

She continued in my direction, although I still felt unseen. She stopped in front of one of the palms along the tree line, where there was a large rock. Gina turned her back toward me and grabbed the hem of the tee shirt on both sides. She pulled the tee shirt over her head and laid it on the rock.

A few of the palms blocked my sight, so I only saw a portion of her back. She settled under the tree, but in the sun, to dry off.

I glanced around to see if there was a way to view her without being blocked by trees, but there didn't seem to be. Still, I watched for a few moments, and she seemed to have settled comfortably.

I needed to decide whether to wait until she got up or go ahead and check on the others. I decided to check. She was stunning, but I had work to do.

I MADE A SLOW LOOP ALONG THE BASE OF THE CLIFF. I HEARD the others before I saw them.

They sat close to the shore. I slipped around behind them until I could see through the trees with the aid of my scope. They gathered around a fire ring. It seemed to be all of them, aside from Gina. They were trying to start a fire with a couple mirrors and the sun. I wondered what happened, since they'd had a fire before. Maybe they'd run out of fuel or matches. It was a humorous sight, but I was relieved just to see them.

One of Antoine's men crouched, working with a small mirror in each hand, angled and directed at the kindling. I watched for several minutes as he jostled the mirrors, trying to reflect them onto the fire starter. He paused several times, then pulled a pair of glasses from his pocket and tried them, still no luck. Back to the mirrors, he changed his position and angle to the sun.

Antoine stood nearby, his features tense. William stood beside him. I didn't notice the third man that had walked down the beach toward me.

The group was milling around, and their frustration was palpable. I viewed the fire pile with the scope, as a trace of smoke curled out. He almost had it. I heard him holler, and the flame popped up. Everyone jumped in closer. The assistant, on his knees, dropped the mirror and threw some additional small kindling on the fire. It started to smoke. There were yells and some shouting. Antoine's face beamed with satisfaction.

Wondering again what happened with their previous fire starters, I was relieved to see they'd made this work. Maybe they could have more than coconuts and water.

I thought this would be an excellent chance to address the whole group. It might be the safest. But, I had an urge to talk to Jamal or Mike first. I wanted to know what was happening with the group. I could help them if Antoine didn't want to retaliate against me. With everything I had found, I could make their lives a lot easier.

33

RETURN TO SENDER

I returned to the trail and headed for the beach camp. Arriving a few minutes later I sat under the trees overlooking the beach. The tide was coming in and sprayed the rocks below. While looking I saw movement in the water, reminding me of Gina. I pulled out my scope and scanned the tide. At first, there was only crashing waves, foam, and water.

Then I saw it, the hull of a small boat. Only the bow emerged from the waves. There was a figure clinging to it.

Wishing I had an easier way down, I grabbed my bag and water, and ran for the trail to the beach. If Gina was still there, I might potentially embarrass her, but it was the only route and I wanted to get to the boat before it capsized or smashed into the rocks.

I'd thought I was tired. As I ran down the trail and tripped over the uneven terrain, struggled to catch my breath, and nearly fell, I was proven wrong.

Gina was gone when I reached the beach and turned for the windward side. The tide wasn't all the way to the cliff, but it was closing in fast. There wasn't much time. I sprinted across the sand.

I didn't see the hull at first, but then it popped up thirty yards away. I turned toward it and ran across the incoming tide, lifting my legs high to not get caught in the waves.

The water got deeper as I got closer. The hull was snagged on the sand as the tide washed in and out. It would lift the boat soon and it would float away. Time was running out.

As I got closer, I recognized one of the young guys who had escaped the island. I didn't know his name and wasn't sure he was conscious. I got to him as he was about to roll off the hull. Looking down at the boat, it wasn't a boat. It was a piece of the hull at the bow, inverted. It had an air pocket underneath that kept it afloat. He clung to the wreck. There was little left of the stolen motor launch.

I slid his arm across my shoulder and hauled him toward the shore. He was near dead weight. We had to get out of the tide. He mumbled as he pressed against me, and I could feel his body was still warm.

We struggled as I pulled and dragged him toward the tip of the island, and out of the tide. He might have taken a step or two, but not many.

We made it beyond the point and to the beach on the leeward side. We both collapsed and sprawled in the sand. I rolled him to his back and grabbed my water bottle. I slid my arm under his neck and supported his head. I splashed water on his face and he moaned softly.

I poured a small sip of the water in his open mouth, trying not to choke him. He jolted a little, and his eyes fluttered. I poured more of the water on his face and spoke, "You're okay. You're back on the island. It'll be alright, hang on."

His eyes fluttered again, and his body jerked. I poured

more water in his mouth, and he coughed and swallowed. He thrashed and I held him still.

"It's okay."

His eyes opened. He squinted at me, trying to register who I was.

"You're back on the island. We've got a nurse. She'll fix you up. You'll be okay. What's your name?"

He mumbled. I gave him another sip and leaned in closer to him. He mumbled again.

I thought I heard him say, "Ben, Benjamin Donner."

I looked at him, "Ben?"

He gave a slight nod.

"Well, Ben, this is your lucky day. You're back in paradise," I said in an attempt to make him feel better. "We're going to get you fixed up."

I looked up the shore, wondering how I was going to get him to them or them to him, and decided it was probably better to go get Angelic and pull Ben up in the shade.

I felt him tug, and I looked down.

His mouth moved, and I leaned in closer again.

"They shot Jared."

I looked at him. He moved his head slightly and repeated, "Shot Jared."

I realized what he meant. That last shot I had heard, and the thud it had made, was the bullet hitting one of them, Jared. He spoke again, "He died, we…overboard," and I saw a tear in the corner of his eye, and it trickled down his cheek.

He went on, "Not enough water, or food, we drifted in circles…never saw anything but water…middle of the night we got bumped by something big, shark or whale, not a boat. We all went into the water. Lost Egan. Jamie and I got on the hull. We tried to figure out how to flip the boat, but it was too large for two of us. We drifted, I woke up, and Jamie was gone…a foolish thing to do, because we got mad. "

"What happened to the boat? You were only on a piece of the hull."

He shook his head slightly, his eyes blank, and he shuddered a second.

I got to get him help, I thought to myself. I slipped my arm under his shoulder and said to him, "Come on, let's get you to some shade."

Ben tightened his grip on me as I lifted him from the sand and started toward the foliage above the beach. "Come on, Ben, we're almost there."

About halfway up the beach, his hold slackened, and I called out to him, "Stay with me, Ben!"

I slipped to my knees and leaned him against a palm tree in the shade. I sat back.

"That's better, Ben, made in the shade. Want some water?"

His eyes were closed, and his head was tilted.

"Ben," I said. I slapped his cheek. He didn't move. "Ben," I repeated more softly. "Don't you die on me."

I touched his hand. I went to his wrist and then his neck, no pulse. I put my fingers to his lips, no breath.

Touching his shoulder, his body slipped from the tree and onto the sand, slumped at an awkward angle. I felt his neck again. No pulse. I think he's dead.

Staying beside him for what seemed like a long time, but was probably only a few minutes, I wondered if I should go get Angelic. I touched him again, and his body was cooling. I don't guess so.

I pulled Ben back against the tree, leaned in and draped him across my shoulder. It was going to be a long, slow climb to the beach camp.

34

THE NEXT DAY

Wanting to get in touch with the group, I needed to check on them, and tell them about Ben. But, this was the tropics, twenty-three and one-half degrees above and below the equator. We were likely within the Tropic of Capricorn. It was hot. I would need to bury Ben soon.

I hadn't seen any wildlife or birds, which meant we were so far outside the normal migratory patterns that none of them flew by. It was a good thing regarding scavengers, a bad thing for rescue, but it was still hot. Decomposition would set in quickly.

Wrapping Ben's body in the fishnet I had made I covered it in fronds early that morning. Then I started for the cliff camp to collect the shovel. That was the only problem with being scattered over three campsites. Whatever you needed was always in another camp.

I made it up the cliff and to the turn for the camp. Checking again I saw there was no sign of activity. I went in fast this time and grabbed the shovel from the pavilion and started back to the beach camp.

. . .

Fifty yards beyond my camp, and the tip of the island, toward the windward side, is where I chose to bury Ben. There was a break in the foliage and a view over the ocean. I wasn't sure Ben would want his eternal resting place overlooking the water that killed him, but it was a peaceful spot, and it was beautiful.

I dug his grave and placed him in it. The ground was soft, and it didn't take long, but I was covered in sweat and grime by the time I finished. Sitting in the stream I rinsed off then walked back to the grave. I'd make a marker of some kind so that he could be identified later if something happened to me.

I work in the music industry, and while I'm not a professional singer, I can carry a tune. I sent him off with a chorus of Amazing Grace, because his story was pretty amazing:

"When we've been here ten thousand years,
Bright shining as the sun,
We've no less days to sing his praise,
Than when we first begun,
Amazing Grace, how sweet the sound
That saved a wretch like me
I once was lost but now I'm found
Was blind but now I see."

I was silent for a moment. I stood and absorbed the stillness of the sea and the whisper of the wind, the sun shining down, time passing us by.

"Vaya con Dios, Ben," I said and turned for the camp.

35

REUNITED

After grabbing the scope and my water bottle, I slipped the Glock into my pocket and left everything else stashed inside the cave. I made my way along the cliff and toward Antoine's camp. I climbed a little higher up the cliff face so that I could see the area and pick up any sound from the group. At one point, I could see the beach and the huts they had constructed. There were four huts and thirteen people. I wondered how they were split up. One hut was surely Antoine and the boys, the one slightly apart from the rest, I guessed. The other three were side by side. As if in answer to my question, Antoine stepped from the far hut, followed by William. They stood looking toward the water. Antoine stretched his arms and took in the day. William looked sullen.

I heard other sounds, and I swung the scope up the beach. I hiked along the cliff and spotted a workgroup.

There were Jamal and Mike, Tom Jones, the skinny guy with the heavy set wife, and the beefy guy with Holly. Beefy guy didn't look too good and was leaning against a tree. I saw Mike go over and put a hand on his shoulder and speak to him. I couldn't tell what he said. The rest of the group was gathering fronds, sticks, and bamboo.

I moved down the cliff side. The entire group had stopped and was gathered around the beefy guy. I stood on a rise in front of Jamal's line of sight. I waved my arms slowly, hoping he would turn and look in my direction. I didn't want to get any closer just yet.

Jamal looked up at me after a few minutes of trying to get his attention. He stood still for a moment, then dropped the material he was gathered and started toward me. Mike noticed his departure and stopped talking to the man against the tree and watched. Mike hadn't looked far enough to see me. I jumped off the rock, took a couple of steps, and stopped. I watched Jamal approach, and I looked back at the group, to check the other men. They were all looking in my direction.

Jamal came within a few steps and then ran up and hugged me. I mean hugged me hard, not one of those "bro hugs." I had to catch my breath.

"Man, we thought you were dead." He pulled his face back and looked at me, "You and that thug, Antoine sent after you."

I smiled at him and saw the others approaching from behind. "Just you guys?"

Jamal took a second to realize the question. "Yeah, Antoine and the boys don't work. They're "central planning." They no longer feel the need to supervise, although they did the first few days."

I nodded to him as the rest of the group settled in behind us.

"Tell me what's going on? "

Mike spoke up, "Antoine and his guys have guns. They haven't used them since the night the boys took the boat. But they don't let us forget."

The beefy guy jumped in, "I'm Jim Satterfield," he extended a hand to shake then continued, "they work us like slaves. I've got medical conditions, I'm not really able. I don't have my medicine." He looked down at the sand.

Tom Jones stepped up and shook my hand. "Good to see you," was all he said.

I looked over at the skinny man, and he said, "I think we met in scuba class, I'm Darryl Johnson," and offered his hand to shake.

They stood in a loose semi-circle around me. They looked tired, sweaty, and defeated. All of them had lost weight.

"What's happened?" I asked.

Jamal replied, "Antoine had us build the huts, which are hot and uncomfortable."

"And flimsy," added Mike. "He just wants to keep us together and keep an eye on us."

"Why?" I asked.

Jamal jumped back in, "We do the work, they watch. They have Satellite phones and have been trying to reach a link, but nothing so far. I think two of the phones are already dead."

"How do they justify not working," I asked, and thought about my nearly dead phone.

"They have guns," piped up Tom Jones.

I grinned at him. *That was a stupid question.*

Mike spoke, "We have fire, and we've been able to net or spear a few fish."

I looked at him.

"They have knives too," he replied.

"How are the women? " I asked.

Jamal replied, "They're okay for now. Antoine's guys look at them real hard sometimes. Antoine seems to be in control, but I don't know how long that will last. We felt like as long as we were compliant, we might have some chance of survival. We were hoping for a quick rescue, but that doesn't seem likely now, as much time has passed. "

I nodded to him, "Yeah, I thought that too, it's been over a week. I don't know how much longer than that they would search for us. We'll be presumed lost at sea, dead."

Darryl spoke up, "Where have you been? We thought you were dead."

"It's a long story," I said. "But, so you know, I found one of the boys, washed up on the other side of the island in what was left of the motor launch. He was alive when I found him, but he died shortly after I got him ashore. Two of the other three were lost at sea. One of Antoine's guys shot the fourth one the night they escaped and stole the boat. He died shortly after that."

They all looked down at the sand.

"When are they expecting you back?" I asked.

"Anytime now," replied Jamal. "We were gathering kindling for the fire. Antoine wants to keep it going. It's a full-time job."

"What does he have the women doing?" I asked.

"Weaving nets, cleaning fish, cutting coconuts, and fetching water," replied Mike.

"How are they responding to that?"

Mike raised his eyebrows.

Tom Jones jumped in again, "They got guns and hungry eyes."

"What kind of guns are they?" I asked.

Jamal looked at me, blankly, and said, "Pistols."

"What make or model?" I asked.

Jim spoke up, "I think they were Glocks, 17's or 19's. Why do you ask?"

"I wondered how many rounds they had. They shot several times the night the boat was taken."

Jim replied, "They were each carrying, probably had backup clips. I think they're well armed. They haven't discharged the weapons otherwise, to the best of my knowledge."

I nodded at him in thanks.

"You going back with us?" asked Jamal.

"Yeah, I think so," I replied.

36

DON'T SAY GOODBYE SAY HELLO

I followed the men, their arms loaded with kindling, back to the camp. Antoine, William, the third guy, and the women were gathered around the fire. I was able to get close to Antoine before anyone noticed me. I had my hand in my pocket with the Glock. The one I found that had no bullets.

The men laid their kindling in piles beside the fire. The women were talking about how to cook the fish. William was the one who noticed me.

"Hey, it's him." William stood and pointed at me.

I pulled the Glock from my pocket and stepped in front of Antoine. I held it about six inches from his face.

"Everybody stay calm, on your knees, hands in the air, everybody!" I shouted out.

They all fell to the sand. Jamal and Mike positioned themselves beside Antoine's men. Only Antoine and I remained standing.

"Well, I see you're still alive. Where's Anthony?"

"Who?"

"I sent a man looking for you, I thought perhaps you were hurt," said Antoine with a smile.

"I haven't seen him lately. Don't know what happened to him," I replied, my face fixed.

Antoine continued to smile, but I could see the harsh coldness in his eyes.

"Why are you holding a gun on me?"

"Because you'd be holding one on me if I wasn't."

"Nonsense," he replied. "Why would I want to do that?"

I just looked at him.

"Well, it hardly matters, the safety is on, and there's nothing you can do," he quipped.

I took a step closer and placed the barrel against his forehead. "Glocks don't have a manual safety, want me to prove it?"

There was a pause. I could hear the ocean, the collective breathing of the group, the breeze coming up the beach.

"That won't be necessary, what do you want?"

"I don't want anything except to leave here when I finish speaking. Yesterday, I found one of the boys who took the boat. He washed up on the other side of the island on what remained of the hull of the motor launch. He died shortly after I found him. He said one of your thugs shot one of them the night they fled. The boy that was shot died. That would be murder."

"Nonsense, they were stealing the boat. Besides, at this point, there's no body, no one saw that happen. Don't be ridiculous."

"I'm not, I'm just not staying here. It wasn't your boat."

"It belonged to all of us. We had a right to defend it."

I continued "You took a man's life for a presumed collective right, for an item that had no real value. I don't think so."

"What are you going to do, shoot me?" Antoine sneered.

"If I need to," I replied.

"My men have guns."

"I know they do, but you die first."

I saw him swallow, his mind raced in calculation.

Jamal got to his knees. "Angelic and I are going with you."

"So are Keno and I," called out Mike.

"Move over behind me."

They rose slowly and made their way across the sand. There was another voice.

"I'm going with you too," said Gina. She looked me in the eyes, rose, and came across to join the group.

"Anyone else?" I looked at the others.

"Thank you," said Tom Jones, "but I'm too old to go traipsing through the jungle, I'll stay."

"We're going to stay," said the heavyset woman and wife of Darry Johnson, "we have huts, and we're close to the water."

I looked at Darryl. He looked dejected but nodded.

Jim Satterfield spoke up, "I'm going to stay. I'm not well enough to go."

I looked at Holly, who was standing next to him. She looked at our group and smiled. She put a hand on Jim's shoulder and said, "I'll stay with Jim, he needs help."

I nodded at her.

I could sense Antoine getting fidgety. Before he could act, I took the opportunity away from him when I stepped sideways and slid the gun around Antoine's temple. I looked over at William and the other thug.

"William, you and your buddy, take one hand, thumb and first finger, very slowly pull your guns out by the butt. Drop them in the sand."

He didn't move. I pressed the barrel of the Glock tighter against Antoine's head.

"Do what he says," called out Antoine.

William didn't look happy, but he did it.

"Jamal, Mike," I called out.

They scrambled over and grabbed the weapons.

"Now," I continued to William and his associate, "undo your belts. Pull them out of your pants and toss them in the sand."

The two men slowly undid the buckles and threw the belts down.

"Face down in the sand, arms behind you. Jamal, tie up their hands."

Mike took the same approach I had. He put a gun to each man's head as Jamal tied their hands behind them with the belts.

I spoke to the group that chose to remain. "Start walking down the beach in that direction." It was the opposite direction from where I stood. "Keep walking until you hear a sound."

"What sound?" asked Tom Jones.

"You'll know it," I replied, and he grinned and got up to start walking.

"Come on," he said to the others. They got up and started slowly away.

"You'll be sorry for this," hissed Antoine.

"Maybe," I replied, "but not as sorry as you. You're coming with me."

I called to the rest of my group, "Start down the beach that way, go!"

They took off.

I pulled Antoine by the arm as we backed away from his men. We got about fifty yards down the beach, and I heard a gunshot.

Antoine turned to me. "They had back up's, and they're coming for you."

I clubbed him over the head with the gun barrel and ran for the tip of the island.

37

TOGETHER AGAIN

When we reached the beach camp, I ushered them into the cave and we sat around the fire pit.

"Mike, Jamal, we can stay in here and hope they pass by, or we can post a guard outside and try to determine what they are doing."

Mike replied, "Let's go outside." Jamal nodded.

We were each armed with a pistol. I also unloaded my scope from my bag.

I put Mike in the tree line and Jamal along the bluff. "I'll go to the trailhead and see if they approach." I pointed to the pistol in Mike's hand. "Think you can hit anything?"

"Not likely," he replied. I turned my attention to Jamal.

"Not me either." He looked at me. "Can't you shoot? Can you hit anything?"

I shrugged. "Maybe the side of a barn if I was lucky." I waved them to their places and went to the trailhead.

When I reached the trailhead I lay next to one of the palms with a clear view of the beach. Once zoomed in with the scope, I could see Antoine and his men headed our way.

Blood oozed down Antoine's head and he held a hand

to it. Beside him, William walked with a pistol in hand. It looked smaller than the Glock we'd taken from him. He still had his belt wrapped around one arm. The other man accompanying them had shed the belt and was jumping in and out of the Chapman stance, taking steps and scanning the trees as he went. They didn't look to the sand for a trail.

About fifty yards from the bluff trail, they stopped. Antoine yelled something to them about returning to their camp. They stood nearly a full minute, scanning the trees, but didn't look toward the tip of the island.

Then they turned and started back, walking three across. The two men's pistols had dropped to their sides.

I didn't look away until they were specks in the distance. Getting up I went to get Mike and Jamal. I waved my arms as I approached. They had bullets. We went back to the cave, where the women were joined together in laughter. They heard us coming and went quiet.

I laughed when I saw what they'd gotten into. They'd found the fruit and one of the knives and were eating mangoes and trying to cut up a pineapple.

Angelic giggled. She had fruit on the side of her face. "We couldn't wait. We thought we were going to die, we'd just as well take the fruit with us."

Mike and Jamal looked disgusted. "There's more. Nobody has to be in a hurry. Let's go outside." I grabbed the fruit bag and the machete, and we went out to the fire ring under the palm, overlooking the tip of the island.

"Everybody sit down," I said. They did. I took the machete, cut the fruit, and tossed it to each one of them. It took the rest of the bag, after what they had already eaten.

"I have fish we can cook too." I pulled out the container of fish and they stared at it with wide eyes. Then I took out the grill and tossed Mike the "one light" fire starter.

"You guys fix something to eat, and I'll watch the trail to make sure Antoine doesn't double back on us."

"He's pretty prissy," Mike said. "He probably wanted to get back to camp. He might send his guys, but I don't think he wants to be alone. He'll want to round up the rest of that group so they don't get too far away. He needs workers, although he and the boys may now have to participate."

"I'll watch until dark. Then we can sleep in the cave. They shouldn't find us there."

I walked off to them cackling about the food and the fire. They sounded better than they looked, but there were smiles on their tired faces. I took my position by the tree and watched the beach. There was no sign of anything through the trees either. Mike was probably right. Antoine would want to regroup before he reacted.

I lay there watching for an hour with the smell of smoke and fish in the distance. I heard an occasional laugh. I was glad to have them with me. I wished the others had come, but they were right. You needed to be fit enough to traipse all over the island, or you needed to stay put and rest and stay out of the heat. We would need to get them food, but Antoine was going to be a problem.

There was a sound behind me. I glanced over my shoulder to see Jamal approaching with a piece of fish in one hand and nibbling on a piece in his other hand.

"Here, I brought you something." He handed me the chunk of fish.

I took it in my free hand and sat up. He settled in next to me.

"I want to hear all about this sometime, maybe in the morning. Right now, I'm just grateful to you. That took some big balls to walk in on Antoine and his goons."

I grinned at him, while I chewed, then reached behind me and pulled out the Glock. I shoved the rest of the fish in my mouth and dropped the slide from the pistol, held it up for him to see. His mouth dropped open.

"That took some big, brass balls! You didn't have any bullets!"

"It happened kind of quickly. Once William saw me and started to act, I didn't have any choice. It was a bluff. I think William knew it. I don't think he knew I didn't have bullets, but that I wouldn't pull the trigger."

"Would you have pulled the trigger, I mean?"

"I don't know. It doesn't matter. I didn't have any bullets."

"Did you get this from the other goon?"

"No, I found it with the stuff you saw in the cave. I'll take us all there tomorrow. Get some distance from Antoine and gather up more food for everyone."

He looked at me and shook his head. "And I thought you were dead."

At full dark, we went back to the group. I poured water on the fire to put it out and keep anyone from spotting us. I doubted they would go out at night.

"Did they have any kind of flashlights, other than their phones?"

Mike jumped in, "Never saw anything, and Antoine didn't want them using the lights and wasting power on the phone. Unless there is a full moon, I don't think they could get far off the beach."

I nodded and packed up the grill, machete, and dive knife. I stirred the ashes to be sure the fire was out and to dissipate the heat.

"Let's go to the cave."

38

CROWDED HOUSE

We spread out around the fire pit in the cave. As I slid into the bed I'd dug out, I said, "It helps if you contour the sand to your frame. Makes it a little more comfortable."

Keno and Mike gathered to my right, while Angelic and Jamal lay across from me, and Gina slid into my immediate left. After a few minutes, we all settled into sleep.

Jamal, recalling the old TV show, called out, "Goodnight, John Boy!"

Everyone laughed, and as I turned my head, Gina was lying on her side facing me and smiling brightly.

"Goodnight," she said.

I nodded at her and smiled.

I woke the following morning with the sun coming through the smoke vent in the ceiling of the cave. I slipped outside while the others slept. Looking back at them, I could see they were tired but more relaxed than they had been the day before.

Everything was quiet and peaceful around the camp, just

as we had left it. I walked out to the trailhead and looked up the beach. There was nothing but slow waves rolling in to shore. It was beautiful. We were in paradise.

I started back toward the cave and saw Mike and Jamal standing outside the entrance.

Mike spoke, "What's the plan today?"

"I think we'll do a little hiking. There's a place I want to show you. It will probably take us an hour or so. It's not really that far, but it's uphill. Everybody needs to get water. It will get hot on the way. There's more water when we get there."

They both nodded, and I heard the women coming out of the cave. I led the way over to the stream, and everybody rinsed their face and drank.

I looked at them and said, "I think we ate all the food last night. I hate to do it to you, but you'll need some energy. Let's gather some coconuts for breakfast. We can fan out toward the windward side. There are coconut palms near the point."

As we started off together, everyone was quiet. We got to the spot where I had buried Ben. The women stopped abruptly.

"It looked like a good place for him." I turned to Angelic. "I was going to come and get you, but he died as I was trying to make him comfortable."

She squeezed my arm. "I'm sure you did all you could."

Mike spoke up, "Tell us what happened when you left. We thought you were dead. Antoine sent one of his thugs after you and he never came back. When you didn't either, we figured he must have found you, struggled, and you both died."

"I was up on the bluff. I saw him down below on the beach. He appeared to be looking for something, and I figured it was me. I stayed out of sight. He walked around the tip of the island on the windward side. The tide was coming in. When it reaches high tide on this side, it's twenty-five feet up." I pointed down to the waterfall. "It's just below that falls, the shoreline is a rock bluff. There is no way off of it or on to it. He likely got caught and slammed into the rocks. It would take an unbelievable swimmer to survive. I never saw him again."

I looked at the group, and the harsh reality of the grave, the power of the ocean, the strength of the tide, the forces of nature and man that we were dealing with, registered on their faces. This wasn't really paradise. It was a large chunk of rock in a remote corner of the ocean. An island that could be cruel and unforgiving, without a way off. They had just escaped a forced labor situation that was becoming unbearable and dangerous. They were scared.

"If he didn't come back, I'm guessing he didn't make it. I guess he caught a wave."

Mike looked up. "I bet he wasn't sitting on top of the world."

I had to smile. That was a line from an old Beach Boys tune. But, you had to be careful around the power of the ocean.

We scattered out from the point and gathered up a dozen coconuts. We walked back to the stream and cut and ate the fruit. Everybody got water.

I addressed the group, "We're going to hike for about an hour. It's mostly uphill and a little rocky. Does everybody have decent shoes?"

Everyone shuffled their feet and eyed the ground. "We got what we got," chimed out Mike, grinning.

"Just be careful, the rock is sharp in places."

I led the way, and we started the climb to the camp.

39

SCALING THE HEIGHTS

We hiked for thirty minutes and were halfway to the cliff camp. It was getting hotter, and the trail was in the direct sun. Still, everyone made good time. They were sweating hard but excited to be on their way someplace new. I stopped them for a minute to rest in the shade of a couple of palms.

"We're halfway. Is everybody holding up okay?" I got out my water bottle and held it up. "Anybody need water?"

Every hand went up.

But then, Mike spoke, "Halfway, plenty of water when they get there?"

"All the water you can drink."

He looked at Jamal, who nodded and said, "I can wait."

Then Jamal motioned to the women. They scrambled over to me. Gina was closest, and I handed the canteen to her. She took a sip and passed it to Keno, who did the same and passed it to Angelic. Angelic sipped and handed the canteen to me. In total, they drank about half of it. I capped the canteen, and we returned to hiking.

Jamal moved forward and walked beside me. He looked at me and grinned.

"Why did you come with me?" I asked.

"If I had to be at gunpoint, I'd rather it be you than Antoine. We were getting tired of the whole thing and talking about what to do when you showed up. The group that stayed behind didn't want to act. Especially Mrs. Johnson, she was very vocal. The others might have acted, but the men weren't able. We thought we'd be rescued quickly, and we could put up with it for a short time. It didn't happen like that, and you came along with a better plan."

"How bad was it?"

"The only food was coconuts. We had to walk to the stream for water. Antoine wanted us to work through the heat of the day. He wanted to build those silly huts. He and the boys didn't work, they supervised. Antoine said it was for the good of all, and that we all needed to work together, except they didn't work."

"Oppressive!"

"Yeah, and I'm not into oppression. I make up my own mind, and nobody tells me what to do." He looked around the island. "We did not land on this rock, it landed on us," he said and grinned.

"I've heard that quote before," I replied and paused. "We could still be at sea, or worse."

"Right on," he chuckled, "another day in paradise. We'll make the best of it."

We reached the fork in the trail, and I stopped the group again. The palm was still marked, and there was no evidence of activity.

I turned to the group. "We follow this ridgeline for a short way, and we'll be there."

Mike looked out the ridge. "It looks like it drops off in the water."

"Yeah, but it doesn't. Come on!" I waved to the group.

We walked along the ridge. As we turned into the valley, everyone stopped to look at the three canyon walls.

"You're right," said Mike, "you'd never know it was here."

"How did you find this place?" asked Jamal. The women were all looking, faces intent.

"By accident."

"Does it have a name?" called out Angelic.

"Not that I could find." I waved them forward.

"We'll have to fix that," she replied, looking at the other women who were grinning broadly.

"What was it, or what is it?" asked Mike.

"Some sort of a camp. I don't know if it was old hippies, or new agers, or preppers, or whatever, but it's very well done."

We marched to the pavilion.

I stopped and had them circle up for a visual tour.

I pointed to the fields and said, "We have fruit out there, pineapple, mango, papaya, and kiwi. Over at that pond, there are stocked fish. The pavilion has tables and chairs. There is a fire ring under the trees. The pavilion also has a few supplies. There are a couple of canteens. The stream for drinking water is over there," I said, changing directions and pointing beyond the pavilion.

They stood and followed my gestures in amazement.

"Who were these people?" asked Jamal.

"I don't know. I haven't seen anyone or any sign of who they might have been. I've been coming and going for several days, and there's been no other activity."

I took a step toward the pavilion. "Let's get some water, I'll grab the canteens."

I came back with three. There were six in the box, so we could take the extras to the others.

"Everybody hungry?" I asked.

There were nods all around.

"Mike, Jamal, who wants to build a fire, and who wants to fish?"

Mike replied, "I'll build a fire."

Jamal added, "I guess I'll fish."

We walked to the pond, and I pulled out the dive knife. I had left the bamboo shaft by the pond. I tied up the knife and showed Jamal how to spear the fish. I left him to the task and bent to get the plastic tub out of my shoulder bag. We walked back to a small fire, in the shade, on a hot day.

"Who wants to cook, and who wants to gather fruit?"

Angelic jumped in, "I'll cook."

Keno and Gina raised their hands. "Fruit!" they shouted out.

We gathered a good sample of everything. When we got back, I could smell the fish. I handed the fruit to Mike and Jamal. "Cut that, while I grab some plates."

I came back with five plates, and there were five hungry faces. I handed them out, and we dug into lunch.

40

SHARING THE WEALTH

We spent the day at the camp. Everybody walked the perimeter and looked it over. Late in the day, we gathered at the fire ring. We'd been on the island for ten days. It'd been seventeen days since we'd left LA. It felt like a lifetime!

Mike spoke, "Why don't we just stay here? We have everything." He glanced around the group. The women were nodding. Jamal looked at me.

"I agree this is a great place, but I have two issues. What happens when whoever built this camp comes back, and I don't think we have as good a chance of being spotted from here. I think we need to be closer to the water, to see a boat, or up on the top, to see a plane or a ship. We can certainly move around between the sites and cover our bases."

Angelic spoke up, "Could we break up in groups, or send a couple of us at a time to patrol the locations?"

"That's a good idea. I'll take us all to the top tomorrow so that everyone can see everything, and we can figure out how to get the best coverage."

.   .   .

"WHAT ARE THE SLEEPING ARRANGEMENTS AT THIS breathtaking accommodation?" asked Jamal, holding his hands out and gesturing around the camp.

"There are four beds and mattresses in the pavilion, no sheets, but I wasn't comfortable there. I kept thinking about whoever set this camp up. I slept by the fire the nights I was here."

"It's beautiful out here," said Keno, holding her hands up to the sky.

"Let's just circle the wagons, like we did in the cave."

Everyone nodded and scattered around the fire ring, beside the bed I had already dug. Unlike the cave, this was more of a foxhole than a shallow pit. They dug in and made themselves comfortable.

We settled in our spaces. Gina was to my left again. I looked at her, and she was beautiful in the fading light. As the stars came out and the moon shone on us, it was nearer to daylight than the dusk it had been at twilight. We laid there looking at the stars and the sky, around and beyond us. We were of the world, but we were in our own world, civilization, unknown miles beyond.

MIKE CLEARED HIS THROAT AND SPOKE UP, "ANYONE WANTS to be serenaded?"

"What you got in mind?" called out Jamal. I could see Angelic punching him in the shoulder.

"Let the man sing. I'm exhausted, but I'm wide awake."

Gina spoke, "Entertain us."

"He's such a ham. Y'all remember you asked for this." Keno giggled.

Mike spoke, "This is my favorite Jimmy Buffett song, maybe you'll recognize it."

It was a song about the ocean, like most Jimmy Buffett songs, about the call of the ocean, and the consequences.

"You're not even forty yet," injected Keno.

"Nearly," replied Mike.

He had a good voice. I was impressed. I hadn't thought about it, but, before cell phones, and radios, and television, people had conversations, they talked, they sang, and here we were again, brave new world.

"If construction goes away, you can come to Nashville. I'll hook you up," I called out.

Mike started laughing.

Jamal chimed in, "He's right. That was good."

"Y'all let the man sing," hollered out Angelic.

We were all tired, and our diction was slipping. Or maybe we had finally spent enough time together, we had become one tribe. We were all now, "Y'all."

There was more good-natured kidding and commentary, but we all slowly slipped away into sleep.

41

TO THE MOUNTAIN TOP

I woke at early light, got up, and started the fire. Gina was awake and smiling at me. I smiled back. She hopped up. "Need any help?"

"Let's go fishing."

We strolled toward the pond as the others began to rise.

At the pond, I fixed the knife on the stake and showed her how to spear. She took the spear, and in a couple tries, had breakfast for us. I put the fish in the container and turned to her. She was watching me.

"Why don't you like me?" she asked.

I was surprised. "Uh, I do like you. Why would you think I don't?"

"You don't talk to me, or look at me, much," she said with a soft smile coming across her face.

I glanced up, and Jamal was halfway between us and the fire pit. "Y'all come on, I'm hungry." He waved and watched us for a second, then turned back to the fire.

"I'll do better, I promise," I said with a smile of my own.

I took a step toward the pavilion, and she turned and slid her arm under my arm, and we started back.

Breakfast was good.

"It's another hour to the top. We can take a look around and camp there tonight. We can start to make plans about coverage. Also, how we can help the others. I don't know what Antoine has in mind for them, but I'm afraid he'll work them to death." There were nods from everyone.

We packed, and I led the way to the cliff opening. As we got close, Angelic spoke up, "This place needs a name, so we know what to call it. What did you call it?"

"The Cliff Camp," I replied.

"No," she said. "That's got no style. We need a name, so we know where we are or where we're going."

I turned to look at her.

She jumped back in, "I think "Shangri-La" would be nice."

Keno followed up, "What about "Bali Hai?""

I couldn't help myself, and said, "What about "Hole in the Wall,"" which got both men laughing.

Gina spoke up, " It's more like "Heaven on Earth.""

"Heaven on Earth, H, O, E for short," said Jamal. "So it's the HOE Camp."

Gina grimaced at him.

I didn't think he could resist. Jamal started marching out of the valley, up the trail, swinging his arms and singing,

"Hi ho

Hi ho

It's off to HOE we go

Hi Ho

Hi Ho"

Everyone got a kick out of that, although the women looked a little aggravated.

We hiked straight through. Everyone had water, and we

made good time. It was late morning and starting to warm up. The closer we got, the more breeze we picked up, so it was still pleasant when we got to the top.

They were impressed with my "help" sign, the signal fires, and the view.

42

ON TOP OF THE WORLD

I pulled the phone out and tried for a signal. There was none, and I was now at a quarter-power. It wouldn't last much longer. I scanned the horizon with the scope and saw nothing but water and sky.

We walked around the peak and checked the view in every direction. It remained unchanged. I showed them the cooking fire pit and the bed I had dug.

"Man, you've been a busy little beaver in the couple of days you were gone," noted Jamal.

I grinned at him. "It was just by chance. I was looking for a way to the top, and an opportunity to see if there were surrounding islands, or a ship, or a plane, anything, that would help us get off this rock."

I LOOKED AT THE GROUP, AND EVERYONE WAS HOT, TIRED, AND hungry. "Let's spend the day here and rest."

There were nods, and a couple of the women sat down. "The stream is over there, for water, and cleaning up. I'll start some lunch." I sat the bags down.

Keno spoke, "Did you weave those?"

"Yes, the first couple of days, I needed to be able to carry things since I was planning to move around. Then I found the cliff camp and really needed them."

"I can weave some," she said. "I'm going to need to do something. My clothes are shredding in the heat, and on the rocks and sand."

Her shorts were tattered. Jamal and Angelic had on linen, which was comfortable, but also shredding. I had gone to the dry-fit, and it was wet all the time. Maybe we could create something.

"Did you use some type of loom?" Keno asked.

I shook my head. "What I've done has been on frames that I build from bamboo sticks. Most of my experience has been on the fly."

"We could make some vests and a kilt or cover for the men, and some halters and a wrap for the women," she replied.

"There's a lot of undergrowth here on top. We can gather it and figure out a few things," I replied.

Keno, Gina, and I gathered the vines, and the others made lunch. We returned a short time later with a large load. Keno sat down and looked at the sticks, sorting them in piles, and doing the same with the vines.

We ate. Everyone relaxed, soaked up the breeze, and rested for several minutes.

"I'm hot," I said. "Anyone want to join me at the stream to cool off?"

Everyone got up and walked to the water. We took our shoes off and found a place to step in and sit in the stream. We lay against the bank or the rocks and let the water run over us. It wasn't that cold, but on a hot day, it felt great. We sat for ten minutes.

"I'm starting to get cold," muttered Angelic.

Jamal replied, "It must be a hundred degrees, girl."

"Not in this water," she said, shaking a finger at him.

"Feels good," said Mike.

While I listened, I watched Gina. She floated a bit, spinning from side to side like a small, shapely fish. She caught me looking and grinned as her face turned above the water.

"How about some grooming, everybody? Maybe a haircut, or a trim, some beard shaping?" called out Keno.

She got our attention. I looked around the group. I had a heavy beard, and it was scruffy, so was Mike's. Jamal was less raggedy. The women looked good. I guess this offer was for the men's benefit.

We got out of the stream and wandered back to the campsite. Keno grabbed a small handbag she had been carrying and opened it. She pulled out a wrap that looked like a bundle of silverware. It was a packaged set of her tools-a comb, mini brush, set of scissors, and a small battery-operated trimmer.

"How do you happen to have those?" I asked,

She smiled. "I never leave home without them."

Mike spoke, "When Antoine wanted to see what we had in our pockets or purses, Keno emptied the bag for him, then held it upside down and shook it, to prove it was empty, but the tool kit fits into a small zippered compartment on the inside. He fell for the purse being empty."

I looked at the others. Jamal spoke, "I didn't have anything but my wallet."

Angelique jumped in, "I had my bag, but it was mostly empty, nothing he could use."

"Same for me," noted Gina. "All I had was some extra clothes and a little makeup."

"I had a small pocket knife that I hid in my shoe," added Mike.

"We didn't have much, but we hid what we could," summarized Jamal. "They had no right to take anything."

"What about the others? I asked.

"Mrs. Johnson had a pair of scissors, and her husband had a four-inch pocket knife. They took both of those," said Mike.

"Yeah, but Mrs. Johnson was the only one who admitted they knew how to weave, and Antoine ended up giving the scissors back to her for the fishnets. Her husband, Daryl and one of Antoine's men did the net casting. They'd pick out the larger fish for Antoine and themselves, and give us what was left. They did share the fire, as long as we kept it going," added Jamal.

"Holly, Jim Satterfield, and Tom Jones didn't have anything. Tom had his hat and cane, but they let him keep those," added Gina.

"They kept talking about the common good, and the fight for survival, but we did all the work, and they supervised and watched," stated Angelic.

"Who is he?" I asked.

"We never were sure. You remember, he told us his company name and title. He was some kind of businessman. The other two or three were associates and bodyguards. It looked dubious. He was a control freak, power happy. He tried to be nice, but it wasn't believable," said Mike.

"How about those haircuts?" said Keno.

It was really the beards and the heat. We hadn't been on the island long, but it was hot, and Mike and I had hair that was below our collars and over our ears.

Mike sat first. Keno looked at him. "You don't have enough hair yet to braid, but you could do a bun. I could run the trimmer over your ears and cut that away, keep you cooler, let the rest of it hang. We probably need to weave some hats or some head covers."

Mike agreed and Keno ran the trimmer along his ears and his neck, cutting the hair to the scalp. He was left with a mop and sidewalls. He shook his head and slung the remaining hair.

"Cooler already," he said.

She punched him in the shoulder. Then, she took the scissors and feathered the ends, so it wasn't quite as blunt, which made the hair fly even more. The other women got a kick out of it and were laughing at him. Keno took the trimmer and ran it over his face, taking away the bulk of his beard, and leaving a five o'clock shadow.

"Jamal, you're next," Keno called out. Jamal sat and looked over at Angelic.

"I like the thicker Afro," she said. "It makes him look more like Shaft. But please, do something with that fuzz on his chin and jaws." Angelic shook her head and smiled.

Keno finished him up and nodded at me. "It's your turn."

I sat, and she studied my hair. I figured I'd get the Mike treatment.

She lifted my hair off the collar of my shirt.

"Leave it in the back," said Gina. "He can braid it before long."

Keno nodded, cut the sides of mine, and feathered it. She ran the trimmer across my face and cut away most of the growth.

Keno shook out the trimmer. "You guys have some tough facial hair. This battery won't last long. You'll have to go to a short beard that I can scissor cut. It will be totally tribal!"

Then she added, "Let's get to work on those new accessories."

Angelic stepped beside Keno, while the rest of us rose

and stretched our legs. I heard her whisper to Keno, as I moved away.

"Do you notice how everyone in our group is pretty good looking?" she asked.

Keno giggled. "Aren't we lucky! Maybe ugly people don't cruise, or maybe they're too smart to get stuck on a deserted island."

"That's cruel," Angelic said and then they laughed together.

EVERYONE GATHERED AROUND KENO, WHO STOOD IN THE center and said, "I think this is what we need to make: some hats with brims, some vests for the men, some halters for the women. They will be lightweight, and they will dry quickly. We need some kind of wrap or cover for the bottoms. We could make bikinis for the women or a bikini with a wrap for when we sit or sleep."

The men agreed on the bikinis but shook their heads at the wrap.

"We have to be practical," she said. Angelic and Gina nodded.

"The tougher part will be the men. I can weave a crotch with two legs, but you'll have no openings or "limited access" I should say. If you wear them against your bare skin, you should be able to manage. "

"Won't that get hot?" asked Mike.

"We have the waterfall by the lower camp, and the streams. We need to rinse often and stay out of the sun in the midday heat. That should keep us cooler, and reduce the wear on our regular clothes. I think we should try it," I said.

"What about shoes?" I had noticed Angelic and Keno in scandals. Gina wore a pair of tennis shoes I hadn't noticed before. She caught me looking.

"I had on sandals too, but I had these in my bag."

"We can make some," answered Keno, "but they won't have much arch support. We probably should try to make them and rotate with our regular shoes, so we don't wear them out. We can go barefoot on the sand or soft ground."

She looked at me. "Can you guys build some frames for weaving the vests? The ladies and I will start on the hats and other things."

I nodded. Mike, Jamal, and I sat and started to assemble the sticks into a frame for weaving. This promised to be entertaining. We should end up looking more like Robinson Crusoe and less like Gilligan's Island.

We worked through the afternoon with Keno giving instructions and supervising. After we started, she left me to manage the men. We stopped weaving late in the day and went to gather more vines. It felt good to be moving. It was warm, but the brightest and hottest part of the day and the sun had passed.

We gathered another large load of vines and got to work making dinner. I noticed the women giggling and comparing several woven items.

The men sat around the fire and watched the fish cook, as Keno announced, "For your viewing pleasure, we have the summer, in this part of the world, swim collection by Keno, Angelic, and Gina."

She waved a hand, and Angelic and Gina stepped from behind her. Keno then turned and pulled her tee-shirt over her head.

The three of them stood in woven bikini tops. Angelic and Keno's went around their necks and tied in the front. When they turned, there was a small braided strand across their mid-backs. The tops didn't cover much, but they looked great and would be a lot more comfortable than what they'd been wearing.

Gina's top was different. It ran across under her breasts and around her back. It had small woven braided straps over the shoulders, which tied to a small woven triangle that covered her in front. It was impressively engineered.

They had on their regular shorts, but it was easy to see the jungle look, when fully developed, changed the game.

"Dinner's ready," I said. "Bon appetite, y'all"

We sat and ate while we discussed what to do next.

"I think we should go to the beach camp and check on the others. We can stop at the HOE camp and gather some food and gear for them."

"How do we keep Antoine and the boys from hoarding everything we give them?" asked Jamal.

"Observe them, I guess. Try to catch the others when they're working. It depends on what Antoine has them doing. We'll have to wing it."

"I think we have to try," Angelic agreed. "I need to check on Jim and see how he is doing. He didn't have his medication. In this heat, with poor hydration, he'll die."

We were all in agreement.

We camped around the fire pit. Everyone was weary and fell asleep quickly.

BACK IN REAL-TIME

We woke with the new light of the day. We'd gone to bed with the fading of the old light of yesterday. It was a natural rhythm. We had gotten away from it in our lives, before the cruise. It made sense here and now.

We ate fruit and packed for the trip to the HOE camp.

Gina kept saying, "It's Heaven on Earth, not HOE," and we laughed at her each time.

When we reached the camp, the group laughed at me for being so cautious upon entering the canyon. You can't be too careful, though, never know when someone might come back, and they'd not be happy with us eating their food and using their camp.

The others gathered fruit while I grabbed two of the rods and reels. I took the other shotgun for backup.

The women had smoked more fish. Gina had speared them. I was impressed.

I spoke to Keno, "We'll need to weave a strap for the other shotgun, make it simple to carry." The women had grown accustomed to me having a shotgun over one shoulder, but I hadn't used it. They looked uneasily at the second one .

"It's a tool, ladies, if we need it. We probably never will, but Antoine's guys are armed, and we need to be on a level footing with them."

Keno nodded. "I have a couple of ideas. I'll make it work."

"Thanks."

We ate, shouldered the bags, and prepared to go.

"We're in the heat of the day. Do we want to go now or wait?" I favored going on but wanted to ask, make sure everyone was comfortable. "We'll need to come back regularly and work the fruit, perform maintenance, and clean up. I'm not a farmer, but we want to look after what we have."

Mike seemed to sense my thinking, and said "Let's head back."

Jamal nodded.

Keno said, "We can get to work on the clothes and shoes, while you guys check on the others."

"Can you think about some type of a rope or ladder that we could use to climb down to the waterfall? I think that would be easier than sitting in the stream. We could go down in pairs." Gina looked over at me and smiled. Jamal raised his eyebrows. I realized what I'd said.

We started for the beach camp and caught a breeze as we came around the cliff to the main trail. We dropped down the cliff face and arrived shortly at the ocean. Keno organized a quick gathering of vines and stakes.

THE WOMEN GROUPED IN THE SHADE TO WORK WHILE Jamal, Mike, and I went to check on the others. I took the scope and the bag with the fruit and reels while Jamal carried the rods. We each had a pistol. I loaded some 9 millimeter rounds Jamal gave me. We had two shotguns and the machete. We were fierce-looking, for three guys from a cruise ship, stuck on a deserted island.

We took the trail along the base of the cliff, toward their camp. I noticed that Antoine and his boys didn't like to wander into the vegetation. Only if they had a work party, would they go inland.

Eventually, I saw Mrs. Johnson and her husband, Daryl, down near the shore with the other thug. I didn't see William. They were casting with the nets. Daryl seemed to manage it well.

I didn't see Antoine, Holly or Jim. We spotted Tom Jones inland, gathering vines.

We approached him. I had Mike and Jamal on my flanks, to watch for any sign of activity.

"Tom," I called out softly. "Tom," I repeated. He stopped what he was doing and stood very still, only his eyes moving. "Over here," I called from under a tree. He spotted me.

A big smile came across his otherwise tired face. I motioned for him to come over. He did, and I had him sit under the tree. He looked frail. I reached into the bag and handed him some water. He drank it gratefully. I gave him some pineapple. His eyes got big.

"Damn, manna from heaven."

"No," I said with a grin, "pineapple from the field."

He ate slowly at first, savoring the flavor, but then pushed the balance of it into his mouth and swallowed. He slumped back against the tree. "That was good. Where'd y'all get it?"

"Found it," I said, being cautious. "A few stray plants we ran across."

"Yeah, okay! How y'all doing?"

"We're good. More importantly, how are you and the others here doing?"

"We're able to catch some fish. Antoine and his guys eat most of them. Jim isn't doing well. Holly tries to help him. Antoine's boys mostly stand around and ogle Holly. Can't say I blame them. Mrs. Johnson and Daryl do most of the work. I help as best I can."

"We got a couple of rods and reels I can give you if you think it will help?"

He looked at me again. "What y'all got, Amazon delivery?"

I grinned and shook my head at him.

"Just one might help. Daryl could use it. Antoine's guys wouldn't use it, and I don't know how. Maybe he could catch something bigger than those baitfish he keeps netting," Tom replied.

"How do you explain it to them?"

He looked up at me. "Take it out of the bag. Lay it down. Take a step back." I did.

He put his hand out and touched it, "I found it on the ground, under a tree. That's the gospel!"

I laughed. He was a survivor. I wished he'd been strong enough to come with us. "You sure you don't want to come with us?"

He smiled this time. "I'm too old, boy, don't have the energy, besides somebody has to keep an eye on these peckerwoods. You never know when you might need a piece of information."

He pushed off the tree and picked up the rod and reel. "I best be getting back to work. I don't want them looking for me."

I gave him another piece of pineapple. "I can leave more of the fruit here if you think you can get it to the others without Antoine or his guys being the wiser."

"I don't know. The rod I can cover. I'll guess that your group left it for us or maybe somebody else was here. There it was, is what I can say. The fruit might be harder. They might come looking for you. We're eating coconut and fish, and drinking water. We're getting by. Don't make it harder than it has to be. They keep an eye out for you and would love to catch you, but they're too busy making us work to look for you."

I shook his hand. "Stack up three coconuts and leave them under this tree as a signal, if you need anything. We'll keep an eye on it and on you guys."

He touched my shoulder. "You're good people. We'll get out of this, and we'll have a beer or two and laugh about it." He hobbled as he started through the trees. I wondered if I could make him a knee brace, would it help.

We started toward the beach camp, and I brought Jamal and Mike up to date on the other group's situation.

Mike was aggravated. He had gotten a good look at Tom. "We should just go in and kick ass. We got guns."

"Yeah, but so do they, and they're probably better with theirs."

"Yeah, but we got shotguns. We don't have to be as good, or as accurate, just close," he commented.

"That's not a bad idea," said Jamal, "but somebody's going to get hurt if we do that. Antoine won't give up power that easy. We have to remember, we will get off this rock one day. What will we have to answer for then."

"Antoine's a tyrant. We need to take him down," Mike replied.

"I don't disagree, but for now, let's keep an eye on the others and try to keep everyone alive until we figure out a bloodless way to go about it."

They both seemed satisfied for the moment.

We got back to the camp and a big surprise.

44

HIGH FASHION WEEK

The ladies had been busy in our absence. They strutted around camp in their new halters, and now they had wraps around their hips. They looked good. Everything was the same color, green and soon to be brown, but they fit nicely.

Keno waved to us. "Have a look."

Angelic and Gina stepped forward and turned a 360-degree circle, showing us their wraps, which tied at one hip and draped to the other side. When they undid them, it revealed a woven bikini that sat high on the hip bones and plunged down between their legs and around in the back. When they turned around, it revealed the backside of a thong.

Mike whistled, and Jamal let out an, "Oh yeah!"

"Very nice," I said, catching Gina's eyes and her smile.

"We thought these would be comfortable and practical, and we can cover up as needed," Keno said. "But, we have more."

Gina and Angelic grabbed a garment and started toward me and Jamal. Keno picked one up and headed for Mike. They looked like something Superman might wear. It was woven shorts that you pulled on and then tied up. It was topped with an open vest. We were looking good…styling, as they would say back in the day.

"We're still working on the shoes and hats, but we wanted to get the basic outfits together," Keno said.

"They look great," I said.

"Absolutely," added Jamal.

"Positively," threw out Mike.

We got a hug in return from each of the ladies. We're just one big happy tribe!

We sat and told them about Tom and the other group.

"How can we best help them?" asked Angelic.

"I think we keep an eye on them, and offer assistance, food, or aid, as needed," I replied. "I don't think we want to get into a power struggle with Antoine and his guys."

"We need a plan, a routine," offered Gina. She didn't speak much, but when she did, it was worthwhile.

"Yes," I agreed, and the others nodded.

45

PLANNING THE WORK AND WORKING
THE PLAN

"I have some ideas for getting to the shower, to the waterfall," Keno said. "We could make a ladder out of bamboo. Cut the length we need, then braid the shorter cross pieces. Or, we could braid a rope ladder that we drop down and roll-up."

"We can pull the ladder up or down if needed," suggested Mike.

"That'll work," added Jamal.

"Bamboo shouldn't be too heavy, and it would be sturdier than a rope ladder," I added.

"Good," Keno said. "That's how we'll do it. You guys get the bamboo together. We've got the vines already."

We did as we were told.

The ladder came together quickly.

When we finished, Jamal, Mike, and I dropped it over the ledge, and it comfortably reached the level below. They secured it at the top, and I climbed down. The landing area was large and ran under the cliff further than we could see from the beach. There was plenty of room to shower and change clothes. We'd have to weave some towels to dry ourselves.

I climbed to the top and nodded to the guys.

"Keno, why don't you and Mike go first, since you designed the access?"

She smiled and grabbed Mike's hand. "I thought you'd never ask."

They climbed down and disappeared below the ledge.

I suspected that if I went to the trailhead leading to the beach on the leeward side, I might see the falls. But I didn't go to the trailhead.

Mike and Keno came back up. I signaled to Jamal. He took Angelic by the hand, and they went to the shower.

Keno had the rest of us gather and sort vines for her next set of projects—shoes, hats, towels, and more shoulder bags.

When Jamal appeared on the ladder, I saw Gina watching him and Angelic. She got up, came over, and took me by the hand. "Let's go."

I know I looked surprised. Jamal was grinning at me. Mike gave the thumbs up. The women didn't pay any attention.

We climbed down the ladder and walked over to the falls. She turned to me, smiling brightly. "Let's get wet."

Don't get me wrong here, it was an amazing offer. *But, I wasn't sure we should get involved in a situation where we'd be trapped together if there was a problem, if it didn't work out.*

"You go ahead," I said and turned toward the ladder. I had my back to her.

She sighed. "Okay, but we need to talk."

We got back to the top, and Keno had everyone weaving. We spent the rest of the day working and made good headway on several of the items.

We stopped, and Mike asked, "What's for dinner?"

The rest of us shouted out in unison, "Fish and fruit!"

. . .

WE SPENT THE NEXT DAY FINISHING UP THE ITEMS. THE FOOD was running out, and we decided to make a trip to the HOE camp for ourselves and to gather some things for the other group.

Jamal made a suggestion, "Why don't Mike, Keno, Angelic and I head for the camp, two of us can gather food and the other two can hike to the top and check the sign and the sights? You and Gina can stay here this time, continue on the garments, and check on the other group. We'll meet back day after tomorrow, compare notes, and decide what to do?"

We all agreed that it was a good plan. The four of them took off the next morning.

AFTER THEY HAD GONE, GINA AND I SAT UNDER ONE OF THE palms for most of the morning, weaving.

"Let's take a break and go from a swim," she said.

It was hot, and I was anxious to talk with her after the fiasco at the waterfall.

"Okay."

She got up and said, "Let me get my towel."

I'd forgotten the day I saw her on the beach she'd had a small towel.

She came back wearing her tee shirt and carrying the towel. I was hoping she'd be in the halter and bikini and was a little disappointed. Maybe I'd made her angry.

We walked to the beach, and she dropped the towel in the shade, by the rock where she had swam and sunned when I'd seen her before.

We took off our shoes and waded into the water. It was warm, but there was a slight breeze, and the sun felt good on our skin. We bobbed in the water, and she swam up in front of me. I had my dry-fit on, and she had on the tee-shirt. I suddenly remembered how that worked. The shirt clung to her curves, and even in the water, I could see every line of her body. So yeah, the tee shirt was good!

We were crouched, facing each other, and she was paddling her arms, her body swaying. I was trying not to stare.

"I think you like me," she said.

I didn't know where this was going, but I decided that being direct was best. "I do, like you. But I didn't think it would be respectful to you," I said. "I mean, if we didn't work out as a couple, or if you weren't interested, that would be awkward for you, me, and for everyone else."

"You know," she said. "You seem like a really decisive kind of guy, a take charge, take no prisoners, kind of guy, but still a nice guy. I'm attracted to that, plus I thought you were cute. Besides, you're the only one left." She laughed and touched my shoulder. "Seriously, what's holding you up? You were by yourself on the ship and here on the island. You don't have a ring or a ring tan. Is there someone else?"

I looked into her eyes for a moment. They sparkled and smiled back at me.

"There was," I paused. "But she was killed in a car accident last year."

Her face grew serious, "I am so sorry." She paused. "I know a little about that. It's miserable, feels hopeless sometimes."

I looked into her eyes. "Yeah," I said and suddenly felt a lot more comfortable with her.

We turned, walked to the sand, and stood at the edge of the water.

"Tell me about you," I said.

This time, she pulled back a little. "I'm a straight shooter."

I believed her.

"Are you sure you want to know?" she asked.

"Yes, I do."

"I'm a dancer," she said, looking me in the eyes. "An exotic dancer, a stripper, before that I worked in the adult film industry, I was a porn star, AVN newcomer of the year."

My face was blank, but I'm sure my eyes got big.

She smiled like a burden had passed. "Yes, I'm good at it, and I enjoyed it, but I only dance now. I'm not in porn anymore."

My mouth moved, but no sound came out.

"I got tired of the "BS" that surrounds it. I mean, many people that work in porn are absolute professionals, but like any industry, many aren't. As a dancer, I control the environment, and they can look, but they can only touch if I say so. I like to be in control." She smiled again.

I looked at her, my face still blank. "I'm sure you do." I paused. "How did you get involved?"

"Like I said, I know a little about loss. My mother was a single mom. I have two brothers and a sister. We never knew our father, or at least I have no memory of him. My mom and her then-boyfriend, she always had a different boyfriend, until they found out she had four kids, they were killed in an accident. They were drunk, and I suspect she was giving him a blow job while he was driving."

"What would make you suspect that?" I asked, perhaps foolishly.

"When the cops pulled them out of the wreck, she had her head between his legs."

"Maybe he forced her?"

She rolled her eyes at me. "She loved oral sex. She loved all sex. She wasn't shy around us. She was naked in the front seat of the car."

I didn't know what to say, so I went with, "I'm sorry."

She looked at me for a moment, and a smile captured her face.

"It was probably best in the long run. We were crushed at the time, but it made me grow up fast, and that was helpful."

"What did you...I mean, what happened?"

"Human services, the department of children's services was going to come and get us and send us to foster homes. I was 16 at the time, but I looked much like I do now. My mother had stripped a few times at a local club, and I knew a couple of her friends. I contacted one of them and asked if she would come and stay with us, so there would be an adult presence. She agreed and got me a job at the club. I started dancing the following week. I paid the bills and kept the kids together. The friend, she was about as crazy as my mother, was no help, but she kept the authorities off of us for a while, and then she ran off with some guy. I learned quickly, and as soon as I got to be eighteen, I jumped to one of the big gentleman's clubs, and started making really good money."

"How did you manage?"

"I worked nights, slept days, dropped the kids off when I got off shift, picked them up before I went on, did what I had to, and slept in between. My oldest brother, just a year younger, joined the military as soon as he was able, and eventually became a Special Forces member and then an instructor. The two younger ones were a couple years behind. My younger brother was a real introvert and spent all his time reading and playing with his computer. He eventually got a degree in engineering and works for a large international firm, travels the world."

"What about your sister?"

"That was the tough one. She wanted to go into porn too. By that time, to get her brother through college, I had to move on to the adult film industry. I had made some contacts while dancing, and it wasn't that hard. I posed a few times for magazines and websites and then got an offer, which I jumped on. I mean, I like sex. I'd always been fascinated by it. I was good at it. I was built for it. What else was I going to do to keep my family together? I don't regret it. I had a good time, but there's a limit to it, and you have to know that and move on when it's over, or when you want it to be over. I went back to dancing. I still make a good living. But, to get back to my sister, she was adamant about getting into the business. I realized by that time it was a short term thing. There's no career path in porn. You might become a producer or something, but I was ready to move on. I managed to get her interested in nursing, and once I got her started, she was hard-headed enough to not let go. She's a fireball though, incredibly sexual, some poor doctor is not going to know what hit him. She has sexual energy and imagination running out of her ears. When I finally got her through school and into her residency, she decided to continue and become an NP. She said she'd pay for it. I think she may have gotten a sugar daddy to help with the bills. The girl won't give up, giving it up!" Gina sighed as she finished.

I just shook my head. "I don't know what to say!"

"Did I answer all your questions," she asked as she turned toward me and smiled.

"I thought all porn performers had tattoos," I said, raising my eyebrows and teasing her.

She looked serious for a minute. She stood, put her arms to her side and grabbed the tee shirt. She pulled it over her head in one fluid motion and held it to one side in her hand. She stood there naked in front of me, less than a foot away. She turned slowly. "Do I look like I need ink?" she asked coyly.

I watched her as she turned, every line, every curve, her skin rippled with goosebumps.

"No, I guess you don't."

She took a step closer. "Would you put a bumper sticker on a Ferrari?"

"I never had a Ferrari."

She slid against my chest, naked, her skin pressed warmly and firmly against mine, her legs entwined, and then she wrapped her arms around my neck. "You got one now!"

THE GIRL FRIEND

Gina was pressed firmly against me so that I couldn't help but respond. Her thigh pressed harder against my groin. She smiled and pressed a soft kiss to my cheek. "I see I have your attention," she said as she stroked my knee. "Is that Mr. Happy and the Twins?"

I broke into a smile. "Yes, and they're glad to see you too!"

We stood for another moment with her wrapped tightly around me. Then I put both my hands under her butt, picked her up, and walked further inland. We sat on the sand and held hands.

"I'm hungry," I said.

"So am I, but not for food," she replied. She dove into the water and swam out a short distance. I sat on the beach for a minute.

"Well," she said, "get out here, and don't be wearing those shorts."

What could I say? I lost the shorts and dove into the water to meet her.

Don't believe what you hear about sex in the water. Try it out for yourself! It can get pretty wet.

GINA BROKE AWAY AND POINTED TO THE SEAFLOOR. SHE DOVE under a wave, and I realized she must have seen something. I followed her.

We drifted toward the tip of the island where the rock ledge with our cave was located. Gina swam along the bottom and grabbed a large conch. As she turned toward me, she looked up and I followed her gaze. There was a ledge above us, and she swam for it.

I had taken a good breath of air when I dove but didn't want to be stuck under a rock with no escape. I pulled her leg, to swim back, when I realized she had broken through the surface of the water. Kicking up beside her, I realized we were in a cave underneath the rock.

We were inside the outer edge of the rock, and fifteen feet from a bank that sloped toward the shore.

I guessed immediately that this, at some point, led to the cave where we slept. The passageway had become filled by sand over time and through storms. The light rippled off the water and shone about the cave. At night it was probably dark, but in the day, there was enough reflection to see.

We swam to the bank and climbed out. We were both naked, and I couldn't resist looking at her from head to toe. She smiled and took my hand.

"Over there," she pointed. "I see something."

We took a couple of steps, and it was an empty box, heavy cardboard, looked new.

"Let's climb toward the ceiling," she said.

We got near the top of the cave, and there was a flat shelf that ran around the perimeter. There were wooden boxes stacked across it. Fortunately, one of them was open.

It was full of automatic weapons. They looked fresh, as in, not rusted, dirty, or as if they had been sitting around a long time. Someone had been here recently. There were a half dozen cases of them and what looked like boxes of ammunition. But, there were also other boxes. I went to move one of them, not a chance. It was heavy.

I wondered what was inside. Gina must've had the same thought, "Can you open one?" she asked.

I stepped to the closest box and pried at the top. It took several tries, but finally I got a board loose, and there was a shiny reflection. I pulled another board and another.

Gina looked in the box and up at me. "Now we know the name of this place, Treasure Island."

"Yes, I guess we do."

They were gold bars. Stamped with a seal in a language I didn't understand and the words South Africa. These weren't old, weren't buried treasure, these were current, and some kind of contraband and inevitably someone would come back for them.

We left everything as we found it. I put the boards from the box of gold bars back in place and hammered them down with the heel of my hand. Gina grabbed the conch.

We walked to the water and took a last look, jumped in, and swam to the outside surface. We didn't speak. It felt good when we broke into the open sunlight. The sky and the sea were just as blue, the few clouds floating above us the same. But it was different now.

Before then, I thought someone might come back eventually, some group that was trying to get away from the world, for some esoteric reason of their own. But they still might have been helpful. Now, I doubted it. This group, searching for guns and gold, would not be helpful. In fact, they'd be deadly.

Gina swam over to me, wrapped her arms around me,

and kissed me firmly. She pulled her head back and said, "I guess this changes the game for us?"

I nodded at her. "I think someone will definitely be coming back. And since we're camped directly above their hiding place, we may be in harm's way. We need to be nearby, but able to hide until we can determine who they are and how hostile they might be. We should sleep in the cave and post a watch."

We swam to the shore, sat on the sand, and watched the small waves roll in and break at our feet.

She took my hand and looked me in the eyes. "A lot has happened in the last few minutes."

I couldn't help but laugh. "Yes, it has," I said, squeezing her hand.

"How about some lunch? I am hungry now," she replied and smiled.

We walked to the camp, hand in hand.

Gina put the conch in her sleep pit while I started the fire. I heated fish, and she cut up fruit. We ate in silence, comfortable in each other's presence. We didn't talk about the gold or the guns. They seemed like part of another world, one that shouldn't have intruded on us here on the island. We sat in the shade and worked on the weaving for the next hour.

As I wove, I scolded myself for not taking one of the automatic weapons and ammunition. I'd never fired one before, but had seen them at the range, and anticipated I could figure it out. The old gunnies called it "spray and pray."

Gina was working quietly. I said, "You want to take a break and see how the others are doing?"

She sat the weaving down and hopped up, brushing off her legs.

I grabbed the scope and the Glock. She watched as I did. "Do you need that?" she said, pointing at the gun.

"Well, I hope not, but it can be effective as a tool if we run into the wrong part of the group."

She nodded, and we started toward the middle of the island.

We went inland as we walked up the beach, and stopped often to listen for sound. We walked along the cliff face so that I could see and use the scope to look for workers. I spotted Tom Jones gathering vines and fire starter. He appeared to be alone.

We approached him with caution and emerged about fifty feet away. I stood and waved slowly. He finally looked up, saw me, and nodded. He glanced over his shoulder at the beach and then made his way toward me.

"Morning, boy!" It was actually midday, but I was glad to see him. On the island, time moved very slowly. I turned and motioned to Gina, who came out from a thicket. He saw her, and his face lit up. They hugged as she reached him.

"How are you doing?" she asked him.

He took off his Panama hat and wiped his forehead. "We manage. Mrs. Johnson maintains and mends the nets, her husband, Daryl, catches the fish. Jim and Holly gather the fruit, and we take turns managing the fire. We gather the food, Antoine and the boys take what they want first. We get whatever is left over. That's the routine."

Gina had removed her shoulder bag while he was speaking and gotten him some pineapple. He dug into it ravenously. It didn't look like they were managing that well. He looked weary, almost haggard and hungry.

"They making any progress with their phones or anything?" I asked.

Tom shook his head. "The phones are dead. They don't want us to know, but I overhead William and the other guy talking. They're getting really frustrated. It's all Antoine can do to control them. They openly eye Holly and flirt with her. Jim would probably kill himself, trying to keep them away from her. She seems torn on what to do. Between that and Antoine's proclivities, they're not happy boys."

"Proclivities," I said. Tom and Gina smiled. Tom looked at her.

"Antoine is gay or bisexual," noted Gina, looking at Tom to confirm.

Tom smiled and replied, "Fortunately, I'm too old, and Daryl and Jim don't appeal to him. William seems to be his primary toy."

I looked at Gina. "How did you know?"

"I didn't really but I watched him closely. I've been around performers that were gay or bisexual and sometimes you can get a sense of it or they tell you after spending a little time with them. It depends on their personality."

"It's how Antoine spends his afternoons, in the hut with William" replied Tom. "Also he has the boys watch over us more, since your last visit."

"Unbelievable," I said.

"No," said Gina, "just human nature."

Tom smiled. He and I heard the sound of someone moving through the brush at the same time. He swung his head toward the brush. I grabbed Gina's hand, and we stepped into the thicket. Tom started toward the sound. In a minute, I heard William.

"Jones, you out here?" William bellowed.

"Yo," Tom called out.

I watched William come toward him and actually cause Tom to back up almost to us.

"I heard voices," said William.

"What?" asked Tom.

"Who were you talking to?" William demanded.

"Myself," said Tom. "I said to myself, self, we have to talk."

William just stared at him.

"I was bored. I talk out loud sometimes, often actually," replied Tom.

William took another step closer to Tom. I heard the snick of a knife locking in place. In East Nashville, we'd call them switchblades. William was not in a good mood. It made me wonder what he'd been up to.

Tom stepped around William and back toward the camp. "I'm hungry. Did they catch anything this morning?" He gathered up the vines and fire starter he had in piles and plodded toward the beach.

William took a final glance around and then turned and followed.

Gina and I stood in silence until they were out of sight. We moved toward the cliff and away from the area.

She took my hand halfway to the camp. "He was clever to lead William away, but it sounds like they aren't doing very well."

"I agree. We need to talk to the others and see what can be done."

We reached camp and prepared dinner. Afterward, we walked out to the point where I had buried Ben and watched the day fade away. It was beautiful as the sun slipped into the ocean, and the moon rose in the night sky. We walked back to the camp and settled into the cave for the night.

Gina removed her halter and bikini, naked she slipped into the pit beside me. It was nice. There was a stronger breeze blowing thru than usual. Even with all the body heat we produced, it was comfortable, or maybe it had something to do with her lying naked upon me.

47

PLAYING UP A STORM

I woke predawn with Gina sleeping beside me, arms and legs draped across mine. I hated to move. I lay there and watched her breathe, the rise and fall of her chest, and listened to her heart beating next to mine. *Why would I want to get up?*

But I did. I was driven by something. I slid from the sleep pit and went to the mouth of the cave. I looked cautiously around the camp and didn't see anything out of place. I stepped from the cave and turned to the sunrise. The sky was a bright, brilliant red. It was positively on fire. I almost got my phone to take a picture.

Then I remembered again the old saying my mother had taught me:

"Red sky at night
Sailors delight
Red sky at morning
Sailors take warning"

It seemed so long ago that I stood on my patio on the ship and glanced out at a similar sky. The breeze was up as I walked to the bluff and looked over to the waterfall and the incoming tide. It was swifter than usual and slapped off the rocks. Could this mean another storm? We'd been here for two weeks with calm weather. Was it time again?

Gina slid up beside me. She had her bikini bottom on but was carrying her halter in her hand. She was magnificent to look at. She was so comfortable naked. I guessed it came from the work she did. But I also think it came from inside her. She wasn't shy or embarrassed about anything, including her body.

"It's beautiful," she said, looking at the sky.

"Yes, it is." I looked from the sky to her and back. "Some say, red sky in morning means a storm."

She looked around and pulled her hands to her shoulder. "The breeze is stronger than usual. Is that a part of it?"

"It could be. We'll have to wait and see."

We went back to camp and ate breakfast. We worked through the morning and talked about going back to the cavern to take another look at the guns and the gold. But, the sea was up. I mean, it was swirling, and the waves were coming quickly. Most mid-days, it was calm as a pond. The sun was out, but there was a haze that wasn't usually present. It felt like a storm.

I expected everyone to be back later. I hoped they would return to camp quickly. If a storm sat in, I wouldn't want to be out in it. Tucked away in the cave would be the safest place.

We gathered coconuts and filled the canteens to do what we could if we had to weather the storm and spend time in the cave.

I looked out at the sea and sky and up to the cliff. Gina put her hands on my shoulders. "They'll be here. You know Angelic and Keno aren't going to get caught out in the weather."

I had to smile at that. I turned to her and said, "What if they don't realize a storm is coming?"

She looked at the sky. "I think anybody could see something is going on and want to get where they were supposed to be."

"Don't worry," she said and pushed me gently to the ground. She climbed over and straddled my lap, pulled off her halter and pushed my face toward her breasts. "I think we should find something to occupy us for a little while…or maybe longer."

Afterward, I had to admit, I did feel better, at least for the time being. The wind picked up through the day, and the sea was churning. I was ready for everybody to come together.

LATE THAT AFTERNOON, MIKE AND KENO CAME TRAMPING into camp. My face lit up. They were fully loaded and struggled to unload the shoulder bags.

"We gathered food while Jamal and Angelic went to the top. I figured we should share more with the other group, and it looks like a storm, so I didn't know when we could get back up there," said Mike.

I nodded to him. "Good plan, I think the storm is definitely coming."

We put the supplies in the cave and made a late lunch, mostly for something to do.

"Do you think they will be okay, down in those huts?" asked Keno.

"They were beyond the tide line in the daily course of things, but I did see debris, probably from a prior storm, ten or fifteen yards beyond them. It was up in the tree line," I replied.

"I think Antoine noticed that when we were building but didn't think it would matter. I think he thought we'd only be here a few days, and building at the back of the beach made sense," said Mike.

"Do you think he might move inland?" asked Gina. "I mean, those huts aren't very stable."

"I doubt it," I said. "He won't want to be bothered to keep an eye on everyone or get wet or windblown."

Mike laughed. "His boys won't want to either, but I bet any amount of wind will blow the roofs off, and they will get wet. We just couldn't build them that solid or stable, and we didn't think we'd be here that long. They were mostly for shade."

"And privacy," added Keno. "Antoine liked to keep to himself, mostly, every afternoon."

The wind continued to rise, and I thought about moving us into the cave. I feared we might be in there for some time and I didn't want to go in until we had to. It was getting darker, and the haze in the sky was replaced by heavy dark clouds. The sea was pounding the rocks on the windward side and rolling in hard on the leeward.

"I think we better move into the cave," I said.

"What about Jamal and Angelic?" asked Mike.

"I think they would know to go into the cave. I'll stand in the opening and watch for them."

He nodded, and we rose to make our way to the cave. Everyone got inside and settled into their sleep pits. The cave drew a good breeze, but by staying down where we slept, we were below it. I stepped back to the door as darkness fell, and rain pelted down with the force of high winds. As I watched the storm, I worried where Jamal and Angelic might be, fearful that someone had returned to the island and found them. I didn't want to think about it and was ready to head back into the cave when I heard a shout.

"Yo!" It was Jamal. He trudged forward slowly with Angelic falling a little behind. They leaned into the wind, burdened by the heavy shoulder bags. I ran to meet them and took Angelic's bags. As I took it, she nearly fell, and I caught her by the arm. She looked up with a grateful smile.

"Get in the cave!" I shouted to her. She nodded and sped up. I struggled along beside Jamal, who looked like he was about to fall over.

"Let's go!" I shouted, leaning low and pushing him from behind.

We got to the mouth of the cave and he dropped the bag off his shoulder and slid against the wall. I went to pick up his bag, and it was a solid weight.

"What do you have in here?" I asked.

He grinned and pushed himself off the wall. "I didn't want to get hungry."

We drug the bags down the cave floor, and Mike jumped up to help. He was grinning at Jamal. "I told you we'd get the food," he said.

Jamal nodded and spoke, "we thought we could bring a bit more, and it looked like a storm, and we just about weren't fast enough."

We slid the bags to the side of the cave, and Mike and Jamal climbed into their sleep pits.

"I'm going to take one more look," I called to the others.

When I got to the opening, I looked at a sky that was the blue-black you see in bad storms. The wind was howling, and the rain was coming down in big sheets. I could hear the sea pounding all around us. At least this time we were on dry ground and not out in a boat.

I went inside and crawled into my sleep pit. I was soaking wet from the wind and rain. I slid next to Gina, who was warm and naked.

The wind whipped through the upper portion of the

cave all night long. Storms in this part of the world had some substance to them, none of those quick shower things. Everyone was huddled up and cuddled up. It was going to be a long, hard night.

48

WRATH OF THE STORM

When I woke, I stepped out of the cave while the others slept. I met a bright sun-filled and high blue cloudless sky. Everything was bathed in a golden light. There was a breeze, slight enough to feel. The blues and greens of the island glittered in their freshness and color. It was as if the storm had washed everything clean.

I realized that we meant nothing to the island. It was here when we landed, and it would be here long after we were gone. It was isolated in the ocean, far from the world, solitary. Only the storm, in its size and power, had any effect, and that was only fleeting.

Jamal approached from behind. He had the food bags and was going over the contents. Gina, Angelic, and Keno were starting a fire and preparing fish.

"Let's eat some breakfast, load up, and go check on the other group," I said.

Everyone nodded. We were unusually quiet as we worked. Everyone was efficient and focused. I guessed we were all worried about the other group and how they fared the storm. The wind had howled all night, and we had heard the rain and the sea.

We ate quickly and packed for the walk to their camp. Jamal and Mike each had a shotgun in their hands. I had the Glock at my back and the machete over my shoulder.

We hiked to the beach and walked along the shore. It was washed clean, although I saw tide lines far up in the trees as we came onto the beach. It didn't look good.

We walked slowly in the bright sunlight, alert, and vigilant to our surroundings. We saw nothing until we reached the camp.

I heard voices and crying.

We reached the area where the huts had been. There were only a few stakes and some woven webbing remaining. The group was standing and sitting around Antoine. I saw William look up quickly as if to react. Mike and Jamal both lowered their shotguns and racked them. William sat very still, his eyes boring in on us.

Antoine sat hunched over in the sand, his clothes soaked and torn. He looked tired, his face blank but hard and intense. As I looked him over, I saw his eyes were hollow and empty underneath. The man was positively evil. I approached him with caution.

"What happened?" I asked.

"The storm washed us out!"

Holly spoke, "Jim is missing. I'm afraid he may have drowned or been washed out to sea."

Antoine continued, "The storm came in great waves. It flooded the huts, tore them to shreds, and washed them out to sea. We scrambled out of them and grabbed trees or one another, whatever we could find. When it finally passed, Jim was missing. We haven't seen him since."

Jamal and Mike set the bags down, and Gina and Keno moved to them, to hand out the supplies.

"Is anyone hurt or feeling bad?" Angelic asked. "I'm a nurse, and will be happy to examine you."

"My shoulder hurts," called out Mrs. Johnson. Her husband stood next to her.

Gina and Keno distributed food and water to everyone. They were a bedraggled looking group. Antoine and William remained sitting in the sand. Tom Jones leaned on his cane. Holly, her blouse soaked and torn along the buttons, watched the surf and glanced along the tree line. The other assistant stood silently beside Antoine and William. The Johnsons stood with Angelic.

Angelic moved the woman's shoulder and gauged the pain caused. "I think you have a severe bruise and not a fracture. How were you hit?"

"The waves crashed into the hut, and I was slammed to the ground. I landed on Daryl, but hit the sand with my shoulder."

"Let's put it in a sling for a day or so and take the pressure off." Angelic pulled a length of vine from the carry bag and began to wrap it about Mrs. Johnson's shoulder.

THE OTHERS SAT IN SILENCE AND ATE.

"My," said Antoine, looking up from the sand, "you are well equipped. Did you have all that in your gym bag?" He nodded to the supplies and to the shotguns.

"We got lucky, found a few things," I replied.

Holly had been staring out to sea. She pointed. "There, what is that?"

I turned and saw something bobbing in the surf. "Jamal, Mike, keep an eye on everyone," I called as I ran for the beach. Holly followed.

She pointed, and I saw a figure bobbing in the outgoing tide. I stripped off my vest and left the Glock inside it. I ran through the surf and dove into the water toward the figure.

I swam for a distance and then floated, to take another look. I didn't see anything. Holly called from the shore and pointed to my right. I caught another glimpse of the figure, definitely a body, white shirt, dark hair, going grey. I swam for it.

Again I surfaced and treaded water. I couldn't see anything nearby. I waved to Holly. She shook her head. "I lost it."

I swam for several more minutes, checking and changing directions. I looked to her several times, only to get a shake of the head. I swam back to the shore.

"What was he wearing?" I asked.

"A white shirt, slacks, boat shoes."

"Describe his hair."

"Dark, turning grey."

"I think that was him. Did you see it?"

She nodded, without reply, and turned to the shore.

I thought I saw her shoulders shake as she walked up the beach. I didn't know how well she knew him, but to lose someone around you is never easy. I hoped she would be alright.

We reached the group, and I saw the others looking at me. No one spoke. I shook my head.

"Tragic," said Antoine from his perch in the sand. He wiped his hands together, dismissing Jim, like he'd never existed. "I think he had a bad heart anyway."

I started to shoot him right then, but I didn't.

"We'll help you," I said to Antoine and his group. Tom Jones and Daryl smiled.

Mrs. Johnson, her arm in a sling, said, "Why would you help us now, you run off, and took the others, left us to fend for ourselves. We don't need your help."

"I'm afraid she's right," parroted Antoine. "We'll manage."

"Any of you want to come with us?" I asked Antoine's remaining group. No one responded.

His men still had guns. I didn't want to waste time or energy arguing with them. I motioned to Mike and Jamal, and they grabbed the shoulder bags after emptying everything left inside.

"Suit yourself," I said as we backed away from them and onto the beach. We walked several yards down the beach, covering our retreat as we went.

When we got back to our camp, I posted Mike at the trailhead that led to the beach.

"Keep an eye out for a few minutes, then come and eat. I don't think they'd follow us, but it's hard to be certain." He nodded in response.

Night had fallen, and we sat around the fire after eating.

"Why wouldn't any of them come with us?" asked Keno.

"I think they were afraid to," responded Jamal.

Gina spoke, "Antoine has them intimidated, at least Mr. and Mrs. Johnson. They're afraid of him, and as long as he has them, he knows the man will fish, and the woman will cook, and Tom will tend the fire. I think Tom stays because he wants to help the couple. Antoine and his goons piggyback off of the others."

"That's sad," commented Angelic.

"The strong intimidate the weak," continued Gina. "That's the world we live in."

"I don't truck with that. It shouldn't be that way," said Jamal.

"It shouldn't, but it is," concluded Gina.

"Well, we'll keep an eye on them and make sure the Johnsons and Tom have enough to eat," said Angelic. Keno nodded first, followed by the rest of us.

We crawled into the sleep pits that night, and as I snuggled up to Gina, I whispered in her ear, "That was impressive, what you were saying about the situation, and how clearly you saw what was happening."

"It's not the first time in my life I've seen it, "she replied and settled in next to me.

The following morning we gathered a few more things. Jamal and I elected to take them to the camp and let Mike keep an eye on the rest of our group. It was most of what we had left, and we would have to make the trek to the HOE (Heaven on Earth) camp to replenish. We also needed to check the "help" sign at the mountain camp.

Jamal and I made our way along the beach. He had one of the shotguns. I had the Glock. Mike had the other shotgun at the camp.

We looked up the beach and saw a cluster of people in the distance. As we got closer, we recognized Holly and Antoine's two men, William and the other one. We didn't even know his name. They were all naked and intermingled near the waterline.

Holly was on her knees, with the one man standing in front of her. William was on his knees behind her. They were grunting or moaning and thrusting against each other.

"Beach orgy," whispered Jamal.

I nodded. "They didn't wait long."

We walked past, and not one of them stopped or noticed. We walked into the campsite. Tom Jones was standing by the fire, separating kindling.

He waved at us.

Jamal and I dropped our bags and dumped food supplies

and water. He dropped to his knees and sorted through it. He shoved some fruit in his mouth.

"Thank you, boys, I'm getting mighty tired of fish and coconuts."

I nodded to the camp. "Where are the others?"

"Well, you probably saw sex on the beach," he said, pointing toward them. "Mrs. Johnson is out with Mr. Johnson fishing, and I'm tending the fire."

"Where's Antoine? " I asked.

"He wandered off down the beach. He was watching, but he seemed to get bored."

"He doesn't participate?" asked Jamal, his back to Tom and me, watching the beach, scanning with the shotgun.

"No," replied Tom. "He prefers William, they go one on one. William seems to be the glue that holds them all together."

"She didn't seem to upset about the two on one or the act itself," Jamal replied.

"I think she knew it was bound to happen," replied Tom. "They had been staring at her since the beginning. Antoine kept them away from her for a time. He maintained a veneer of propriety, despite the powerful intimidation he supported. Since the storm, he just doesn't seem to care. You fellas hadn't been gone an hour when they took her down to the beach. She called out at first, but in a couple of minutes, they were all naked and going at it. They've been naked ever since, Antoine, too, gratifying themselves every chance they get. As long as we provide food, water, and fire, they don't pay any attention to us. We get whatever food's leftover. "

"Did they ever actually threaten you or her?" I asked.

"Early on, Kyle—he's the other thug beside William—grabbed Holly, and Jim jumped up to protect her. They beat him pretty bad, which led to his health deteriorating even worse. He had a bad heart. He told me himself."

"Come with us," I said.

"No, I got to keep an eye on the couple. Besides, I'm your inside man," he replied. "Just keep some of this food coming, if you can, I'm wearing out myself."

We nodded to him and started back to our camp. The naked trio was lounging now. At least we didn't have to worry about their guns. One of them had his hands on Holly's shoulders, and the other one had her by the thighs.

When we got back to camp, we didn't share what we had learned or seen. It seemed best for the moment.

PART III

———

THE THIRD HOUR

49

THE PIRATES

We rose early the next morning and started for the HOE camp. No one spoke during the climb, and we arrived mid-morning. Everyone relaxed as we rolled into camp. I checked again for any signs of activity, but there were none. Everything was as we left it.

I wanted to spend a few days, but I worried about Tom and the others, even about Antoine and his boys. Things had gotten primal for all of them.

We spent the day gathering food and planning on what to do next. We decided, before we turned in that evening, to leave most of the food at the trail split. Then we'd hike to the top of the cliff to check the sign and surrounding area.

Waking early, we started the climb for the top. By late morning we arrived. Almost three weeks on the island and we'd become good hikers, efficient and strong.

Nothing had changed at the top. The sign was there, the fire pits, the sea, and, most importantly, with the sign flat against the sand, no damage from the storm. The sky was clear. It faded from a light pale to a deep, dark blue. High up and far back, I could see the moon. As I looked at the darker blue beyond, it was so vast and empty, I felt completely disconnected from the world I had known.

As I stared at the sky, the wind whispered across my face, and the water glistened and shimmered in the distance. We were displaced and alone.

"Hey, it's a ship. At least I think it is. I can only see the mast!" Jamal yelled.

He gestured in the direction of Antoine's camp, and there appeared a large shape that looked like the top of a mast.

"We need to get down there quickly," said Mike. I nodded and waved to gather everyone.

"That could be whoever built the HOE camp. They may not be happy to see us."

Gina and I hadn't told the others about the underwater cave or the guns or the gold. Whoever was on that ship might be coming back for them, if it wasn't the same group that built the cliff camp. Either way, I felt like it wasn't a Good Samaritan or a random chance. I didn't think it was someone who'd be willing to help us. We'd been on the island too long without a sighting of any kind.

We were isolated in the world. Based upon the cruise ship's direction, Honolulu to Tahiti, due south, we could be somewhere in the Marquesas Islands, which were north of the Society Islands, home to Tahiti.

Or, Tahiti is about as far below the equator as Hawaii is above it. We weren't quite halfway between the two when we got separated from the ship. If we drifted east, we could still be north of the equator. But the heat, and the location of the sun, for the time of year, made me think we drifted south into open, empty ocean, and below the equator. Either way, anybody coming here would have a good reason. It wouldn't be by chance.

"Look, we don't know who this is, but we do know that it's a remote island. Let's proceed with caution. Hopefully it's just someone passing by and they can help us. It's hard to imagine what they might think, seeing Antoine and his group."

We gathered our gear and started for the trail. We stopped at the fork and retrieved the extra food. If these were friendly people, maybe they'd appreciate some pineapple. We moved quickly down the trail. From our location, I couldn't see the ship once we dropped off the clifftop.

By mid-afternoon, we arrived at the beach camp. We stashed everything in the cave and, as a group, moved to see what was happening.

We followed the foot of the cliff and made our way toward their drinking pool. I stopped everyone when we were still thirty yards from the stream.

"Jamal and I will work our way to the beach and see if we can spot anything through the scope. We'll circle back here and advise you what we see, and what we might do. Stay put, unless you're forced to move."

The others nodded.

Jamal and I started for the beach. We made our way to a small rise in the tree line at the edge of the beach. We could see the ship clearly. It was a three-mast barquentine.

"Surely it's motorized, too," said Jamal.

"I imagine they use the wind to save fuel," I replied.

I eyed the ship through the scope and couldn't see anyone. I scanned the deck and then the rigging. I swore as I lay there, the ship was flying a Jolly Rodger. *Seriously,* I thought to myself. There was a Panamanian flag, and some other pennants, but there hung the "skull and crossbones". *Maybe they just had a wicked sense of humor.* I went back to the decks and looked again. The ship was worn and much of it needed to be repainted. It didn't have the look of a luxury yacht or a weekender. It looked like a working ship.

Maybe it was the people who had built the camp, or the people looking for the guns and gold. I swung the scope to the shore, and it got worse.

Holly was staked between two palms with her feet on the ground, legs spread wide, and arms tied to a crossbar above her. She was naked. Every few seconds, a different man approached to ogle her.

It wasn't just a few men, either. There were a lot of them. I tried to get a total count and lost track after twenty.

I CHANGED POSITIONS AND SAW ANTOINE, WHO WAS TALKING to a light-skinned black man in a flamboyant costume, complete with a feathered hat. He had on a wide sleeved shirt, striped pants, and knee-high boots. He waved his hands vigorously at Antoine, who didn't seem bothered. In fact, Antoine looked quite comfortable.

Settling in place, I continued to survey the camp to get an idea of what was going on. Tom and the Johnsons were down by the water, fishing. A couple of men from the ship, armed with AK-47's, watched them. So, the sailors could be here for the gold and the guns but probably not for the HOE camp.

I handed the scope to Jamal. He scanned the area quickly, nodded, and we started back to our group.

50

THE PREVIEW

We found the group where we had left them. I filled them in on what we had seen.

"Seriously?" asked Keno. "Pirates!"

"Absolutely," responded Jamal.

"What are we going to do?" asked Mike.

"We have to help Tom and the others," said Angelic.

I looked over at Gina. She was smiling at me.

"I don't know. I'm not sure the best way to help them. They have guns."

"Lots of them," threw in Jamal.

"We have guns," said Mike, shaking a shotgun.

"I expect they know how to use them better than we do. They're pirates. We're tourists," I replied.

"We're islanders. They're intruders. Doesn't that count?" asked Gina.

I grinned at her and said, "Probably not enough. They may have been here before we were." I paused. "They surely have a radio on the ship. Maybe we could get to that."

"How?" asked Mike.

"Carefully," added Jamal, with a grin.

"I think we should observe them a bit more," I said.

"Is there time?" asked Angelic. "What are they going to do to their hostages?"

"How long will they stay?" asked Keno.

"Based on having the woman tied up and the others providing food, I think they might stay a while," added Gina.

Everyone turned to look at her. She shrugged.

"That's just how men are. Most men, anyway!" She looked at Jamal, Mike, and me.

"She's right," noted Angelic. "If what you said is true, and they have a reason to be here, they'll stay for at least a few days. Until they get bored or get what they need."

"You said Antoine was discussing something with them. What could that be about?" asked Mike.

"I don't know," I replied, looking at Gina. She took the cue.

"A couple of days ago, Dee and I were swimming by the point. I dove underwater to get a shell, a conch, and I thought I saw a reflection above me. When I swam for it, I came up in a cave. Dee followed me. We explored it. At the top, which is probably right underneath our cave, we found guns, AK-47's like these guys are carrying. Also, we found gold, lots of it, gold bars."

"Why didn't you tell us?" asked Keno.

"We were going to, and the storm came in and everything that happened with that, and now this. There wasn't any way to get it out of there, and what were we going to do with it? We have guns, and the gold was heavy, and what would we have done with it on the island anyway?" Gina replied.

Mike put his hand on Keno's shoulder and squeezed. "I'm sorry," she said. "It was just the first thing that came to mind."

Gina smiled at her, and they hugged. Angelic smiled.

"We need to work together," she said.

"I agree, but I still think we need to observe them for a little while, to get an idea of what they're doing," I responded. "We'll go armed and intervene if needed."

"So you think they're here for the guns and the gold?" asked Mike.

"More than likely. There are too many of them for the HOE camp. There were only four beds."

"They could be brutal," Mike answered.

"Very," said Jamal.

"Do you think Antoine will tell them about us?" asked Angelic.

"I don't think he'd hesitate to," I answered. "It would depend on what purpose he thought we could serve. He didn't seem uncomfortable or act like he'd been captured. He may have bartered with them using us as bait."

"Bait, for what?" asked Keno.

I could only shrug. "I don't know. We'd be able to tell pretty quickly if Antoine told them. If it looks like they're searching for us. We need to be very careful. Keep down the noise, only light a fire at night. Sleep in the cave. These guys are probably better trackers than Antoine's boys."

We started for camp. Angelic said to Gina, "Can I see the shell you found?"

Gina nodded.

When we got to camp, Gina ran into the cave and brought out the conch. She handed it to Angelic.

Angelic turned it over in her hands a couple of times, examining it. She held it to her lips and softly blew a scale. We all turned in surprise.

Jamal was grinning and pointing at Angelic. She played French horn for four years in high school and four more in college. She was in the marching band, the whole deal. Angelic blew a little riff and pulled the conch down.

Mike held his hand out and asked, "May I?"

Angelic nodded and handed the conch over.

Mike held it to his lips and blew a few notes in a bass line. Again we were all nodding.

Keno jumped in and pointed at Mike, "Four years of high school tuba and marching band."

Mike pulled the conch down and handed it to me. I shook my head.

"Go on," he said. The others turned to me expectantly.

I held the conch up and blew as hard as I could. There was one long note that howled, then whimpered, then died away. Everyone in the group doubled up laughing.

"All I got is hot air," I said. I held it up for anyone else to try. Jamal, Keno, and Gina all waved it off.

Angelic took the conch back from me and held it up. "We could use this as a signal when we are separated. We'll have to blow louder but it should be easy to tell who is blowing it."

"Can we hear it from that far away?" asked Keno.

"I think Mike and I can make it ring out enough to be heard from a distance. Dee may have to practice a little."

"I'll make a sling for it. Make it easy to carry," said Keno.

Everyone laughed and nodded.

We ate fruit for dinner and turned in at the cave. No one slept well.

Just after midnight, I crept to the trailhead and down to the beach. Sounds and voices drifted from the pirate camp. There was a glow from a huge bonfire.

There was a sound behind me, and I turned quickly, reaching for the Glock. It was Jamal with one of the shotguns.

I relaxed and exhaled.

"I didn't want you out here by yourself, might get caught," he said, pulling up beside me.

I nodded and pointed to the glow of the bonfire.

"Got your scope?" he asked.

"Yes."

"Let's take a look."

I glanced back at the cave.

"Mike's got it," Jamal answered. "Let's just not be too long."

We walked up the beach, inside the tree line. Moving a few feet at a time, we looked and listened for any sound. If Antoine had sold us out, the pirates didn't care or couldn't be bothered to look for us, yet.

The glow grew brighter, and Jamal and I took a position behind the last stand of trees that gave way to the beach. I pulled the scope and sighted the fire. It took a second for my eyes to adjust.

About a dozen pirates were seated in a circle on the sand. They had cut Holly down from the trees, and she was in the middle of the group, dancing to music one of them had playing. They were all naked. Holly gyrated, thrusting her hips toward the men, shaking her shoulders and breasts. Her hair flowed down her back. Its movement kept time to her rhythm. She stroked her thighs and groped her hips, teasing the men. They came forward, one or two at a time, to fondle her. She made no sound. They'd finish quickly and be replaced. Some left the circle and others took their places.

Antoine was nowhere to be seen, nor was the pirate leader.

"Damn," said Jamal. "She's got stamina, and a strong constitution."

"Appears that way," I replied.

Everyone was awake and waiting for us when we

returned to the cave. I described what we had seen. Angelic and Keno drew in short breaths.

Gina spoke, "She's a survivor. She's doing what she has to. Sometimes it's that way. Back in the real world, a hot shower and a cold beer and she could put it behind her."

"But we're not in the real world," said Angelic. "We're on an island, on a three-hour tour, the boatman said. That was such a long time ago. Can she manage it here?"

"She has to, if she wants to live," replied Gina.

"For how long?" asked Keno.

There was silence. "Until we figure out how to help them, how to save them," I said. There were nods all around. "Let's get some sleep."

I WOKE EARLY THE NEXT MORNING AND DECIDED TO GO FOR A swim. I wanted to think about what needed to be done.

Barely out of the cave, I heard a whisper from behind. It was Gina. "I want to go, too."

I smiled. I couldn't help it. I liked her, a lot. "Come on."

We swam, then, afterward lay on the beach, near the tree line, side by side. It was nice, warmed by the sun and our proximity.

I asked about her brother and sister. "Why didn't you let Human Services take them?"

She looked at me, incredulously. "And have them carried off, never to be seen again?"

"They would have kept you in touch."

"I don't think so," she answered. "The agency would have fed them a bunch of empty lies, and trapped them in a prison of promises they'd never fulfill. I kept them with me. We were family, we stayed together. We found a way to make it work."

I had to admire her. She had balls, and brains, and

beauty, and a big heart. I tickled her nose, and she giggled, suddenly a little girl, and not the fearsome adult she'd been seconds before.

I sang to her in jest. It was the background rap from an old Chaka Khan song.

"Let me take you in my arms, let me fill you with my charms."

She raised her eyebrows. "Did you really just say that?"

"What's the matter, you don't like Chaka Khan?"

"Of course I do, but that is ridiculous."

"Yeah, I guess so, but you could dance to it!"

She rolled her eyes at me. "I have danced to it, on stage, wearing nothing but five-inch stilettos, a feather boa, and a smile." She wasn't smiling when she said it.

I looked back at her. She was serious. I guess she saw my expression.

She put her hand out and touched my chest, above my heart.

"I can feel your heartbeat," she said as she looked me in the eyes. "But you got me all wrong." She paused. "This is not a game. I'm not here flirting with you, or dancing for you. I'm here because I like you, whether you like it or not."

I kept looking at her, my face softening. She leaned in close, her lips near mine but stopping short, waiting.

I leaned in and kissed her softly. "I like you too!"

Then I pulled back and paused.

She looked at me, quizzically. "Are you having a black moment?" she asked.

I looked at her and thought for a second. "No, I'm good."

She smiled and took my hand. "I'm glad that's over with!"

51

A PIRATE TALE

We walked back to camp and sat for a quick breakfast. Mike and I left to spy on the pirates. Jamal stayed in camp. I answered a few questions on the way and told him what we'd try to do. I wanted to find Tom Jones and see what he knew. I also wanted to see if the pirates were looking for us.

We climbed the cliff face to where we could look down over the camp. The pirates seemed to be in no hurry. Holly was tied to the trees again. Antoine and the chief pirate sat in a meeting, a parlay, no doubt, by the burned-out fire. Antoine's guys sat near him. A few of the pirates backed their leader.

We scanned the surrounding area until we saw Tom and the Johnsons near the tide line. I wanted to catch Tom alone, if possible. We slipped toward the beach.

Tom and the others were fishing. Actually, Daryl was fishing, Tom and Mrs. Johnson were watching. We stood a few yards away in a clump of trees. There were no pirates, although I kept Mike on lookout just in case. I watched Tom and Mrs. Johnson and tried to figure out how I might get his attention. They talked and talked and talked, while Daryl fished.

Tom finally turned toward the camp. I acted quickly, stepped out from the trees, and waved at him. Soon as he saw me, I stepped back into the trees.

He turned to Mrs. Johnson and spoke a few words. Then he started toward the camp. He collected sticks and small debris as he wandered in our direction. He ambled along until he got close, and with a last look at the sea, and the couple—she was now watching her husband intently—he stepped into the trees with us. We shook hands. I pulled a couple of pineapples from the shoulder bag for him. His face lit up in a big smile.

I pointed to the couple. "What's her first name?"

He glanced toward them and was thoughtful for a moment. "I don't know. I always call her Mrs. Johnson."

Then he grabbed my arm. "Good to see you boys. As you notice, we now have company," he added as I cut open the pineapple for him.

"When did they get here?" I asked.

"What do they want?" asked Mike.

Tom grinned and waved a hand, watching me cut the pineapple. "One thing at a time, boys."

I handed him a chunk of pineapple and cut one for Mike as well. Tom savored the pineapple for a moment and then sat in the sand against the trunk of a palm.

"Let me tell you a story," he said. "They got here two days ago, and I think they've been here before, and they're looking for something or are here to pick something up."

"What about Antoine and his men?" asked Mike.

"How are they treating you?" I asked.

"One at a time. " He paused and resumed, "Antoine seems to be trying to make a deal. So far, it's kept him and the boys from having to work. The Johnsons and I are managing the fishing, food, and fire. Holly is servicing them, much like she was doing Antoine's boys, except there are more of them. It's the only reason we're still alive. She seems to be holding up for now." He looked at us. "I think they may be exploring the island. I saw a party this morning, looked like they were getting some food and water together."

"Any idea what they're looking for?" I asked.

"Not really. I heard a couple of them saying this place, the island, was turning into a real parking lot, that this was the second time they had sailed in and found people on the beach. I couldn't tell what else was said."

Mike and I looked at each other. More people on the beach. Who could that have been? Then it dawned on me, the HOE camp. Whoever set that up could have been down on the beach. What really bad timing that would have been. You would have thought that both groups could have been here for years without running into one another. But then, maybe they had been.

"Did they say anything else about the people on the beach?" I asked.

Tom thought for a moment, then said, "One of them said something about taking care of the men and having fun with the woman but she wasn't a looker like this one, something to that effect."

I looked at Mike, and he nodded. It could have been them, from the HOE camp. They must've been down on the beach and ran into the pirates.

"Do they have names? Where are they from?" I asked.

Tom shook his head. "They're just pirates, smugglers, dopers, gun runners, who knows what all. They are from everywhere, all nationalities and races. There aren't any women with them. That's why they seemed so glad to find us. That and Antoine. He's up to something with them."

I heard talking and saw the couple coming up the beach

carrying fish. "You'd better go," I said to Tom. "Try to overhear what you can. Why they're here, how long they'll stay, what kind of deal they make with Antoine. Can we meet you here again? How about late tomorrow?"

Tom shook his head. "I don't know how fast I can learn anything. I wouldn't want you fellows to get caught." He pointed to his head. "Can you see me from far off with that spyglass?" I nodded. "I wear this hat all the time, except when I sleep. If I have it off, that means I have something to tell you. If it's on, stay clear. You can check me out each day that way from far off and not run any risk. Be aware, they have scopes, too! I've not seen them used any, but I've seen them. They seem very comfortable here. I don't think Antoine's told them about your group. "

"Why not?" asked Mike.

"I don't think he's protecting you or anything, I think he's just trying to make his own deal, leave you behind. I did hear some of them talking about the island being remote."

The voices moved closer, and we fell silent. Tom nodded to us and strolled out with his armload of kindling. He fell in with the couple, admiring their catch. We watched for several minutes and turned to go when we heard more voices coming from behind us. We settled back in the trees.

There was a group of three pirates coming our way, and they had Keno with them. Her hands were tied behind her back.

I grabbed Mike by the shoulder as he started to react.

"They have AK-47's. We have a shotgun and a pistol that we aren't very good with. Keno could get hurt," I whispered.

"She's alive and unhurt for now. They're coming our way," I continued. "Here's what we do, there's two in front and one behind trailing Keno. I'll step out on the two in front and hold the pistol on them. You club the one in back over the head then rack the shotgun on the other one.

"Be sure I have the pistol in the third's one face, close in, or they may open up with those AK's."

"We have to get Keno!"

"Yes, we do," I answered. "Move back about six or eight feet to the next tree. Move when I move, okay?"

He nodded and stepped away.

Here goes nothing.

The two in front drew alongside the trees I was behind. I stepped out and put the pistol to the cheek of the man on the right.

"Don't move."

He stopped in mid-stride. I heard a loud thump as Mike clubbed the rear pirate, who fell to the trail, unconscious. Keno stepped away. Mike leaned in and racked the shotgun. I couldn't help but smile, as I repeated, for the benefit of the pirate on the left who had started to twitch, "Don't move."

He didn't.

"Drop the weapon." His eyes widened. Mike stepped in and caught him under the chin with the shotgun stock. He went down. I slid around the one on the right, keeping the pistol on his face.

"You're coming with us."

"What if I don't?"

I stuck the pistol in his mouth. "You'll have 9 mil for lunch."

He nodded and gurgled, "Who are you?"

"Welcome wagon."

Mike took his pocket knife and cut Keno free. Then he bound and gagged the two unconscious pirates. When they came around, we started back toward our camp.

We got to the tip of the island, and I marched them around to the windward side. I sat them in the sand against the cliff.

Mike pulled the belt off the one I had at gunpoint and

looped it around his ankles and then his wrists. They were bound together and could not move. We pulled the gags out of their mouths. One of them shouted immediately.

I laughed at him. "Make all the noise you want. Between the wind and the sea, no one is going to hear you. You're on the windward side now. When the tide comes in, it reaches halfway up that bluff," I said, pointing upward to the clifftop. "You'll drown if we leave you here."

I stepped aside with Mike and Keno. "Take Keno back. Find out what happened."

Keno jumped in, "I was coming to warn you. Jamal and I saw a group of them along the stream. They were hiking up the cliff side. We backed away from them, and Jamal went to check on the others, while I came to tell you. We were out gathering coconuts."

"Head back and check on the others, but be careful until we know what is going on," I said. "Mike, come back as quick as you can. I'll hold them here. If you're not back by dark, I'll walk away and come find you. In the meantime, I'll see what I can learn."

They started around the tip of the island.

"What do you want?" One of the pirates snarled as soon as Mike and Keno were out of sight.

"We can be friends," said one of the others. The third one was still groggy. He had a stuffed panda bear, in a sling, on his back. Its head stuck up beside his ear.

"I want to know what you know," I said, pointing the tip of the AK at them.

"You're not going to shoot us," said the snarly one.

"I don't have to. I'll leave you for the tide. We've drowned two already, what's three more?"

One of them paled, the other two's eyes widened.

"What you want to know?" the snarly one repeated.

"Who are you, and why are you here?"

"We was passing by," said the groggy one with the bear.

I raised the tip of the AK. "Bullshit, this is the middle of nowhere, the end of the earth. No one just passes by."

The pale one came back quickly, "Okay, man. This is our base, one of them. We come here to relax, to recharge, and to chill."

"What's here?" I asked.

"It's more like, what's not here," said the snarly one. "No law, no hassle. You're right, this is the end of the world."

"So, you didn't come here for something?"

Their eyes narrowed, and the pale one looked at the other two. The snarly one was shaking his head.

I held the AK up. "Nice weapon, bet there's a lot more of them around here somewhere. I bet there's some heavy, shiny stuff too. It only makes sense."

"What you talking about?" said the groggy one.

"Shut up," said the snarly one.

"Look, we know about the guns," I said. Their eyes got huge, and I knew I had them. "And the gold."

"How?" said the pale one.

"Magic," I replied. "What we want is to get off this island. Maybe we can help each other. You got a radio on that tub?"

The snarly one laughed. "The coverage out here is spotty. You got to sail a ways to get good radio."

"How'd you find this place?"

The snarly one said, "Our navigator was sick, and we got lost. It was the perfect place. No traffic, no radio, freshwater, it couldn't have been better."

"Until you started running into people?"

He looked at me.

"You ran into four people on the beach."

"How do you know that?" he asked.

"Maybe we found the bodies."

"Maybe," he said. "We threw the men behind a pile of rocks a little further up the beach from where your group was camped. We kept the woman for a while. Threw her overboard later. She started whining, and she wasn't that good looking or that skilled." "That blonde, she knows her stuff. We may keep her!"

"Tell me about your group," I said.

I noticed that he noticed the tide was starting to creep closer.

"Leader's name is Beaujeax."

"The light-skinned black guy in the funny hat and clothes?"

He actually smiled. "Yeah, that's him. He dresses funny. He's always playing with his hair and his hat. He likes golf and ice cream. Damndest pirate I've ever seen. But, if he doesn't like you or doesn't have a use for you, he'll kill you in a heartbeat."

"How'd he get to be leader?"

"He had the boat. Nobody else wanted to do it. He collected us all. He can be smart. We call him Bozo most of the time. Makes him mad. He calls himself "Black Jesus" sometimes."

"Help me, Jesus, help me," the groggy one with the panda chimed in. Then he turned and whispered to the panda.

The snarly one laughed. "He picked us up at different ports of call. We plunder luxury yachts, steal the women, peddle drugs in a few ports, run a few guns, whatever needs doing. Crew come and go, get killed, or busted, or move on. There's just a core of us that knows about the gold and the guns."

"How did you decide where to hide it?"

He leaned back against the cliff face, eyeing the water as the tide came to our feet. "We found the cave by accident when we were messing around in the water. He had us chasing golf balls he was hitting off the deck. He's got a little AstroTurf tee. He's the worst golfer ever. We were diving after the balls and came up in the cave."

"Has it ever flooded on you?"

"We wondered about that. We figured the gold was so heavy it wouldn't go far."

"How did you come by that gold?"

He just smiled.

"What's it worth?"

He smiled again. "Depends on who you sell it to. It's not worth much to some, and quite a bit to others."

"Like I said before, how do we get off this island? We'll help you, if you help us."

He nodded his head as the tide came in over his feet. "Maybe there's a way."

I was deciding what to do when Mike got back. I had him cover them with the AK while I separated their hands from their feet. Still strapped at the wrists, I had them get up. We gagged them again and started toward the point.

52

A NEW PLAN

When we got to the leeward side, I had Mike tie them to a couple of palms that were inland from the beach. I covered him with the AK. I didn't want the pirates to know about our beach camp on the bluff line above.

I tossed Mike the AK I was holding and picked up the other two AK's and the shotgun. I motioned him aside.

"I'll go check on the others and get Jamal. The three of us can talk to these guys and see if we can develop a plan. I'll help you blindfold them and plug their ears before I go. Keep a sharp eye in case anyone is searching for them."

I left, walked to the beach, and turned toward the windward side. I waited a few minutes and doubled back on the path to our camp.

I walked slowly so that anyone on watch would see and recognize me. Jamal, holding a shotgun, was on lookout. "Yo," he called. "Good to see you." I nodded at him.

We found everyone gathered by the fire pit. I explained what had happened and where we were holding the pirates. I asked if anyone had ideas about a deal. The general response was, "Let's see what they can offer."

I described the pirates to them.

"There are three of them. The first one, who seemed to be the leader, is a heavily tattooed black guy. What you'll notice when you look at him is the globe tattooed on his neck with a banner across it that says *fuck the world*. Tats run up and down both arms, almost full sleeves. There are skulls, snakes, spider webs, and women. There appears to be no rhyme or reason to the design. His teeth are perfect, a brilliant bright white. When you look at him, the contrast between the white of his eyes and his teeth, against his face, it's almost blinding. He has a pile of dreadlocks that are pulled up in a short ponytail. I don't know his name yet, but I call him the "Snarly One." I paused before continuing on. "He is a little over six feet tall, wiry, and quick. He is very polite and speaks well, but he snarls at everything." I think, by everyone's blank stare, they were shocked, except for Jamal who looked disgusted.

"I call the second one "Huggy Bear." He's also black but shorter than Snarly and very muscular. His head is shaved and he's got this penetrating stare. He wore all black and was heavily tatted on both arms. He carried a stuffed panda bear, about half his size, in a sling on his back. He talked to the bear, although he didn't have much to say to anyone else. All of his front teeth are wrapped in gold. It's all you can see when he smiles. Jamal laughed while the women just stared.

"Really?" Angelic said as she turned to face me.

"Hello, real world," whispered Gina. Angelic and Keno looked at her and nodded.

I continued, "The third guy was a pale white boy. Tall and skinny and he seemed very affable. He talked a lot and agreed to our suggestions. He smiled a lot, too, revealing snaggly teeth and a lot of gum line. He's got big, bright, watery blue eyes hidden behind clear, plastic-frame glasses.

And he's dressed in some baggy, garish clothes and sandals with socks. I called him the "Scraggly One." I stopped and shrugged. "Now you know what they look like."

"What do we do with them?" asked Jamal.

"Try to make a deal to get us off the island."

"They came for the gold and the guns, right?" said Gina.

I nodded.

Angelic spoke, "Then why would they take us off the island, why wouldn't they just kill us if they find us?"

Keno shook her head and said, "I don't know about this. I don't know what they would have done to me. How could we ever trust them?"

"If we had something they wanted, or they needed to cooperate with us," I suggested.

"What would that be, I mean, unless they were stuck here, too. What are we going to do, sink the boat? They'd probably kill us all," said Jamal.

"Sinking the boat is a thought, I bet there's a seacock if we could get to it," I replied. "I'm not sure if that would help us. The pirates are bartering with Antoine about something. He may be making a deal to get him and his boys off the island, and leave us behind."

"What do we really know about him?" asked Gina.

"He's creepy," said Keno.

"Treacherous, I suspect," noted Angelic. "We need to know what deal he's trying to make."

"I agree. I'm worried they'll be looking for these guys soon. Keno, were they part of the group you saw?"

She thought for a moment, then said, "I think so, don't you, Jamal?"

He nodded. "Yeah, the guy with the bear is hard to miss."

"So it's possible that the leader, Beaujeax, won't be

looking for them for a while. He might think they're still out exploring. There's nowhere for them to go. They don't seem very worried about anything."

"Unless Antoine told them about us," noted Jamal.

"I think he's holding that card, waiting to see how to play it," added Gina. "He knows we're out here, but if he tells Beaujeax, that might change the tone of things. Right now, the boys seem relaxed and are entertaining themselves. If he has to put them on alert, that might change the circumstances. Antoine probably thinks we'll hide until the pirates leave. If he can cut a deal to go, he'll leave us, and no one will be the wiser."

I had to admit, that was a clear insight.

"I agree. Let's see if Tom can tell us anything tomorrow. In the meantime, Jamal and I will relieve Mike. The three of us can see what the captives know or what deal they offer." The women gave me a hard look. "Angelic, you, Keno, and Gina stay here in the cave with the shotguns. Stay out of sight. One thing that might get them riled up is to think that there are three more attractive women on the island. We don't need them going on attack mode until we're ready."

They nodded in understanding.

Jamal and I walked to the beach. Mike was crouched behind a tree AK pointed our way until he identified us. I leaned and whispered in his ear, "Let's pull the gags and see what else we can learn from them. Keep the barrel right in their faces."

"How long do you usually stay?" I asked them.

"As long as we want," replied the Scraggly One.

"Shut up," snapped the Snarly One. "We're usually here for a week, tops, I mean there's normally nothing to do here unless we have a captive. We were on the run from a job off Palmyra, northwest of here. We don't normally operate that close to one of our bases, but there was a sweet deal, and Bozo didn't want to pass it up. We almost got burned." Huggy Bear glared at Snarly, who continued. "We beat it out of there before the job went down. Bozo was pretty pissed off. That's why he was so excited to find someone here on the island. It wasn't a total loss after all."

"Where is here?"

He looked at me and grinned. "North of the Marquesas and south of the equator."

I looked at Huggy Bear and asked, "What can you tell us?" He turned away.

The Snarly One spoke again," "He doesn't talk to people much, but he is a stone-cold killer, hooked up with us on a job. Bozo admired his fighting skill so much he let him stay. We became friends of a sort. He only talks to blonde girls. He really seems to like them, and he has some success bedding them. The brother must have other skills besides fighting. He tore that blonde on the beach up. She was begging him, first to stop, then to go on."

It was quite a story, a sad one.

The Scraggly One jumped in, "We can work something out, get you off the island."

I looked at the Snarly One. He rolled his eyes.

"What's the deal Bozo is making with Antoine?"

The Snarly One smiled. "He wants off the island, too! He's making a deal for him and his boys. He hasn't mentioned your group. He plans to leave the other three."

"What's the deal?"

He smiled again. "This is the part where you tell me how you're going to help us."

"You want the gold? We'll help you get it."

"We know where the gold is, we don't need your help for that."

"What if we moved it, or better yet, how many of you are there to share it? What if there were less of you?"

I could see Jamal and Mike stirring.

"You going to drown them all?" Snarly asked.

"No, maybe just divide them up, turn them against one another. Antoine's men have guns already. What if they suddenly discovered a couple of AK's and a few thousand rounds of ammunition?"

"Bozo took their pistols when we landed. They rushed out to the ship, thinking we were going to save them. That fat woman was hysterical. Bozo disarmed everyone. We were all carrying AK's. His guys didn't make a move."

"Would you take a pistol to an AK party?"

He grinned. "Antoine went directly into a negotiating mode."

"What did he promise?"

"Money!" spit out the Scraggly One, anxious to contribute.

"Money and guns," added the Snarly One.

"Money, I can see. But he promised guns?" There was surprise in my voice, and I'm sure my eyes got bigger.

The Snarly One knew he had me. "You don't know who he is?"

"He appears to be a wealthy businessman, chairman of something or other."

Snarly spoke after a second, "He may have business interests, but his primary occupation is arms dealer and human trafficker."

Mike, Jamal, and I looked at each other.

"Antoine?" I said.

"Yes," said the Snarly One, grinning. "I never met him,

but I recognized his name. We heard of him. The guns in the cave probably belonged to him originally, before we stole them. He's big in this part of the world, Southeast Asia and Africa. That's the only reason Bozo didn't kill everyone except the blonde as soon as we landed."

53

LET'S MAKE A DEAL

"How could we turn the crew against one another, or how could we turn Antoine and Bozo against one another?" I asked the Snarly One.

"Tell them about the gold, but you'd better be prepared to kill them all because they won't stop until they get it."

"We could flood the ship, let them kill one another."

"That might thin the crowd, but it would be too hard to refloat the ship," he replied. "We need something else to turn them."

The Scraggly One piped in, "Tell Antoine about the gold. He'd want it for himself, and Bozo sure wouldn't give it up."

"Maybe," said the Snarly One. Huggy Bear was watching in silence, the stuffed panda at his feet.

"Could we get the AK's out of the cave and into Antoine's hands?" I asked.

"Normally we'd do scuba and waterproof containers, but we could get a few out, dry them off, check the ammo. The AK is one of the simplest and most reliable weapons available. It could withstand a little water if we were quick," replied the Snarly One.

"We'd still have to let Antoine know about the gold," I said. "He's going to be really suspicious if he just stumbles across a cache of weapons and a gold bar."

The Scraggly One spoke again, "What if we," he nodded his head back and forth between himself and the other two," went to Antoine with a couple of AK's and one of the gold bars and said, let's make a deal, we'll split this with you. Then we go tell the crew about the gold and tell them Bozo is making a deal with Antoine to cut them out. Stir them up. We turn Antoine against Bozo, turn the crew against Antoine and Bozo, and turn Bozo against the crew. That'd get violent quickly!"

Huggy Bear was waving one of the panda arms at me. The Snarly One spoke, "That's a lot of variables, but it might work. It would certainly be chaos."

"Who navigates the ship?" I asked. "We need them alive, to get out of here."

"He knows about the gold, Bozo had to tell him. He's really the only one that can navigate. Bozo has talked about a backup, but we don't really have one. I don't know what's between them, if there's a side deal. I don't know if we could turn him or not," replied the Snarly One.

"Did you ever see *Mutiny on the Bounty*?" I asked them.

"They were on an island," answered the Snarly One.

"Pitcairn."

"You think that's where we are?"

"No, I was thinking of the part where the crew revolted, threw out the tyrant captain. Maybe we could make that work for us."

"You could do it," said the Scraggly One to the Snarly One. Huggy Bear was still waving the panda arms at us.

"I'm hungry," said Huggy Bear.

"Let's take a break." Turning to Mike and Jamal, I said, "Put the gags and earplugs back on."

When we finished with that, I took Jamal and Mike aside. "What do you think?"

"There's a lot that could go wrong," said Jamal.

"I think it's crazy," said Mike. "But I don't have a better idea. I mean, what are the options? Stay here and let them leave, then wait for someone else to come along. The most likely candidate sounds like these guys coming back. I think we have to mix it up. It's a cluster for sure."

"It could be really dangerous," noted Jamal, "and can we really trust these guys? Why would they help us?"

"A bigger share of the gold."

"Is it worth our lives?" Jamal asked.. "You said it yourself, we're tourists, what are we doing mixing it up with pirates?"

"I understand. It's dangerous, but I'm afraid we may die anyway if they find us." I said. "If we do this, we need to bring up AK's and ammunition for ourselves as well. We could retreat to the HOE camp and let them fight it out."

"Do you think they would track us?" asked Jamal.

"Maybe, but if we leave the gold and take the guns we need, that canyon will be pretty easy to defend, and they'd have no reason to care whether we live or die. They'd want to take the gold and get away. We might survive it all by staying neutral."

"How could we count on getting away?" asked Mike.

"That is a drawback. We could be stuck here."

"We could keep the bulk of our group at the camp and try to observe with a couple of scouts. See how it develops. We flee for the camp if there are problems, or approach the situation if it looks manageable," stated Jamal.

"That could be dangerous," I said.

"Yeah, it could, but we want off this rock," Jamal said.

"Let's tell the women and get their opinions. "

Jamal nodded. "You and Mike go talk with them. I'll watch these guys. Angelic will know how I feel, and she'll have her own opinion."

MIKE AND I STARTED FOR THE CAMP.

We got back and called out toward the cave as we approached. Keno stuck her head outside, shotgun in hand, and verified it was us. She waved to us with the gun.

We entered the cave with her and sat in the sleep pits to tell them what was happening.

They were amazed and confused.

"It sounds like a lot of potential double-crosses," said Angelic.

"Way too many," added Keno.

"But the confusion might allow it to work if we were proactive," added Gina.

Everyone looked at her. She blushed.

She put her hand to her face and twirled her hair for a moment. "I mean, we have three different groups who all want off the island on the same ship. We have guns and gold to work with. Turning the groups against each other is probably the only way, if we want to live. There's no reaching an agreement with either of the other two groups. They will kill us. We have to turn them on each other and stay out of harm's way while we're doing it."

"I agree with that," I said and saw Mike nodding.

"How do we do it?" asked Keno.

"We need a plan!" I replied.

. . .

THE LADIES AGREED IT WOULD BE DANGEROUS BUT WE SHOULD try, or else run the risk of being trapped on the island forever. While Mike and I gathered food and water for the prisoners, the women stayed behind to discuss what supplies we'd need to take back to the HOE camp.

Jamal lowered his AK when he saw us emerge from behind a clump of palms. Mike moved closer to cover him and Jamal set about ungagging and removing the blindfolds from the pirates.

I lowered the bag of provisions and removed the items. Huggy Bear actually smiled and the other two looked relieved. They sat on the ground, arms untied but feet still bound.

As I handed over some dried fish, coconut, and water to Snarly, he said, "There's more of you, aren't there?"

I kept my face neutral, even quizzical. "Why do you say that?"

"Because you weren't gone very long. Not long enough to prep this without help or you're camped very close, or both," he said with a knowing smile.

"It's a small island. Nothing is very far away or takes very long. We were prepared," I said and smiled back at him. I think we understood one another.

"You're going to need our help," said the Snarly One. "Like he said," he nodded toward the Scraggly One, "we can initiate this from the inside, you can't. It's your only chance."

"Maybe," I replied. I nodded to Jamal and said, "Tie them, gag them, and blindfold them."

Mike and I covered him, and Jamal hooked them all up.

I drew Jamal and Mike aside. "Let's go find Tom Jones and see what he knows." I nodded to the prisoners. "Do you think we could leave them alone?"

"Maybe," replied Mike, "but I'd feel better if they were under guard."

"Bozo and his people may have organized a search. I'd hate to lose them now. Two of us can go and take a look."

"I'll stay," offered Mike.

Jamal and I nodded and started toward the pirate camp.

54

COME ON DOWN

Jamal and I approached the beach area with caution. Through my scope I saw the Johnsons fishing by the water's edge. There was no sign of Tom. We worked our way back toward the cliff face and finally spotted him gathering coconuts, closer to our camp. Apparently, he'd been looking for us as we looked for him. He had his hat off.

We approached slowly and carefully, though we'd seen no sign of an escort or guard. I motioned for Tom through the trees and he made his way toward us. I took the last of the food from the bag and offered it over. He smiled and sat to eat.

"Thanks, good to see you boys." He put his hat back on. "It's about time you showed up. My head was getting burned." He smiled weakly, and I could see that he was exhausted.

"What's going on?" I asked. "You look worn out."

"Yeah, I'm getting too old for this. They keep me and the Johnsons really busy. All they do is eat, sleep, and diddle with Holly."

"How's she holding up?"

"They took her down from where they had her hanging suspended and tied her to a tree. She's got some shade now. We take her food and water several times a day. They have her naked all the time, and one of them brought a dog collar from the ship. They put her in that and a chain and lead her down to the beach a couple of times a day. She washes off, relieves herself, and they bring her back. They've taken quite a shine to her. But, after everything they've done, I think they'll kill her before they go."

"Have they said something about leaving?" Jamal asked.

"Not from what I hear. Of course, I'm not privy to Bozo and Antoine's conversations, but the crew seems to think they're going to stay a few more days. Bozo says to let the heat die down, but I think he's working Antoine for some kind of deal."

"Have you heard anything on that?" I asked.

"Not specifically," he replied. "They have food and water, cooking slaves, and sex. They're in no hurry!"

"Are they looking for anything or anybody? Are there any issues with them?"

"There don't seem to be, they're pretty informal. Except Bozo, he's always prancing around in some fancy outfit saying things like, "damn, I'm looking fine," or some other fool thing. I have to help him, be his valet, in the mornings before I start gathering food and firewood. He holds up a mirror to his face every morning and says, "I'm so pretty," then he kisses the mirror."

"How you like doing that?" asked Jamal.

Tom looked at him and grinned. "I look away, so I don't puke on his shoes."

"Do you see any signs of discontent? Do you think they might ever turn on one another?" I asked.

Tom gave me a long look. "They're pretty much one big happy family right now, except when two of them get to messing with Holly, it can get a little ugly. But yeah, I'm sure they'd turn on one another. Like I said, I don't hear the conversations, but you can see from the body language that there's tension between Antoine and Bozo. Antoine is used to being in charge, and Bozo is having a good time not letting him."

"So it could get ugly?" injected Jamal.

"In my opinion, absolutely." He looked back toward the camp. "They don't really pay much attention, but I should be getting back. The Johnsons will be more curious than the pirates if I'm gone too long. I'll come this way for coconuts each day. You should be able to find me somewhere in this neighborhood." He pushed off the ground and stood up slowly. He threw up a hand in waving and walked away, his back to us.

Jamal looked at me and asked, "What do you think?"

"Lack of trust, turmoil, and trouble, look like the answer."

We started back for the prisoners.

MIKE WAS LEANING AGAINST A PALM WITH AK IN HAND WHEN we returned.

"No problems, no signs of any kind," he replied.

I pointed to the Snarly one. "Pull the gag, untie his feet, leave his hands."

Mike nodded and set about it. "I'll stay here this time," Jamal said.

"We'll probably need your help when we get to the surface. There are several things, and we'll want to be quick. We can leave the other two alone for a few minutes."

He nodded.

Mike and I led the Snarly One down toward the beach. We stopped at the tree line.

"We're going to go swimming and shopping," I said. "We're going to pick up a few things."

He smiled. "So you're going with our plan?"

I smiled back.

"You're going to be between us. Your arms are going to remain tied, and your feet will be free to help kick when we swim," I said to him.

His eyes got a little large. "I don't really swim that well."

"We'll try not to stay under too long. Don't struggle, or we'll let you drown. Kick when we push off."

We walked into the water with him between us, and when we got positioned off the rock, I pushed his head under, and we kicked off the sand. It took less than thirty seconds to swim under the cliff and into the cave. We broke the surface, and he was sputtering, coughing, and spitting.

"You okay?" I asked.

"I damn near drowned."

I punched him lightly in the head. "You weren't under that long."

Mike climbed ashore and then pulled the Snarly One out. I followed them. We put Snarly between us and climbed the cave to the top rim. His eyes were shining as he saw the guns and the gold.

"Come to poppa," he whispered.

I feared this was the part where he'd try something. We were unarmed as we'd left the guns on the beach. I had my diving knife, and Mike had a chunk of stone he'd picked up, but Snarly didn't make a move. He just turned around and looked at us.

"How do we play it?"

I squatted next to him. "We'll take a few of the rifles, ammunition, and one of the gold bars. We'll turn you and the others loose to return to camp. You make a deal with Antoine, set the problem in motion."

"And if I don't do that?"

"You can come after us, but we have guns too, and we don't have the gold, so why would you bother. You make a deal, you have a chance for a big payoff. Otherwise, you're just a pirate."

He smiled. "I'm a pirate anyway! But this might work, and that's a lot of gold."

"What do we need?" asked Mike.

"There's Antoine, his two guys, and the three of us, so six weapons. We need the navigator, and he might need a weapon if I can turn him. A box of ammunition and there should be a box of supplies, and a gold bar or two," he replied.

"I think one gold bar should do it," I replied and smiled.

"No harm asking, Mon."

We dug around and collected everything he requested.

"How much maintenance?" I asked, "after we've had them in water?"

"Wipe them down, check the ammunition, if we're quick."

We carried everything to the water. We took the AK's and him first.

We broke the surface outside the cave and marched him to the beach. Mike picked up the weapons we had left behind and walked the Snarly One to the holding area.

I went back for the ammunition boxes and the gold bar. When I broke the surface on the second trip, Jamal was waiting for me. We carried the items ashore.

MIKE HAD THE SNARLY ONE TIED TO A PALM.

Jamal got in close with the 9mil and held it to his head.

"What do we need to do here?" I asked.

"Relax," said the Snarly One, eyeing Jamal. "Break open

that supply crate. There should be some gun oil and a box of rags and some other things. Pull those out and field strip the AK's and wipe them down."

We followed his directions for the next several minutes and cleaned all the weapons.

"Check the ammunition," he said.

Mike broke open the box, and it was sealed on the inside in plastic.

The Snarly One broke into a grin. "I love it," he said. "How very thoughtful of Antoine's distributors to seal the ammunition. Break it open and load up. We're ready."

We collected everything and removed the gags and blindfolds from the other two.

"Snarly," I said to him, "tell Huggy and Scraggly the plan."

He looked at me and grinned. "So that's what you call us?" I nodded.

Then he told the others the plan.

WE MARCHED ALL THREE OF THEM, NOW BLINDFOLDED AND gagged, down the beach. We stashed the clips along the way.

When we got to a safe spot, we untied their hands but left their feet bound, their gags and blindfolds on. We removed the earplugs.

I whispered quietly to them. "We'll leave the frames and the gold bar at your feet. The clips are further down the beach in the direction we came from. You'll see them. Come after us, we have the high ground, we'll shoot you. Go make your deal. We'll have an eye on you. Good luck. "

They all nodded.

We backed away from them slowly and disappeared into the trees.

55

WATCH IT UNFOLD

When we got to camp, the women were still hidden in the cave, but they were working. Gina had decided they should be able to reach the lower underwater cave, from the upper cave where we slept. It seemed reasonable, but we might be in a different shaft, or it might be fifteen or twenty feet down.

"Based on how far we climbed up the rock, inside the cave, and how far this winds down, I can't think it's more than a few feet between them," she explained.

They had already dug several feet using the shovel I had brought from the HOE camp. "Be careful as you go down," I said. "You might be over the water or several feet above the rock."

She nodded. "We could be, but I think this is the path at the top of the cave. Sand from storms and high water has plugged it up over time."

It seemed reasonable. "Just be careful."

"We needed something to do. If this works, we have quicker access, and we don't have to get in the water."

I watched them work for a moment then spoke, "We

want to move all of you to the HOE camp. Things are about to get ugly."

We explained to them what had happened.

"Shouldn't we have a little time before they strike the deal?" asked Gina. "I'd like to get a couple more feet before we go. Did you get guns for us, or are you going back in the water to get them?"

"We were planning on going back in the water."

"I'll stay and help them," said Mike. "You and Jamal go see what's happening."

JAMAL AND I MADE OUR WAY TOWARD THE PIRATE CAMP. WE stayed close to the base of the cliff, well back from the water. We stopped every few minutes, and I checked with the scope and listened. Nothing.

As we got closer, we climbed the cliff face a few feet and stopped behind a clump of palms. The rise in elevation made us look like we were in the treetops. I figured if any of the pirates were scanning, they'd be looking at ground level.

We could see activity in the camp. The pirates scurried around like they suddenly had a purpose. They weren't wandering or lazing around like they had been all week. It looked like something was buzzing. Nobody looked happy. Nobody was with Holly. She lay slumped against the tree in the shade. We needed to talk to Tom if we could. I doubted he'd had time to learn anything.

I turned to Jamal and said, "Let's go back to camp and see about getting everyone moved."

We got to camp, and no one was waiting outside. We approached the cave cautiously and ducked inside.

They were all in the lower shaft. It looked like they had dug their way through to the underground cave.

The women were bent over with their backs to us, and

suddenly Mike's head appeared from the hole. He had a handful of AK's in his arms. He saw us first.

"Good thing you weren't the pirates, or Antoine," he called out.

Keno stood with her hand to her mouth. "Ugh, I was supposed to be watching, but I got excited when they called out they had broken through, and I had to come and see."

I grinned at her. "That is exciting." Jamal and I stepped closer. "Where did you come out?"

"We're just to the left of the guns and gold, basically at the top of the trail," Mike replied.

I turned and looked at Gina. "You were right."

She was all smiles. "Now, you don't have to get wet, and the pirates think you do."

"Should we move the gold?" asked Mike.

We conferred as a group for a few minutes and decided for our own safety, and maybe secrecy, it was best left where it was.

I called out to Mike, "Grab more guns and ammunition. We need to get everyone to the HOE camp."

We collected everything we needed and bedded down. Everyone was tired, but no one was sleepy.

WE LEFT FOR THE HOE CAMP EARLY THE NEXT MORNING. We hiked quickly, everyone armed. Our intent, since none of us were soldiers, was to look fierce, and fully armed, and to rely on the "spray and pray method" if we had to shoot. Keno and Gina had the shotguns, Angelic and the rest of us had AK's.

We got to the camp, and nothing was disturbed. I sent Jamal on to the peak, to check the hilltop for any activity or visuals. The rest of us gathered food.

. . .

When Jamal returned, we had a group meeting.

"Two of us will go back and scout," I said. "The other six will stay here and provide backup and support coverage if we have to retreat. I want two on guard, one high in the pass and one low at the entrance. Two others should be working, and the last two should be sleeping. Work in four-hour shifts and then rotate. Go from guard duty to work and from work to sleep and from sleep to guard duty. That should keep everyone fresh."

Jamal, Mike, and I drew straws for who would return. Jamal and I were the lucky ones. It worked out well. I was going no matter what, so at least we didn't have to argue about it.

Early the next morning, we left for the pirate camp.

56

THINGS GO AWRY

Jamal and I arrived at the beach camp and saw no evidence that anyone had discovered us. From there, we worked our way toward the pirate camp, with an eye open for Tom Jones. We found him sitting under a palm, his hat off, fanning.

He didn't stop fanning as he spoke. "I don't know what you boys been up to, but the camp is in a tizzy. The crew is pissed off at Bozo for something. Antoine and his boys have gotten real quiet and standoffish, and Bozo is angry at Antoine and his crew. Rumors are all I'm hearing. I don't know what it's about, but they're all stirred up."

I noticed he was rubbing his knee, and when he saw me watching, he spoke, "I didn't get out of the way of one of them, and he kicked me. I dropped my cane and bent to retrieve it, and he came storming around a tree and kicked me while I was bent over."

"We'll gather you some coconuts. "

"Much obliged, I can't walk very well right now."

Jamal and I quickly rounded up a handful and stuffed

them into his bag. We had just sat beside him when there was a noise behind us.

There were three pirates we had only seen from a distance, with AK's of their own, pointing at us.

"Up with the hands, fellows," said the one in the middle. "Well, Mr. Tom, what did you find here?" he asked as the other two fanned out around us, while the one in the middle slipped in to take our guns.

"Up," he said. "Let's do some walking, then we'll do some talking. Bozo is going to want to hear your story."

He marched us toward the pirate camp. One of them flanked us on each side, and Tom shuffled along behind.

BOZO STOOD IN THE CENTER OF THE CAMP. HE WAS WEARING heavily-creased, striped, purple pants, chocolate suede boots that came up over his knees, a matching belt, a flowing, white, long-sleeved shirt, and a purple hat with a white plume. I was sure he thought himself magnificent.

He saw us approach and watched as we were marched toward him. We stopped a few feet away.

"And who might you be?" he thundered.

I looked him in the eyes. "We were just passing by. Stopped to talk to the old guy!"

"Passing by on a deserted island?"

"We were in the neighborhood." I could see his fury building.

Suddenly Antoine appeared. "They were with our group originally. They disappeared, and I thought they were dead." He didn't mention the others in our group.

Bozo took off his hat and rubbed his hair. "Why wasn't I told of this?"

Antoine looked at us and said, "Dead men tell no tales."

"That's right," replied Bozo, looking at Antoine.

Antoine turned away and called over his shoulder, "They are of no value. Do with them whatever you wish."

Bozo watched Antoine walk away, a smile on his lips. He turned to us and said, "Tie them to a tree near the blonde." He poked me. "We gonna have some fun with this wonder bread. Search them." The guards patted us down and collected our knives. They put them in a small canvas bag one of them pulled from his pocket.

The guards started to walk us toward a tree when the Snarly One and Huggy Bear appeared.

"What do you want?" said the guard in front.

The Snarly One smiled and held up two fingers on his right hand. "Wishing you love, peace, and soul…my brother," he said, stepping toward us and putting a hand on my shoulder.

The guard looked sullen, and the Snarly One said, "We got this." He took the bag from the guard and they all stood down.

Snarly and Huggy walked us to the tree.

"What the hell you doing getting caught, you sure gonna mess up the plan. We're going with our part anyway," Snarly whispered in my ear.

"What's the status?" I asked.

"We went to Antoine and showed him the guns and the gold, let him think about it. We kept the clips, he's still unarmed. We got a handful of the crew with us, including the navigator, he hates Bozo. We're all armed and dangerous."

We got to the tree, and Snarly pushed me down and tied me up. Holly was a few feet over, on the next tree with her back to us. She wasn't moving.

Huggy tied up Jamal.

Snarly shook his head. "We'll help you if we can, but if we can't, we can't." They started to walk away.

The three original guards approached us.

Huggy suddenly broke into a song. I recognized it as "It is Well with my Soul."

"When peace like a river, attendeth my way,

When sorrows like sea billows roll,

Whatever my lot, Thou has taught me to say,

It is well. It is well, with my soul."

While he was singing, Huggy cranked the arms of the stuffed panda bear that sat around his neck and waved them at the guards. They stopped in their tracks, and then turned away, muttering.

Huggy looked at Jamal and me and smiled. The sunlight gleamed off his teeth.

He and Snarly walked away.

I LOOKED UP TO SEE HOLLY STARING AT US.

"How are you doing?"

"How do you think?"

"I'm sorry, that was a stupid question."

She smiled wearily. "It's like when you've been sick. You're hot, you're cold, your fever has come and gone, it breaks, you're sweating, you're frustrated and in pain. Sickness has a smell, and when it passes, you feel like you need to take a bath or a swim. It's a chemical reaction that leaves you covered in a by-product that you just want to get away from and come out clean."

She paused. "My choices were the devil," she glanced to the camp, "or the deep blue sea," then to the ocean, "and my conscience was my only guide. For a time, I chose the devil. Now, I pray I come out clean on the other side. When I signed up for a sea cruise, I never expected to die on a deserted island, raped to death."

"You're not going to die, we'll get out of here, and we'll take you with us," I replied.

She almost smiled, but her eyes were blank. She turned her back to us and didn't reply.

Tom brought us some fish and water shortly after that. The Johnsons took the same to Holly. Neither of them looked at us.

Tom spoke, "The Johnsons aren't happy with you leaving the group. Be careful of them. There seems to be a lot going on in camp, and there's tension. The crew is starting to fight among themselves. Antoine and his boys are keeping separate. Bozo seems to be mad at everyone. I'll try to find something to cut you loose. We have utensils for cooking, but they collect them after every meal. There's going to be a party. I think that's when it's going to happen. Bozo is planning something, but then I think Antoine may be too. Keep your heads down. I'll try to get you loose. There will be some entertainment first."

Jamal and I looked at one another.

Tom continued, "There are six guys that call themselves K5J. Five guys whose name starts with "J" and Kazam. Kazam likes to be different and to stand apart from the others. It's a good thing to know and keep in mind if you deal with him. They remind me of Gladys Knight and the Pips. Kazam raps and the others dance and sing background. They're always singing something around the camp."

Tom shuffled away.

Jamal whispered to me, "You think he can help?"

"I think he'll try."

. . .

WE SAT FOR SEVERAL HOURS WHILE NOTHING HAPPENED. As the light began to fade, the activity in the camp increased.

Nobody bothered Holly, so I knew something was going on.

There was a sound toward the shore, and I saw our old friend, the Scraggly One, walk into view. He was talking to someone and glanced toward the camp, then toward us. Another sound came, and then silence. Bozo stepped into view and drew the Scraggly One close to him, and I had a bad feeling. I was sure we'd just been sold out.

After a moment, Bozo strode in front of us. "I'll be dealing with the two of you myself, very soon." Then he walked away.

Jamal looked at me, anxiously. "It's gonna be a long night."

I nodded to him and then looked toward the camp. I could see a small stage had been set up. We were going to have a view.

57

LET'S GET THIS PARTY STARTED

As the sun was setting, fires were lit all around the camp. The darkness was not as absolute as usual. Most nights there was starlight, and some ambient reflection from the moon off the water. Some nights it was just black, you couldn't see a thing. That night, we could actually see, but there were lots of shadows. There was energy in the air. Treachery and deceit were about, along with havoc and chaos. You could actually feel it, or sense it so strongly, that you thought you felt it.

No one had come around Jamal and me for several hours. Holly appeared to be asleep.

A crowd gathered in front of the makeshift stage. They were a colorful lot, in scarves, hats, beards, and assorted jewelry. Some wore cut-offs, board shorts, even capris, paired with sandals, tennis shoes, or boots. They were an eclectic looking group of pirates.

Bozo and his posse stood to one side. A few of the men were scattered toward the middle of the stage. Antoine and his crew appeared on the other side. The two perimeter groups stared at one another.

The pirate that had caught us with Tom got up on stage and began to speak. I thought of him as "MC Pirate".

"Tonight is party night! We have live entertainment and some fine food and drink set aside for everybody."

We hadn't seen Tom or the Johnsons, and I guessed they had been kept busy all afternoon. I didn't see the Snarly One or Huggy Bear either.

MC Pirate continued, "Live from "Deserted Island" we have tonight," there was a drum roll behind him, "K5J for your entertainment. Kazam and the five Jams, let's get this party started!" He clapped and stepped out of the way as six big men came out on stage. They were sort of dressed alike, except for the one in front. He had a big pile of Gerry curls and wore tight, white stretch pants. Bozo gazed at him admiringly.

The lead singer stepped to the front and called out, "We're K5J, and I am Kazam."

The others, lined up behind him, sang out their names, "Jerome," "Jajuan," "Jermaine,"" Jamont," and "Jamari."

They could actually sing. Each one called out his name, twirled, and took a dance step to the left. Then they took a step to the right and twirled, and then back to the left and twirled again. Their hands and shoulders were swinging, and they clapped out a beat and sang what sounded like "Humpty, Humpty Dump."

Kazam strode forward and shouted out, "We're going to do a song called "Break Me Up, the Humpty Dumpty rap.""

Kazam rapped and the 5J's harmonized.

"I can't sing and I can't dance," Kazam rapped.

In the background, the 5Js came in with, "Humpty, you can call me Humpty."

"Ain't got enough ass to hold up my pants," continued Kazam.

"Humpty, you can call me Humpty, call me Humpy, Humpty Dump," sang the 5Js.

The 5Js sidestepped, they twirled, they spun in place, and they sidestepped back, all the while clapping and singing the chorus.

"I got no rhythm and I got no soul," Kazam rapped.

In the background, the 5Js came in with, "Humpty, you can call me Humpty."

"I ain't got no self-control," continued Kazam.

"Humpty, you can call me Humpty, call me Humpy, Humpty Dump," sang the 5Js.

"I sat on the wall, and I took a big fall," Kazam rapped.

In the background, the 5Js came in with, "Humpty, you can call me Humpty."

"But that ain't all, cause I still like to ball, with you," continued Kazam.

"Humpty, you can call me Humpty, call me Humpy, Humpty Dump," sang the 5Js.

"When I sit on my throne, and I get you alone," Kazam rapped.

In the background, the 5Js came in with, "Humpty, you can call me Humpty."

"I throw my XL bone, in yo' red hot zone. Throw it baby, throw it," continued Kazam.

"Humpty, you can call me Humpty, call me Humpy, Humpty Dump," sang the 5Js.

"That's what I'm talking about," Kazam rapped.

"Dump it, Baby, dump it," he continued. "I know that's right."

"Humpty, you can call me Humpty, call me Humpy, Humpty Dump," sang the 5Js.

"My name is Humpty," rapped Kazam. "Break me up!"

"Humpty, you can call me Humpty, call me Humpy, Humpty Dump," sang the 5Js.

THEY ENDED WITH A FLOURISH AND A DOUBLE SPIN BY Kazam, a long slide across the stage by the 5Js, and a big final hand clap. There was silence for just a second, and then thunderous applause.

Jamal turned to me and snidely remarked, "That was enchanting. You think they wrote it themselves?"

I nodded. "Probably, I never heard it before."

"Wished I hadn't heard it then," he sighed.

Kazam and the 5Jams broke into another rap. We turned our attention away.

58

JUST BEFORE THE BULLETS FLY

There was a table to the side of the stage where food was served. During the concert, the pirates and Antoine's men had come and gone to help themselves. Tom and the Johnsons must have been busy all day or maybe all week. The table was loaded, and we saw them scurrying back and forth with new supplies of fish and fruit. Apparently, there was alcohol on the ship, as there was a punch bowl that kept many of the men returning. Their volume and enthusiasm grew as the night proceeded.

So far, no one had come to bother Holly. In fact, we, as prisoners, had been ignored all evening.

As we watched the crowd mill about, it was as if they were waiting for the next event, the main event. K5J had stopped rapping and withdrawn from the stage. The crowd finished their food and drinking. They stood in small groups, murmuring and checking each other out.

Antoine and Bozo stood in the middle of the crowd. One on one, each was flanked by a group of their supporters.

Neither of them looked happy. We couldn't hear from our distance, but the expressions, facial features, and body language looked tense. We saw the Snarly One and Huggy Bear near the stage, almost in the middle of the group. As if they could spring in either direction, if and when, and just before the bullets fly.

I felt it was going to be soon.

Bozo raised his arms and pushed Antoine backwards. Antoine's men sprang forward around their boss. All the noise stopped. Bozo and Antoine glared at one another. I could see William, with his hand in his pocket. I think Bozo saw him too.

Antoine held up a hand, and all eyes were upon it. I could see his head turn slightly as he took in the crowd. His gaze encompassing. He dropped the hand and dove to the ground as William pulled a pistol and shot.

Bozo dove when he saw Antoine dive. The bullet from William, meant for Bozo, hit the man behind him, who went down quickly.

Shouts and shooting broke out from both sides. I could hear the sound of the AK's. Jamal and I couldn't help but flinch at the flashes of light and smoke that drifted around us.

Then we saw him. It was Tom, making his way toward us. He had his hat on and his cane in one hand, the small canvas bag in the other.

TOM DROPPED DOWN TO HIS KNEES AS THE SOUND OF BULLETS continued, and the shouts and screams increased. He slid on the sand next to us.

"Good to see you, boys! I think it's time to go!" He dropped the bag. "I thought you could use these."

We both stared at him. The knives would be helpful.

"Where'd you get the bag?" I whispered to him.

Tom smiled. "Huggy and Snarly gave it to me." Then he

took his cane in both hands and felt around the knob. I heard a small click. He grabbed the handle and pulled a two-foot blade from the cane.

Our eyes got big. "I got something that will work," he replied.

He sliced at the rope binding Jamal. "You had that all along?" I asked.

He smiled, and I could see his eyes twinkling.

"I never leave home without it."

"You should have come with us," I countered.

He shook his head. "It would have been an odd number, besides I needed to look after the Johnsons, although they would never admit it, and Holly, once Jim died."

I looked him in the eyes and could see he was dead serious. He turned to work on my bindings as Jamal jumped up and went to check on Holly.

"I used to stand over behind the trees when the pirates would come to her. I didn't watch it. I couldn't, but I listened. I figured if I heard her scream, I could put a stop to at least one of them," he whispered.

I looked at him as he cut. "They'd have killed you."

"Probably, I was just trying to look out for her," he paused. "It wasn't like that. I'm old enough to be her father, your grandfather. I was just trying to help her survive."

"Hey," called out Jamal. "This is not good." He was standing beside Holly as Tom finished cutting my bindings, and we crawled over to where Jamal was crouched.

Jamal held his fingers to her face and turned it slightly. Her head turned at an odd angle.

"Her neck is broken. The body is still warm. Did you see anything? I didn't," he stammered.

I looked at Tom, who dropped his head and his eyes. "Looks like I failed her," he whispered.

I took him by the shoulder. "We were right here, and we

didn't see a thing. There's no way you could have known. We never heard a sound. You were busy with the food all afternoon. I don't know how or when it could have happened."

"Bozo," whispered Tom. "He did it, or he's responsible for it."

"Yeah," whispered Jamal.

The shots were getting closer, and we couldn't see well enough to tell what was happening.

Tom grabbed each of us by the arm. "Come with me."

He led us to the beach and then in the direction of our camp.

"Where are we going?" asked Jamal.

Tom just waved his arm forward and kept moving. A hundred yards down the beach, he turned inland. We went a few yards and stopped.

Out from behind a stand of palms stepped the rest of our group. They were armed to the teeth and looked fierce. I couldn't help but smile.

Gina, who carried one of the 20 gauge shotguns, had her chin down but turned her eyes up to look at me. I was happier to see her than I realized.

Before I could say it, Jamal burst out, "What are y'all doing here? Can't you hear the shooting?"

Angelic looked at him, her face fixed. "That's exactly why we're here."

Jamal paused, looked down at the ground and then back up, and broke into a grin. "It's good to see you, too!"

Angelic smiled back at him.

Mike jumped in, "When you guys didn't come back, we thought we'd better check on you. I worked point, and everyone else followed at a distance. I saw Tom, and he told me what happened."

Tom chimed up, "I went to the trees where we meet,

hoping you'd told some of the others, and maybe they'd show up looking for you."

"When he told me, I went and got the others, and now here we are," Mike added.

Gina spoke, she and Keno and Angelic were shoulder to shoulder, gun to gun, they looked impressive,

"What do we do now?"

"Retreat to our camp and let them kill each other," offered Mike.

I was surprised when Tom interjected, "I'm going back, I need to check on the couple and bury Holly."

I nodded at him. "I'll go with you and keep an eye on who is winning."

"Does it matter?" asked Keno.

We all looked at her.

Keno had a point. But it did matter. The pirates were pulling a skiff behind the ship. While we'd never pilot the ship, we could manage the skiff. If we could separate it from the ship and then destroy the ship, the pirates and Antoine would fight it out to the death. We could survive in the HOE camp, disappear into the island. If we let them kill each other, it might solve our problem and leave us a way off the island.

"It does matter." I quickly explained to them what we needed to do. They looked grim, but they all nodded. Everyone had a job to do. It would take all of us.

"Here's what we're going to do," I said to them. "I'll go after the skiff, and destroy the ship. I want all of you to flank the pirates and lay down suppressing fire."

I was interrupted by Keno. I could see Angelic and Gina looking at me as well. "What's suppressing fire?"

I stopped for a second. *We are tourists. That's a reasonable question.*

"I want a pair of you to sneak up from each side, behind the pirates, and fire at them to drive them toward one another and Antoine."

"Do we have to shoot them?" Keno asked.

"No, just shoot at them. I think they'll run."

"That's good. I don't want to shoot anyone."

"None of us do, but we want to stay alive."

I went back to the overview. "I think if we climb the cliff face, we can shoot down at them and drive them toward the beach. There's less cover, and they'll see one another better, and hopefully take care of the problem for us. We have to stay out of sight and herd them together."

They all looked at me, waiting.

"Mike, I want you and Keno to flank them from this side. Gina, Angelic, and Jamal, I want you to go down the island and flank them from the far side, push them back this way. Stay out of sight. Use the AK's to drive them. Be careful that they have retreated before you move forward. Stay in sight of one another. Retreat if there is an issue. Head back to the HOE camp. We'll all meet there when it's over."

Mike and Jamal shared a look and shook their heads.

"I don't like it," said Jamal. "You're taking a huge risk going after the skiff, and how are you going to destroy the ship?"

"That's the easy part. I'll unhook the skiff and drive it away. Beach it down on our end of the island. I'll set the ship on fire, or blow a hole in it, or something, before I go. "

"That ain't much of a plan. I don't know, sounds like a cluster," said Mike.

"Look, we can do this," I said. "Just remember, you're not John Wayne, Clint Eastwood, or the Rock, you're just you. Be the best you, you can be and get back to camp alive and unhurt. Do what you have to do. This is not about fair. There is no such thing as fair. You shoot them in the back. You shoot them in the head, you win, they lose, you live, they die, to do it any other way, you die."

I stepped away to let them talk, and I addressed the women. "Lay down your cover fire and keep your distance. Watch out for one another, stay in sight." I looked at Keno, then Angelic, and finally, Gina. "Don't hesitate if you have to defend yourself, shoot them. If you don't, they will rape you repeatedly and then kill you, if you're lucky. If not, they'll keep you alive and just keep raping you repeatedly. There is no politically correct here, there's win or lose, live or die. It's up to you."

Their faces were ashen. I saw Mike and Jamal standing a few feet away. Keno and Angelic turned from me and looked at their husbands, then ran to them. Gina stood next to me. I looked at her, touched her shoulder, took her hand, and kissed her fingers. After a second, she pulled them away and clenched the AK Jamal had handed her. She looked up at me, her eyes bright.

"Stay alive, then we can go home again," I said to her.

"We can never go home again!"

"You read that in a book?"

"No, it's just common sense," she replied. "Nothing is like it was before." She looked down, and I saw a tear trickle from her eye. I reached across and took her face in both hands. I kissed her quickly.

"I'll be back, and I want you to be here!" I kissed her hard. She melted into me and responded with an intensity of her own, her mouth on mine.

We separated and set out on our mission. I watched Gina walk away, my heart pounding. With my deceased wife, I had learned a lesson, it left a scar. I didn't want it to happen again.

. . .

Tom and I started toward the fight.

As we got closer, shots rang out. They were scattered, and it was going to be difficult to follow what was happening.

As we circled the group, it appeared that Bozo's men had Antoine and his group pinned down and were attempting to flank them. It was going to be tough to tell who was who and on which side, not that it really mattered. As we circled the camp and the stage where the show had been, Tom wanted to go check the remains of one of the huts to look for the Johnsons. He motioned to me and said, "I'm going after them."

"I'll catch up later," I said and started toward the water.

I'd taken only a few steps when I heard someone approaching. It was Bozo. I ducked behind a palm until he passed. He was looking down and talking to himself.

I stepped from behind the tree, my pistol to his head. I didn't see the pistol in his hand, which he quickly pulled up to my face. There we stood, pistol to pistol.

"Put it down, and I'll let you live," said Bozo, his eyes bright.

"Why don't you, and I might let you live."

He laughed. "You're a bloody tourist wanker. You won't kill me."

"Let's find out." I pushed the gun up to his nose.

"I could kill you at any time," he replied.

"Don't piss down my leg and tell me it's raining." I heard a sound and glanced quickly down and back. "Piss down your own leg." Bozo had peed himself, and there was a bright wet spot running from his groin down the leg of his purple pants. He was just a frightened bully.

Men burst from the trees and shots slammed into the sand around us. Bozo dove one way, and I dove the other. We each rolled away. I thought they were his men, so I scrambled on all fours and scurried toward the water as fast as I could. I'd deal with him later, maybe, stay alive and stick with the plan.

I WAS HEADED FOR THE BEACH WHEN I SAW THEM. THE Snarly One and Huggy Bear appeared from out of the darkness and smoke.

Shots rang out from behind me. Bozo must have been marshaling his troops. I turned toward Snarly and Huggy.

They slid to the ground next to me. They both had AK's in hand.

"Where you been?" whispered Snarly.

"Trying to stay out of harm's way, but not having much luck."

He actually grinned. "Looks like Bozo has Antoine pinned down in a group of trees and is trying to flank him on both sides. It'll be a real kill zone if he succeeds. If that happens and anyone survives and talks, it could be trouble for me and Huggy."

He looked at me.

"You think this will last through the night?" I asked.

He nodded. "Bozo would prefer to finish it off, while everyone is still liquored up, but it's too hard to see. He'll probably try to pin Antoine down, flush them out in the morning."

I took a chance.

"We got a plan," I said. "Free the skiff and sink the ship. Let them all kill one another, then sail away."

"With the gold?" he asked.

"If it's possible. There's plenty to go around, I could use your help." I looked at him and Huggy. They were both grinning.

Snarly looked at me.

"Okay!" The three of us did a quick fist bump.

"Let's get to the ship, free the skiff, set the ship on fire, or blow it up, or whatever we can do to sink it," I said.

He kept looking at me.

"We let the rest of them kill one another, stay out of it."

"And if they don't all die and come after you?"

"We defend ourselves if we have to."

He nodded at me and laughed. "Let's go fishing."

59

SHE'S A LADY

I followed Snarly and Huggy toward the ship. There was shooting between us and the beach, so we circled back through the camp. As we crossed the camp, I saw Tom and Bozo in the clearing. They were face to face and yelling at one another. In my mind, it was Deja vu for Bozo, but I was surprised Tom was involved. Then I saw the sword. Tom pointed it at Bozo. I stopped, frozen, watching as if I was in a dream. Huggy saw me and stopped, which caused Snarly to stop.

"What's wrong with you?" he snarled, then followed our gazes.

Bozo tried to push Tom away, but Tom didn't budge and brought the sword closer to Bozo, who tensed and pulled back. He tried to bat the sword away with his arm, but Tom held firm.

A group of pirates burst from out of the trees, their backs to us, and stumbled into Tom and Bozo. Tom tried to hold steady, but Bozo flinched as he was hit and thrown forward, onto Tom's sword. The blade pierced his chest, emerged out his back, and his whole body stiffened. Tom's face was stricken in shock.

We started toward them as the pirates turned to see who they had run into. Before they could react, Huggy swept them with the AK, and they dropped dead in the sand.

Tom stood frozen in place, holding the sword, with Bozo impaled on the other end.

I got close enough to hear, but too far away to help, as I heard Bozo say, "A heart for a heart, you old fart." He pulled a pistol and shot Tom in the chest.

They both dropped to their knees and fell to the sand.

When we reached them, I went to Tom, and Snarly went to Bozo. Huggy stood guard with his AK.

Tom was bleeding out in the sand, but he fixed me with a weak smile and croaked out, "He killed Holly, for no reason other than he was tired of her."

I nodded.

He continued, "I didn't mean to kill him, I wanted to, but I couldn't."

"It's okay," I said. "I saw it, it was an accident."

His mouth was open, and his breathing labored, but I thought I saw his eyes twinkle. "You be sure and get off this rock," he said and his head rolled back.

I put a finger to his neck, there was no pulse.

I glanced up to see Snarly beside me and then turned my attention to Bozo.

"He's dead," said Snarly. "The tide may have turned here, without him. There'll be chaos among the pirates. I think Antoine could pull it out now. We'd better get to work. I'll put Bozo's body out of sight so they'll continue to look for him and keep fighting. They'll bolt for the ship if they see him dead."

I nodded. He heaved Bozo over his shoulder and headed toward the remains of one of the huts.

I grabbed Tom by the shoulders and pulled him toward the trees. Huggy surprised me by grabbing Tom's feet and helping me carry him. I nodded to Huggy, and he smiled, his teeth shining in the moonlight.

We met Snarly and started for the ship.

"How you planning to disable The Lady?" he asked.

"The Lady?"

"That's the name of the ship. That's what Bozo christened her," Snarly replied.

"As in, *The Lady is mine?*" I asked.

Snarly shrugged his shoulders. "It was his ship, who knows?"

I shrugged. "I don't know the best way to disable it."

Snarly grunted at me, "It would be easiest to sink it. Open the seacocks in the engine room and the cargo hold. There are several of them."

"Will that get the job done?"

"A couple of feet of water will flood the engines, and in time the ship will settle to the bottom of the lagoon. It won't be going anywhere. It could be refloated later if it doesn't sit for too long, or get damaged on the rocks, or by a storm. That's a pretty nice little harbor. We're sitting in twelve or fifteen feet of water. It'll go down." He looked over at me.

"Sounds good. Can the three of us get it done?"

"Huggy can grab the skiff. You and I should be able to open the seacocks. We can be in and out quickly. Shouldn't be a problem. Bozo didn't leave anyone on board, once things got tense with Antoine. He usually has a guard on the supplies. We'll want to grab a few things, supplies for the skiff. It's about two days to the nearest civilization. I'm no navigator, but I can get us to there." He paused for a moment, as we drew near the water and looked up and down the beach for any activity. The shooting was still behind us. All seemed clear.

"So, do other people know about this island?" I asked.

He motioned to Huggy, who had been bringing up the rear, and watching our backs.

"A few of the old-timers know of it, the thing is this place isn't on the way to anywhere. It's just out here isolated in the water," Snarly replied.

"What about casual sailors, or the locals?"

"They have everything on their island that you have here, why bother? They don't tell tourists because they don't want to have to come and look for them. There were a few people when we first started to come here, but Bozo ran them off, except for those hippies. They pissed him off, and you saw what happened to them." He turned to Huggy and put a hand on his shoulder.

"Grab supplies for the skiff. Get extra fuel cans, water jugs, and dry food. Strap it down and tarp it. Run the skiff down the shore toward the point."

Snarly pointed in the direction of our camp.

"There's a little inlet, a hundred yards or so before you get to the point, you can tie up there or beach it," I offered.

They looked at me. "I spent some time on that end of the island."

They both grinned.

We got to the ship and split up. Huggy went for the supplies, while Snarly and I went to the engine room.

We clambered down the steps and into the dark. Snarly turned on lights and pointed to the seacocks. "We use those to let a little water in if the engines start to run hot. This time we're going to let a lot of water in." He grinned, bent over, and started to turn.

A few rotations and I heard water seeping and saw it pool onto the deck.

He stood. "That's not a lot of water flow. Let's go to the cargo hold. Those are bigger."

I followed him to the hold, and he led us to a larger seacock. He pointed across the hold and said, "There should be another one on that side. There is a lever that unlocks it and then spin it as far as you can. After that, we're out of here. It'll take some time, but I don't want to be around if any of them head this way."

We spun the wheels, and water began to seep in. We made our way topside and looked for Huggy. He waved to us and went over the side to the skiff. I heard the motor start just before shots rang out overhead. A handful of pirates were streaming toward the beach from out of the darkness.

"Go!" shouted Snarly. He dove over one side, and I dove over the other. I jumped to the ocean side, and he jumped to the beachside. Maybe he was going to slow them down. I kept swimming.

I reached the shore a hundred yards or so down the beach. I started toward the pirate camp. As I looked out to the harbor, I saw several pirates climbing aboard the ship. I hoped it took on enough water before they noticed. I heard gunshots from that direction, and I dropped to the sand. I turned my head, and there was other gunfire coming from down the beach and inland.

I scrambled a few more feet and decided to circle around to link up with Mike or Jamal. I saw a figure several yards down the beach, so I crawled into the shadows and sat still. The figure came slowly toward me, carrying an AK. He paralleled with my position. I was trying hard to be quiet, not to move, or even breathe. Then I recognized Jamal.

"Jamal," I whispered and rolled flat to the ground as he swung the gun around. "It's Dee."

He swung the AK around fast but managed not to fire.

"Dee!" he called.

I pulled my head up slightly. "It's me."

He lowered the AK. "I just about shot you."

"Yeah," I said as I climbed up. "What are you doing here?"

"Gina and Angelic are herding the pirates this way. Looks like Antoine and his guys are held up in a grove of palms. We're pushing them slowly together. I figured you might need some help."

"I ran into Snarly and Huggy. They helped me sink the ship and steal the skiff."

"And they took the skiff, and the gold, and sailed away?"

"Maybe," I replied. "We'll manage. Let's find Mike and Keno."

We started inland and only got a short distance when we were caught in a hail of bullets. Pirates emerged. I'd lost my rifle, but Jamal sprayed and prayed as they came at us. Then he stopped, and I heard a click.

"Damn, I thought you said these things never jammed," he called.

We took shelter behind a couple palms. With my back to the tree, I stopped to dig around in my pockets. I pulled out one knife, then another, and then a third.

"How many knives you got?" asked Jamal.

I didn't bother to look up as I said, "As many as I need."

A pounding of footsteps rushed toward us. Jamal raised his AK. I pulled the diving knife from my waist strap, flipped the blade into my hand, and in one continuous motion, hurled it at the oncoming pirate. It buried to the hilt just above his heart.

Jamal's eye's got big, and his mouth fell open. I pulled Jamal back to the ground.

"Who are you?" he mumbled. I was still watching the other pirates. I reached out and grabbed the AK from the impaled one.

He leaned toward me. "Special forces?"

I was scanning with the AK, trying to determine if I needed to fire. "Boy Scouts."

"Boy Scouts," he said. His voice was dubious.

"Sort of," I said as I continued watching the trees beyond us. The pirates seemed to be hunkered down.

"When I was in the scouts, I had a scout knife. Over time I ended up with four or five other scout knives that were given to me, or I found when we were camping. My family had a detached garage with a wooden door. I drew a silhouette on the door and took my knives and practiced throwing them. You should have seen those knives. The blades were wobbly, and the handles beat up from where I miss-hit so many times. I finally figured it out and got the blades to stick. It's kind of like riding a bike, it stays with you. Once you learn."

"Unbelievable," replied Jamal, shaking his head.

"They seem to have pulled back," I whispered.

"We going after them?" he asked.

I nodded and we stepped out from behind the trees and started that way.

THE TIDE TURNS

We glided through the darkness, toward the sound of the shots. They were periodic, and I worried about our group. I hoped they'd keep firing the AKs, move the opposing forces together so they'd shoot at one another.

We'd crossed most of the camp when shots rang out again. We dropped to the sand, not knowing who was shooting or what they were shooting at.

A pirate came running out of the brush. Jamal swung the AK up and sprayed him. The pirate screamed and fell to the sand. At the same time, Jamal fired, there had been another round of shots. Mike burst out of the trees on our right.

"Mike, it's Dee and Jamal!"

Mike slid into the sand next to us. "You got to help me," he panted. "I got separated from Keno. I haven't seen her for about twenty minutes."

"What happened?" I asked.

He was breathing hard. "We were about twenty yards apart, firing steadily behind the pirates and moving them toward the beach. A small group turned and tried to back out and split us. I think Keno panicked when they turned their guns on us. She ran for cover, so did I. I guess we got too close."

I looked at Jamal, then back to Mike. "Lead the way."

We scrambled back in the direction Mike had come. We didn't have to go far. There were four pirates standing in an open space in a grove of palms. One of them was behind Keno, holding her by the arms. Another was in front of her, asking questions. One each was to the left and right, a few feet away, AK's in hand.

We dropped to the sand and crawled. The pirates threatened Keno and backhanded her across the face. Mike moved to rise, but Jamal and I grabbed onto his arms and held him down. He struggled, until I held a finger to my lips and whispered, "Just a second."

"Jamal, you get the one on the right. Mike, lend me your AK, and I'll get the one on the left. You gang tackle the group in the middle and we'll jump in to help." We started to rise.

The pirate holding Keno by the arms slid his hands to her shoulders, and she bent to pick up something. It was her purse. She flipped it open while the one who had been asking questions stood and watched. The one holding her was looking over her shoulders.

She discarded a couple of things we couldn't see. Then I saw her unrolling a pouch. It held her salon tools, specifically the big pair of scissors that she had used to cut our hair and trim our beards. She unrolled the pouch slowly while they watched her closely. I wondered what she had told them. I bumped Jamal and Mike, and said, "Get ready!"

Keno reached inside the pouch and grabbed the scissors out by the handles. She did it with her thumb facing down and her palm in so that when she pulled them out, the tips were pointed at the man behind her. She quickly rammed the point into the back of his hand. He yelped and turned away. She pulled the scissors back in front of her as the pirate who had been questioning her lunged forward to grab her.

I punched Jamal, and we sprang up and sprayed the two pirates on each side of the group. We were close, and the sound was deafening. We were able to control the muzzles blast to shoot from where each of the flanking pirates was standing, and sweep outward, so as not to hit Keno, or the other pirates. Mike sprang forward and tackled the one Keno had stabbed in the hand. He planted an enormous fist to the jaw, and I saw the pirate's head snap. Mike retracted his hand, shaking it in pain.

We turned to Keno and the remaining pirate. His eyes were big, and blood was trickling from his mouth. Keno stepped back, shrieking, and pulled her hands to her face. I saw the scissors buried to the hilt just above the pirate's heart. He gurgled, stepped back, and fell. Mike grabbed Keno with his good hand and pulled her to him. Jamal and I looked at one another, then at the pirate.

He gripped onto the scissors and craned his neck to see. He fell back in the sand, head rolling to one side. Jamal stepped in to check his pulse. He shook his head and moved on to the one Mike had hit. No pulse there either.

Keno had stopped screaming and clung to Mike.

I looked at Jamal. He said, "We'd better check on Angelic and Gina." I could see he was nervous, so was I.

We pushed inland and started for the far side of the skirmish. Jamal ran point, Mike shepherded Keno in the middle, and I provided rear guard. Just like that, we had gone from being tourists to being a real team.

As we moved inland and gained a little elevation, we could see the harbor. We stopped. The pirate ship was on fire. Shots were ringing, and we couldn't tell what was happening. The fire looked to be growing. The whole ship was going to burn. I had a quick thought.

"Mike, you and Keno make your way to the cliff top and set the fire on the "help" message. Grab the conch from the cave on your way and sound it when you have the fire lit. Maybe between the harbor fire and the mountain top, we can catch someone's attention."

"And bring them into a war zone," piped up Keno.

"We have to hope that anyone who sees it will approach with caution. It may be our best or only chance."

Mike nodded and grabbed Keno by the hand. She turned for a second and hugged Jamal and then me.

"Thank you," she said, tears still in her eyes. We nodded and squeezed her arms.

Mike pulled her away, and they started toward the mountain camp.

Jamal and I watched them for a second before we turned and started back toward the fighting.

"We need to go in slow," said Jamal. "The girls were pretty jumpy. We don't want them shooting us."

"Were they staying back?"

"Yeah, when I left we were spraying from a distance, I warned them not to get much closer."

It took us some time. Random shots were coming from the beach. I was afraid everyone had scattered out. It might be morning before anyone could see. I figured it was best to find Angelic and Gina and retreat to the HOE camp. We could catch Mike and Keno as they came down from the clifftop.

"What do you figure happened on the ship?" asked Jamal.

"No idea. Snarly jumped over the side toward the group that was headed for it. Maybe they got into it."

"What about Huggy?"

"He was running the skiff down the island, maybe he came back."

We heard a couple of isolated shots below us.

"Be cautious," I said as I punched Jamal on the arm and pointed toward the sound.

We moved slow and silent. There was light reflected in the sky, from the burning ship, but nothing else. It was pitch dark. We felt our way along. I thought I saw movement, and then heard a slight sound in front of us. I tapped Jamal on the shoulder. He had stopped, as he heard or saw it too.

I looked at the sky, hoping for some light from the mountain top, but it was too soon for Mike and Keno. A sliver of moon might be helpful, something to show us the way.

We edged closer.

"Angelic," I heard Jamal half-call, half-whisper.

The movement turned our way. There was a pause, and I feared shots were going to ring out. But instead, a lone reply, "Jamal."

"Angie, baby." He jumped up and ran toward her. I hopped up and followed.

They were huddled behind a palm. Gina was leaning against it and had blood all over her shirt. I dropped the AK and bent over her, my eyes big, my face slack.

She held up a hand. "I'm okay, it's not mine."

I leaned back for a second, my eyes adjusting to the light. I saw the 20 gauge beside her, my eyes drifted out, and I saw the dead pirate a few feet away.

Angelic and Jamal were embracing. Angelic pulled back and spoke, "We were well behind the pirates, we thought. Suddenly there were two of them, stragglers or deserters, and they jumped us as we moved forward. I sprayed mine since he wasn't quite as close to me. Gina's got ahold of her and knocked the AK out of her hands."

"I didn't have the strap on the AK, but I had the 20 gauge. He knocked me down and was bending over for me when I emptied the shotgun in his stomach. It rained on me." She looked down.

"How long ago?" asked Jamal.

"Ten minutes, maybe less," replied Angelic.

I leaned over and pulled Gina into my arms. She melted into my embrace, and trembled against me as she lifted her head from my shoulder and gestured to the sky.

"Look," she said. "There's a light in the sky, on the mountain top."

I followed her gesture. Mike and Keno made it. Fire lit up the whole sky. And though it was faint, I heard it. Angelic must have, too, because she said, "I hear it! The conch!"

I looked at Jamal and said, "We'd better get started for camp, so we can catch them on their way down."

He nodded and took Angelic's hand. I helped Gina to her feet. We grabbed the guns and set out.

Much of the shooting had died away. I wanted to get an idea of what had happened. I figured, from a distance, with a view, would be best. I'd find a high point on the way to the HOE camp.

We started toward the camp. We went inland and gained elevation on the cliff face.

The ship continued to burn, and between it and the light from the cliff top, there was a smoky, eerie, surreal quality to the night. I pulled out the scope and struggled to see. Pirates gathered in the water and on the beach, but I didn't see any of Antoine's men. I didn't know who was on which side at that point. I didn't see Snarly or Huggy, either, but it was hard to tell.

Then I heard something, like a clanging, and wondered what it might be.

Pulling through the smoke and into the hazy light was a

Coast Guard cutter, a small one, but still relief flooded over me.

I gestured to the others.

"It's the Coast Guard, in the harbor!" I exclaimed.

I swung the telescope around, and there were pirates on the beach with their hands in the air. I wondered if they'd found Bozo and were deserting to a burning ship. There was nowhere for them to go now.

The Coast Guard shone lights into the water and onto the shore.

"Put down your weapons! Down on your knees and put your hands on your heads! Do it right now!" a voice echoed through their com system.

The pirates dropped to their knees. I wondered about Antoine and his group, if they would comply or if they would try something.

A few shots rang out from inland, and the Coast Guard must've decided that was enough. A small rocket shot out from their ship, zoomed inland, and exploded. The rocket was probably similar to what we'd seen on the yacht. The night sky was flooded with light, fire, and sound. Screams and shrapnel filled the air. Several more bodies wandered to the beach from inland, including William and Antoine, but none of the others. I'd have to score it-Coast Guard 2, Antoine 0. I guess he opted for "live to fight another day."

"What now?!" shouted Jamal.

"We wait."

61

WHEN THE WHIP COMES DOWN

We started toward the HOE camp. We stayed along the cliff edge until we got near our beach camp on the tip of the island.

I held up a hand, and everyone stopped. "I want to go see if the skiff is sheltered down there," I said, pointing to the beach. "Y'all go ahead."

Jamal shook his head. "I'll go with you, or we'll wait here. You got ten minutes, or we're coming after you. I'm not confident in Snarly or Huggy."

I nodded at them and headed out. After I made it to the camp, I spotted the skiff beached and tied on the sheltered inlet. I didn't see Snarly or Huggy.

I watched for three minutes and saw nothing. Mindful of the time, I decided to get a little closer.

I followed the path leading to the beach and saw them, standing in the shadows and observing the activity along the harbor, passing a small telescope back and forth. Huggy's bear sat on his shoulder.

"Gentlemen!" I called out.

"Who you calling gentlemen?" snarled Snarly as they

turned to face me, then he broke into a smile. Huggy waved the bear's arms at me.

"Perhaps I was mistaken," I said. I grinned and walked toward them. "Who set the ship on fire?"

Snarly turned toward Huggy, who was still waving the panda arms.

"I swung the skiff around to see the firefight, and as I turned back for the inlet, I saw you both go over the side. I throttled down and watched the ship. I saw a group of the guys climb on board. He was with them," Huggy replied and pointed to Snarly.

Snarly jumped in, "I went over the side and splashed around until they got close to the ship. Apparently, they had found Bozo and were going to make a run for it. I started questioning them, and they got suspicious and pulled a pistol on me. I shot them and went back over the side."

Huggy took over again, "By that time, I'd drifted close to the ship. I saw him shoot and go over the side." He grinned. "I found a small stash of dynamite when I loaded the skiff. I tossed a piece on board and cranked it out of there. "

Snarly interjected again, "I saw him head toward the inlet, and I swam that direction."

Huggy came back in, "The dynamite blew a hole in the deck. It looked like it killed a couple of them and caught the ship on fire. It went fast and spread. I tied up the skiff at the inlet, and was watching from the beach when he swam up."

"So, you guys decided to stick around?" I asked.

Snarly looked at me and grinned. "I wasn't sure I could find the gold in the dark, and I sure couldn't navigate in the dark. We got nowhere to go!"

I pointed behind us. "There's a camp there, did you see it?"

"Not yet, we were heading that way when we stopped to look."

"There are a couple of hammocks between the trees, water in the canteens and some coconuts and other fruit in the bin. Make yourselves comfortable. I'm going to go find my friends. We'll be back."

They looked at one another. "You going to give us the run of your camp?" Snarly asked.

"I think you'd better stay away from the Coast Guard, don't you?" I pointed toward the ship, and we could see landing craft in the water, prisoners being rounded up.

They nodded at me and started toward the camp. I followed behind, then took a side route. I went a little way until I felt they weren't following me. I turned back toward Jamal and started running.

I caught Jamal and the girls as they were starting toward the beach camp.

I held a finger to my lips. I waved them in close and whispered, "Snarly and Huggy are at the beach camp. Let's head for the HOE camp until morning." We started up the trail. We hadn't gone far until we saw Mike and Keno coming down the trail.

Jamal explained to them what had happened. Keno squealed, "So it worked, the fire drew in the Coast Guard."

I nodded. "Sure looks that way. We're letting them round up prisoners. We'll contact them in the morning."

62

MR. CLEAN

His name was Ivan Perez, Captain Ivan Perez. He was a native of Puerto Rico and proud of it, as he let us know. Gina and I approached him under a white flag early the next morning. I wasn't sure at first how to go about it, but he seemed to be in charge and larger than life. I didn't figure we could go wrong.

He was immediately suspicious of us. That's why it was Gina and me. Our group had talked at great length over who should go. We didn't want to seem too aggressive, but we didn't want to get left behind. So, we sent a male and a female, a couple.

He approached us cautiously, eyeing our flag. "And who might you be?" he boomed out.

I told him. I started with the cruise ship, which he had heard about, and how we were here on the island minding our own business until the pirates arrived. He asked about Antoine and his men. I explained that Antoine was on the ship, and on the motor launch and that there had initially been four of them. He grinned. "Yes, I've heard that."

He went on, "I transferred here from Puerto Rico, I miss

Puerto Rico. I would rather be in Puerto Rico. We don't have this kind of problem in Puerto Rico."

I looked at him wryly.

"We may have issues with hurricanes, but not this."

I told him there were six of us, and we had set the fire on the mountaintop when the pirate ship had started burning. He replied that it was a good thing for us, as while. they didn't see the pirate ship until they got closer, they saw the fire from the mountain top, several miles away.

"You realize you are in the middle of nowhere?" he asked.

"We didn't know it, but we suspected it," I said. "We've been here four weeks, and nobody but those pirates has come around. There were no cell or satellite signals, nothing!"

It was his turn to elaborate, "We were on a mission out of Honolulu. We were way south and cutting across what's supposed to be open ocean, on our way back to Pearl. We saw the fire on the mountain top and drew a bead on it. When we approached the harbor, we saw the ship on fire and heard the shooting."

He paused, then added, "This is the part where you can help me out."

We nodded.

"I've spoken to pirates," he said, and gestured to some of the remaining men they were rounding up. "Also, to a gentleman named Antoine Debaucher and his," he paused, "assistant." He grimaced on the last word.

"His name may be William," I offered.

"I believe it is," replied Captain Perez nodding curtly.

"They were on the ship with us and the motor launch. We split into two groups when we landed. There was a middle-aged couple that stayed with Antoine, and an older gentleman. There was also a middle-aged blonde and a heavy set gentleman. I can give you names. They're probably all dead."

"Why do you say that?" asked Captain Perez.

"The heavyset man drowned. The blonde was killed by the pirates. The older man, Tom Jones, to be specific, we saw get shot, from a distance. The other couple we don't know what happened."

"We found them shot to death behind what might have once been a hut."

I looked down and away. "That saddens you?" he said.

"We didn't know them, but yes, it is unfortunate. We hoped they were hiding somewhere."

"I expect they were, hiding that is, around what was left of the hut. They chose," he paused again, "unwisely."

I thought for sure he was going to say "poorly."

"Now," he stated, going on, "tell me about the guns and the gold!"

I looked up at him. Gina stood very still, looking at me.

"What do you want to know?"

"So, you admit to knowing about them!"

I nodded to Gina. "She and I found them."

"How?" he purred.

"Accidentally."

"You can show my crew the location?"

"If you like! What have you been told about it?" I asked.

He did not respond at first and seemed to be weighing the question. Finally, he spoke.

"One of the pirates mentioned it. He didn't seem to know a lot about it. I think perhaps he thought he could make a deal. When I asked several of the others, none of them knew anything. Then I spoke to Antoine and his assistant, and they didn't just not know about it, they denied its existence, at which moment, of course, I knew it existed. Clearly, there were guns about, and one of my men thought to dig up the floor in the hut Antoine had occupied and he found a single bar of gold about half a foot down in the sand. Any deeper, we probably wouldn't have found it."

I stared at him. He broke into a small smile.

"How is it you found these things, and how did the others find out about it?"

I sighed and then pointed to Gina. "We were swimming and saw a conch below a school of fish. We dove down into them. When we looked up, there was a lip above us, like a rock jutting out into the water, only we could swim under it. We did, and when we surfaced, we were in a small cave. We got out of the water and explored. It wasn't very big, and near the top, on a flat plane, were several boxes of guns and gold." I paused. "Jamal, another one of our group, and I were out gathering fruit sometime later, and we were captured by the pirates. They wanted to know where we had gotten our guns." I felt Gina's stare. I was trying to stay close to the truth, without complicating things, or outright lying. I mean, he didn't need all the details, the result was the same.

"They threatened us. We told them where we got the guns. We took them to see. Word got out, apparently, at least among some of them. We escaped with the help of the old man."

"So, they were fighting among themselves over the gold and the guns?"

I nodded again. "Apparently! We weren't really involved." I glanced at Gina. "We're a bunch of tourists. We were just trying not to get killed."

He laughed. "You appear to have succeeded!" Then he narrowed his eyes on us.

"But, there's more," he said.

I looked at him and shrugged my shoulders. "What do you mean?"

"We were not traveling alone. On our ship, we have

international law enforcement authorities. Your man, Antoine, is an arms dealer and a human trafficker."

Gina spoke for the first time, "I knew he was a son of a bitch."

Captain Ivan Perez laughed again. "Quite so, plus the pirate group is notorious in these waters. It's quite the party you stumbled into. We presume they were in a fight for control of the island, the guns, and the gold, and possibly for you. That's how it will be written up anyway."

"So, what happens now?" I asked.

"Well, you're fortunate I knew about the cruise ship. I might think you were a pirate otherwise," he said, winking at Gina.

She smiled back at him and even blushed.

He continued, "We're holding the survivors in custody. They will be remanded when we reach port. Would you like to see them?"

I looked at Gina. She shrugged her shoulders.

"Yes, I would."

"This way, please."

We reached the beach, and the Coast Guard launch was idling just offshore. The prisoners were being assembled in a long line, each of them in shackles. It was both impressive and formidable.

A group of the pirates held Bozo's body aloft on a series of planks. It looked like a Viking funeral pyre. I wondered if they planned to burn his corpse and send him off to Valhalla, as some kind of tribute.

Captain Perez saw me watching and cocked an eyebrow.

"Some of the pirates used to call him the Black Jesus," I replied.

"Actually, I think he called himself that."

Captain Perez then turned toward them and back to me.

"Riding high up on those planks," he said, grinning "is as close to God as he's ever going to get."

I had to smile.

The procession moved along.

As they did, Captain Perez pointed to Antoine, who turned and saw me.

"He should be in jail for a very long time," said the Captain.

"You," Antoine said, raising his shackled hand and pointing a finger at me. "I'll be out of custody by this time next week. Do you know how many politicians I own? Greed always wins."

I nodded at him while Captain Perez stood beside me and laughed.

"I'll find you," said Antoine.

"I'll be waiting," I replied.

The prisoners continued to march toward the Coast Guard launch.

Captain Perez turned to me and said, "Perhaps I underestimated you, or overestimated? He is a dangerous man. If he finds you, he'll cut off your head and stick it on a pike."

I turned to the Captain. "He'll have to find me first. You said yourself, he'll be in jail for a very long time."

"Let us hope so," replied the Captain. He turned and took Gina lightly by the arm. "We were a full ship before we stopped here. With these prisoners, we are very overcrowded. Would it be possible to send another ship for you? It could be here in a day or so."

"That's fine," I replied.

"Good," he said. "I've already made arrangements."

I turned to look at him and thought to myself, *what if it hadn't been acceptable?*

He smiled.

"We'd like to bury our dead. I notice you collecting the bodies."

He paused for a moment, as if in deep thought, then said, "As you wish, please identify them, and they will remain behind. Do you have everything you need for a couple of days?"

"Yes."

Gina interjected, "You wouldn't have a case of cold adult beverages on hand, would you, we're pretty thirsty."

Captain Perez smiled.

"From my own personal collection, I'll be happy to leave you a case of Medalla Light, Puerto Rico's finest."

She gave him a huge smile. "That'd be great!" she said, then kissed him on the cheek. He stood an inch taller.

63

GOOD DAY SUNSHINE

After they finished loading the prisoners, Gina and I escorted Captain Perez and his men to the water. We made no mention of our camp above the beach or the passage from our cave.

He had divers and dive gear, and we all outfitted up and swam into the cave, including the captain. We led him and two of his men up the path. He quickly ascertained the gold and the guns.

"This is amazing," he said, looking at us.

We didn't know what to say.

"This gold is the property of the government of South Africa. The guns may be likewise."

"It's a long way from home, isn't it?" asked Gina.

The captain nodded. "I doubt this is the work of those pirates, especially since they didn't seem to know much about it. By the way, when we found Bozo, he was behind what was left of another of the huts. He appeared to have been stabbed to death. Would you know anything about that?"

"Part of the conflict?" I asked.

"I hoped you might be able to tell me," replied the

captain. "There was a sword hidden in the shaft of the cane the old man carried. It seemed odd."

"You got pirates, you got gun runners, you got gold, and you got guns, what more could there be."

"Tourists," he said.

"Yes," replied Gina.

He smiled at her again. "You know there will be a reward for this gold."

Gina and I looked at one another and shook our heads before replying in unison, "No, really?"

"Yes, actually, it's probably in the neighborhood of 10%."

Gina jumped in, "Why would they pay us, how will they find us? I'm not sure I believe that."

Captain Perez looked at her. "I understand, and I will leave the one gold bar, that Mr. Antoine had in his possession, with you. I feel confident they will then come and find you, wherever you might be. Just a little insurance, you could say."

Gina exhaled. "It all seems unbelievable, anyway!"

"Gold and guns do strange things to people," noted the Captain, nodding at us.

We made our way to the launch and watched as the Coast Guard made final preparations to depart.

I pointed out the bodies of Tom Jones and Holly Smithson, so they could be left behind. I also claimed Tom's cane and sword, which the captain allowed me to have. He had one of the crewmen turn over the gold bar.

"When you get to Honolulu, wait a day or so. I'll tell the South Africans they can find you there."

Most of his crew had boarded, when one of his men brought us a cardboard box with Puerto Rico emblazoned on its top, and a cooler full of ice.

"Enjoy with my compliments," he said, leaned forward

and shook my hand, then hugged Gina. "Two days or less, and the other cutter will be here for you. When you return to Honolulu, I'd like to meet the remainder of your party. Perhaps we can have lunch on Waikiki." He said it as a statement, and I looked forward to seeing him again.

I nodded at him. "Vaya con Dios."

He smiled. "Always."

Gina and I stood on the beach and watched them motor away. We stood there a long time until they were a speck on the horizon.

Behind us, I heard the rest of our group approaching. Guns still in hand, they followed where I gestured to the box.

"Party time," said Mike. "That's good stuff."

We gathered the box and the cooler. Mike shouldered Tom, and Jamal shouldered Holly. We made our way to the beach camp.

WE BURIED THEM AT SUNRISE THE NEXT MORNING. WE DUG the graves the afternoon before and covered the bodies lightly in netting. We placed them in line with the young boy, Ben, I had buried weeks before. It seemed so long ago. We stood, as the sun rose over the water, and light began to fill the air, the darkness of the night seeping away. The ocean was calm as a pond, the sky and the sea the same blue, and the air, golden in color. We stood in a circle holding hands, a light breeze in our faces.

Mike blew a series of bass notes in a riff on the conch, which he repeated twice. He lowered it to his side, as the wind blew the last of the sound away. Angelic stepped forward.

She sang a verse of *Turn Your Eyes upon Jesus* for Holly Smithson.

"O soul, are you weary and troubled?
No light in the darkness you see?
There's light for a look at the Savior,
And life more abundant and free
(Refrain)
Turn your eyes upon Jesus,
Look full in His wonderful face,
And the things of earth will grow strangely dim,
In the light of his glory and grace."

SHE PAUSED, AND WE STOOD TOGETHER, SILENTLY FROZEN IN
time.

THEN SHE SANG A VERSE OF *JUST A CLOSER WALK WITH THEE*
for Tom Jones.
I am weak, but Thou art strong;
Jesus, keep me from all wrong;
I'll be satisfied for as long
As I walk, let me walk close to Thee.
(Refrain)
Just a closer walk with Thee,
Grant it, Jesus is my plea,
Daily walking close to Thee,
Let it be, dear Lord, let it be.

AS THE SOUND OF HER VOICE DRIFTED AWAY, WE LOOKED OUT
to the sea as a group. The sun was shining and shimmering
on the water, not a cloud in the sky. The island remained.
Nothing had changed in the world around us, but we knew
that our time there was coming to an end. We thought that
we could go home again, the same, but different.

EPILOGUE

We were sitting in the shade at the beach camp, making plans for the evening when we heard them.

"If I had a low IQ, I'd be a pirate just like you."

"Pirate, pirate," a second voice rang out.

It was Snarly and Huggy, in tandem. Huggy waved the panda's arms as they walked up to us and stopped.

I reached to shake hands, a big grin on my face.

"We're about ready to go," said Snarly.

Huggy turned and waved the panda arms at the rest of the group.

Snarly spoke again, "We got the skiff ready. We got fuel, food, and water for several days. Coast Guard's coming back for you, right?"

I nodded.

"We best be gone before they return. It'll take us two days or so to get to the closest island. But I think we can make it. We'll take our chances."

"Thanks," I said. "I don't think it would have worked out if we hadn't had your help."

They both nodded. "We got out alive, and we ain't going to prison, it's all good," said Snarly.

"I got something for you," I replied. "Hold on just a minute."

I went over and picked up my shoulder bag from under the palms and walked back. I pulled out two cases and held them up.

"Chewing gum," said Jamal.

"It's a special blend," I noted, handing one to Snarly and one to Huggy.

Snarly opened the case, pulled out a box, and took out one of the plastic gum holders. He looked at me, and then he looked at the gum.

"Take a look," I said.

He opened the plastic top, and his eyes got big. "That sure is a whole lot of gum. Where did you get this?"

I looked at him solemnly. "The hippies y'all killed."

"Damn, I didn't kill no hippies. They sure did like their gum."

"Yeah," I said. "There are about a million pieces in each case. Don 't chew it all at one time." Huggy smiled and shook the case.

Snarly wiped his face. He held an arm up, forearm toward us. Huggy, Jamal, and I were standing closest, three brothers and a whiter shade of pale.

Snarly pushed his arm out a little further. Huggy raised his arm and looked at Jamal, and me. Jamal raised his arm, and finally, so did I, fist to elbow. They made a square among the four of us.

He spoke, "Skin tone's just pigment, soul ain't got no color."

Huggy rang out with an "Amen." Jamal glanced between them, nodded, and said, "That's right." I looked at all three and murmured, "I reckon so, but it goes good with green."

They laughed and then nodded to the group. Huggy waved the panda's arms, and they started down the path to the beach. We wandered over to the cliff face and watched them hop in the skiff, motor out of the harbor, and into the sea.

Mike turned to me. Angelic, Keno, and Gina stood behind him. Jamal was off to one side. They were all staring at me.

"What's with the gum?" he asked.

I smiled at them. "There's some for everybody. About three cases each. We'll go get it in the morning."

WE STOOD IN FRONT OF THE SUPPLY ROOM AT THE HOE camp. I passed out the crates, everybody got three each. They stood and pulled the tubs, from the boxes, from the crates, and examined the contents.

"Those hippies did this," said Mike while holding up one of the tubs to the light.

"Yes," I replied. "I don't know who they were or where they came from, only that they are all dead. There are 250 one hundred dollar bills in each tub. They are eight tubs in a box and five boxes in a crate. That makes one million dollars."

"You gave one to each of those pirates," said Keno.

"I did, that made it easy to do the math. We get three million each. They got one million apiece for helping us."

Angelic held one of the boxes in her hand and shook it. "And everybody goes home happy."

"And rich," added Gina, who was checking each of her crates. She looked up at me.

"By the way," she continued, "Captain Perez," she paused and looked at me as if to see whether I would speak. I smiled back at her, nodded, and she continued.

"Captain Perez said that we would be receiving a reward for finding the lost gold. We can split that six ways as well."

"How much do you think it will be?" asked Mike.

"No idea," I replied. "Captain Perez said it's typically around 10%."

Keno held up one of her boxes. "That could be this much or more."

"Yes!" shouted out the entire group.

WE PACKED OUR CRATES, TOOK ONE LAST LOOK AROUND THE HOE camp, and headed for the beach. We were going to have a bonfire and a party. We grilled fish, hopefully for the last time, for a while. We had the captain's Puerto Rican beverages and fruit from the HOE camp. It promised to be a good time.

We built a fire on the point near the graves and watched as the sun sank in the sky. We ate and toasted one another, the friends we had lost, the hippies who'd made us rich, whoever left the gold and guns, and the Coast Guard, mostly the Coast Guard.

Darkness had fallen, and the moon shone on the water, reflecting back its soft shimmer in the sky. Jamal stood and waved his arms.

"Some entertainment?" he asked.

We all clapped.

He snapped his fingers a couple of times and clapped his hands on his legs to set a rhythm. "Y'all join in now."

He broke into an old Al Green song. You know the one that gives such good advice about the people you love, and the time you spend with them.

Angelic jumped up and joined in, adding harmony and clapping her hands.

The other four of us got to our feet, stood in a line, and

began to clap, sing along and sway. Who could forget the swaying!

It was a fine time, as we stood counting down our remaining moments on the island.

After Jamal finished, we were standing talking, and Mike asked, "Do you suppose we could come back one day?"

"Wouldn't see why not," I replied.

"We'll come back in our own ship," threw out Jamal.

The women slipped their fingers into the hands of each man and started back to the cave.

THE NEXT MORNING WE WERE WOKEN TO THE SOUND OF A massive horn blasting across the water. Jamal jumped up and ran for the top of the trail to the beach. He came back, shouting, "It's the Coast Guard! It's the Coast Guard!"

Mike and Keno scrambled up and started for the trail.

Jamal was shouting and waving at Angelic, who was pushing herself up. She smiled at Gina and me and nodded her head. "Let's go." She jumped up, and she and Jamal took off.

I stood, held my hand out to Gina, and she took it. We strolled along the trail to the beach.

About halfway down the trail, she spoke. "What are you going to do next?"

I looked at her and smiled. "I'm not going back," I said. "I'm going surfing in Costa Rica."

"Why?" she asked.

"Because I can…you want to come along?"

She smiled and pressed herself closer to me. It felt good.

"I thought you'd never ask!"

She took me by the other hand, led me out into the sunlight, and down to the water.

. . .

THE END

———

BONUS CONTENT -

Extended Epilogue

Sign up for LP's email newsletter and receive a FREE extended epilogue that follows the continued adventures of Dee Sanders and his friends:

3 Hour Tour - Extended Epilogue
www.lpsnyder.com

ENJOY THIS BOOK?

If you've enjoyed this book, I would be very grateful if you could spend just five minutes leaving a review (it can be as short as you like) on the book's Amazon page and on Goodreads or BookBub.

Thank you very much.

ALSO BY LP SNYDER

COMING NEXT

Mason Bennett, Boston Operative

Dee's friend Mason Bennett is the Boston Operative.
Mason lives in a darker and more dangerous world as he
works for the agency. Hop on board and see for yourself if
he can save the world!

Sign up for LP's email newsletter at www.lpsnyder.com to be
notified when *Mason Bennett, Boston Operative* is available to
purchase.

ACKNOWLEDGMENTS

From Author L.P. Snyder

I want to thank the "Indie" community who made writing books possible for many of us. Traditional publishing was never going to be a possibility for me. I didn't have the patience for it! But this, this is a brave new world or a brand new day, pick your cliché! But, I am grateful to be here, and I hope you enjoy the story.

I want to thank Vince Conti for the beautiful cover, Elizabeth Mackey for cover consultation, the editors at Frostbite Publishing for their invaluable assistance, my friends and fellow authors Kelly Utt and Shannon Brown for extensive insight, support, and patience, and finally my wife, Diana. She told me I could do it!

ABOUT THE AUTHOR

LP Snyder is a life-long reader who, at the last minute, decided to become a writer. It's been a great experience, and he wonders why it took so long to decide! Having read a little of most genres, LP decided to stick with his favorites—adventure, espionage, and crime thrillers! If you like fast-paced, humorous, action-filled, suspense thrillers, he's your Huckleberry!

Newsletter subscribers receive bonus content, including short stories and extended epilogues. Don't be afraid to ride that train!

Sign up at www.lpsnyder.com.